"Not every line is a lie, Dana,"

Griff told her. "Can I help it if I think you're beautiful? Or that you walk with an incredible grace that I've never seen in another woman?"

Dana's eyes were wide with wonder—and trust. "Sometimes I have a tough time telling a line from the truth," she admitted.

His hand tightened on her arm and he drew her to a halt. Inches separated them. "There's one way to tell," he whispered.

She saw the look in his eyes. His intention was unmistakable.

"Your heart will never lead you wrong," he whispered. "Dana, I want to kiss you...and I promised I'd never take unless you wanted to give. I meant that...."

Leaning upward, she pressed her hands against his chest and whispered unsteadily, "Yes, I want to kiss you...."

A groan vibrated through him as his strong mouth eased her lips apart.

Dear Reader,

Welcome to Silhouette **Special Edition** . . . welcome to romance. Each month Silhouette **Special Edition** publishes six novels with you in mind—stories of love and life, tales that you can identify with— romance with that little ''something special'' added in.

And this month is no exception to the rule. May 1991 brings *No Quarter Given* by Lindsay McKenna—the first in the thrilling WOMEN OF GLORY series. Don't miss more of this compelling collection coming in June and July. Stories by wonderful writers Curtiss Ann Matlock, Tracy Sinclair, Sherryl Woods, Diana Stuart and Lorraine Carroll (with her first **Special Edition**!) round out this merry month.

In each Silhouette **Special Edition**, we're dedicated to bringing you the romances that you dream about— the type of stories that delight as well as bring a tear to the eye. And that's what Silhouette **Special Edition** is all about—special books by special authors for special readers!

I hope you enjoy this book and all of the stories to come.

Sincerely,

Tara Gavin
Senior Editor

LINDSAY McKENNA
No Quarter Given

Silhouette Special Edition

Published by Silhouette Books New York

America's Publisher of Contemporary Romance

To the women of all Services...
who serve our country equally well as any man.
You unsung heroines who never receive the accolades
or press that you do, indeed, deserve:
I salute you and your commitment.
And
Ursula and Robert Langford
and
Anne Parsons, my editor
and
Lieutenant Scott Prator, U.S.N.R.

SILHOUETTE BOOKS
300 East 42nd St., New York, N.Y. 10017

NO QUARTER GIVEN

ISBN: 0-373-09667-4

First Silhouette Books printing May 1991

Printed in the U.S.A.

Books by Lindsay McKenna

LINDSAY McKENNA

spent three years serving her country as a meteorologist in the U.S. Navy, so much of her knowledge about the military people and practices featured in her novels comes from direct experience. In addition, she spends a great deal of time researching each book, whether it be at the Pentagon or at military bases, extensively interviewing key personnel. She views the military as her second family and hopes that her novels will help dispel the "unfeeling machine" image that haunts it, allowing readers glimpses of the flesh-and-blood people who comprise the Services.

Lindsay is also a pilot. She and her husband of fifteen years, both avid rock hounds and hikers, live in Arizona.

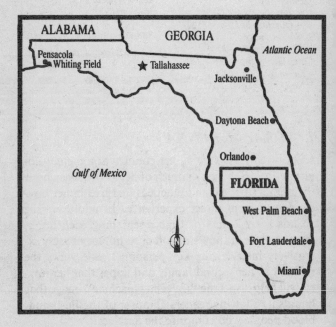

Prologue

"When a man graduates from Annapolis, he becomes a part of the Brotherhood, an elite group that has made it through the academy. The men who wear this ring take an oath to help their brothers at any time in their naval careers." Maggie Donovan looked solemnly at her two best friends, Dana Coulter and Molly Rutledge. "We're three women graduating from Annapolis," she continued. "We've made it. But we're forming the Sisterhood, a place where women graduates can turn for help and support from other women who have got through the academy."

Dana held out her small hand, the heavy Annapolis ring looking huge on her slender finger. "Let's take the vow that from this day on, the Sisterhood is a living entity among the three of us," she said, her soft voice firm with intent.

Molly placed her slim hand over Dana's and looked at her friends. "The Sisterhood will start with us, but this is only the beginning. We'll be there for our sisters who have graduated before us, and for those who will graduate in years to come.''

Maggie reached out her long, slender hand to cover the other two. "Women helping women in a military world ruled by men. I vow to be there for any sister who is an Annapolis graduate. I'll do what I can to help her in an honorable way."

"I vow the same thing," Dana said.

"I vow it also," Molly whispered.

Maggie placed her free hand over their joined ones, squeezing lightly for a moment. "It's done," she said with satisfaction. "The Sisterhood is formed."

As Dana withdrew her hand, she reminded, "Although we've all heard about the Brotherhood, it's an unofficial organization—it never has been proved to exist or operate within the Navy. I know those who aren't Annapolis graduates see it as a discriminatory thing. I don't know about you, but my vow includes *any* woman in *any* service I happen to work with. I don't care whether she's enlisted or an officer. Women need to support and help each other."

Maggie stood a moment, digesting her friend's fervent statement. Then, running a hand through her thick red hair, she grinned. "I like the concept, Dana. Yes, I'll support the Sisterhood as more than an elitist unit."

"Maybe," Molly added, "the three of us can be an example of positive action by women for women. Our actions will speak louder than words."

Dana grimaced. "We've already had four years of harassment by men who didn't want us going through this military academy. Most of them didn't believe we could hack it, but we did. Still, I don't think being a woman Annapolis graduate is going to make things any easier out there. They'll be expecting us to fail."

"But we won't," Maggie said, her smile widening. "We're winners. And now we're all going for the brass ring: our naval aviator wings. Ninety percent of those who try get washed out in the first six weeks of flight school," she warned.

"The pressure is going to be worse," Molly agreed. "But a lot of Annapolis officers tried to fail us, and we stuck together and made it through."

"It won't be any different at Whiting Field down in Florida," Dana said determinedly. "We'll get an apartment together, study together and make it through—together. Just like we did at Annapolis. Women helping women. It's the future—our future..."

Chapter One

"Look out!" Dana's cry pierced the crowd of milling people at the Tallahassee airport. She dropped her two bags on the sidewalk, just outside the main doors. A tiny elderly woman, wearing a beige dress that hung nearly to her ankles, approached the multiple lanes of unrelenting traffic. Her thick glasses had slid down her nose, and she felt her way with a wooden cane, tapping it along the curb as she prepared to step off. Although Dana weighed barely more than a hundred pounds herself, she managed to wedge between two businessmen and lurch ahead toward the woman. Her cane poised, the little steel-grey haired lady was on the verge of stepping forward.

Dana shouted another warning, but the woman didn't seem to hear. Desperate now, her mouth tightening, Dana extended her short stride. Her eyes widened when suddenly a young man with long, unkempt brown hair jerked the old woman's purse from her shoulder, as she still tottered uncertainly on the curb.

The woman gave a startled cry, trying to hold on to her handbag, but the young man yanked it from her savagely, flinging the tiny lady to the concrete sidewalk. *Damn him!* Anger surged through Dana. No way in hell was the purse snatcher going to get away. Not if she could help it.

If she'd had time to consider her reaction, Dana might ruefully have shaken her head. But her response now was the same as it had been so many years ago when her father beat up on her mother and herself. Dana tensed the small shoulders that had carried so many burdens in silence for twenty-two years. This man was no different from her father. He had the same insane look on his face, the same dark and wild eyes. Probably on drugs and needing a fix, he'd picked on the weakest, most likely victim. And wasn't it always a woman—whether child, adult or elderly person—being abused by a man?

Although the thief was at least six foot three and built like a center for a football team, Dana put herself in a direct collision course with him. Her eyes narrowing, she monitored the culprit's sudden sprint in her direction. He didn't even see her in the crowd of taller people surrounding her. Her stomach tightening, her muscles tensing to take the coming blow, Dana prepared herself for a head-on collision.

Suddenly, as it had whenever her father had come at her with a belt in his hand, everything seemed to slow to single frames in vivid color and focus. Dana heard nothing of the commotion around her. An emptiness took over inside her, along with the cool detachment she'd learned to depend on. Long ago, Dana had figured out that it was the adrenaline pumping through her bloodstream that had helped her to survive those hellish years. She never felt the thick leather belt biting into her sensitive flesh, or the impact of her father's fist as he struck her when he lost his temper. As she positioned herself now, her feet slightly spread for maximum balance, she knew she wouldn't feel anything—until afterward.

It was as if a hurricane had erupted around Dana as she stood calmly, watching people being pushed aside by the purse snatcher. Startled, angry shouts filled the air, but they seemed dim and faraway. Dana realized with a trickle of triumph that the thief hadn't even seen her yet. Flexing her elbows to act as shock absorbers when he struck her, Dana took a deep breath.

The man was running full tilt, the purse in his left hand. His mouth was open, and he was sucking in huge gulps of air. Too late, his eyes registered Dana in his path.

The impact knocked Dana off her feet. Instinctively she wrapped her arms around the thief, grabbing his legs. They both became airborne for a split second. Her eyes had automatically squeezed shut as she gripped his extremities. Dana slammed onto the concrete, a cry torn from her as the man landed on top of her. He'd knocked the wind out of her, but she clung to his legs, knowing he'd get away if she let go.

"Let go!" he shrieked, thrashing to break free of her grip. Managing to loosen one foot, he struck out at her with the heel of his boot.

Dana felt the jarring impact on her shoulder. He rolled over, dragging her along. Her breathing was ragged, and she couldn't cry out for help. Would anyone help her? Opening her eyes, Dana saw the thief release the purse. Enraged, his lips curling away from his teeth, he reared into a sitting position and doubled his right hand into a huge fist. Dana tried to prepare herself for the blow. She knew now, as she had known growing up, that no one would come to her rescue. Stoically, sheltered in some inner place deep within herself, she accepted that reality and refused to release the culprit.

Lieutenant Griff Turcotte stood with his baggage in hand as the sequence of events unfolded before him with explosive fury. His mouth dropped open when a tiny woman in white slacks and a flowery print blouse deliberately placed herself in the path of the desperate purse snatcher. Though as a Navy fighter pilot Griff's reflexes were fast, they weren't quick enough to help the young woman. Women were a sore spot in Griff's life lately, but this one was different, he acknowledged as he automatically dropped his bags and surged forward through the crowd of stunned onlookers. She had guts. She weighed about as much as a feather against the hulking young man.

If he didn't get there in a hurry, she might be killed. She had heart, Griff had to give her that—and stupidity. He saw the bloody scrapes on her lower arms and elbows. His heart quickening, Griff moved through the crowd like the football player he'd been before entering the U.S. Navy. He saw the thief sit up, his fist cocked. He was going to throw a punch at her. Cursing, Griff sprinted, thundering at the gawking onlookers to move aside.

Many impressions assailed Griff as he closed the final ten feet between them. The woman clung like a wolverine to the man's leg, though clearly she knew he was going to strike her. Her small, heart-shaped face was pale, her huge blue eyes narrowed and defiant. It was the set of her full lips, shouting her resolve, that made Griff want to applaud her courage despite the circumstances. Her short black hair, touched with cobalt highlights, glistened like a raven's wing. Everything about her spoke of frailty. Yet she was the only one who had challenged the thief.

Griff wanted to cry out a warning to her as the man's fist hurtled forward. She could have released him and avoided being hit. But she didn't. Wincing, Griff saw the blow strike her cheekbone. He heard the pulverizing connection, and his stomach turned queasy.

"You bastard," Griff growled, catching the purse snatcher's arm before he could take another swing. It gave him great satisfaction to hit the thief in the face, just as the man had done to the woman. Pain soared up Griff's hand into his wrist and lower arm at the contact, and he heard the man's nose break. Good! He had it coming! Dragging the culprit off the semiconscious woman, Griff jerked him onto his stomach, pinning his arms behind his back.

"Get the police!" he gasped to the nearest onlooker. Twisting his head to the right, Griff worriedly took in the young woman, who lay on the concrete several feet away. Blood was running from her nose, and her cheek was bruised, already beginning to swell. In anger, he tightened his hold on the thief. "Get an ambulance! Someone call an ambulance for her!" he thundered.

Pain. It always came afterward. Dana bit back a groan, light-headed as the pain began to work its way in a radiating pattern out from her cheek. Slowly she sat up, pressing her hands to her temples. Lowering her head between her legs, she staved off faintness and allowed the blood to return so that she could think coherently.

Someone had helped her. Who? Aware of the agitated crowd surrounding her, Dana lifted her head. Her vision blurred momentarily, and then it cleared. A man had helped her. A *man*. Swallowing against her dry throat, her heart banging away inside it, Dana stared over at him. He was rugged looking, with stormy gray eyes that were thundercloud black with anger, and his mouth was drawn into a tight line. His square face had a strong, stubborn chin. She couldn't tell if he was in his late twenties or early thirties. Dressed in jeans and a white short-sleeved shirt, he looked like a bird of prey perched over his trapped quarry. His clothes offered only a thin veneer of civilization—there was a primal savagery about him.

He was deeply tanned, his walnut-colored hair cut short, his movements fluid. As a champion swimmer, Dana immediately recognized a fellow athlete. He had a boneless kind of grace that shouted his top physical condition.

As a teenager growing up in Carlsbad, California, Dana once had seen an eagle at the L.A. zoo. This man had those same kind of eyes, she realized suddenly—huge, intense and all-seeing. She'd never forgotten that raptor sitting proudly on his zoo perch and the way his predatory look had knifed *through* her, as if the eagle knew her deepest, darkest, most painful secrets. The eagle's bearing somehow had made her feel safe. Now, as the man raised his head, his gray eyes widening with concern when they settled on her, Dana felt a cry shatter deep within her, as if this man could evoke that same feeling of security.

Unable to meet his questioning stare, Dana turned her head away. His eyes reminded her of the turbulent, powerful storm-clouds that had appeared each summer over Annapolis. Something ordered her to look up again, to turn and hold his gaze. Reluctantly, Dana followed the unspoken directive. The man had huge black pupils, but his eyes were now a dove-gray color as they gently held hers.

Peace. The feeling flowed through her, startling and unexpected. She'd never found peace with any man. Drowning in the warmth exuding from his eyes, Dana's gaze clung helplessly to his as some silent, invisible strength seemed to flow from him to her. She felt the power of his caring and allowed it to wash through her, cleansing her of fear and momentarily taking away her pain.

And then, the weight of her past rushed up within her to crush the new experience. No man gave without wanting something first. No man gave anything without extracting a price and payment, an internal voice reminded her. They always took. Bitterness coated Dana's mouth, and she tore her gaze from his. Looking up, she saw people crowding close around her, curiosity written on their faces. Two policemen were working their way forward. Good. The thief would get his due. Her hands shaking, Dana pressed her fingers to the bridge of her nose and tipped her head back to stop the bleeding. She'd learned this trick when she was seven years old after her father had struck her for not getting him the Sunday-morning newspaper fast enough.

She had to get out of here. Trying to ignore the crowd, Dana keyed in on the conversation between the police officers and the man who had helped her apprehend the thief. His voice was low and modulated, sending a ribbon of calm through the chaos roiling inside her. It was a deep voice, belonging to someone who was very sure of himself. For an instant the desire to open her eyes and simply watch him was nearly overwhelming. And then she laughed at herself. The last time she'd been drawn to a man, she'd allowed his lies to become her reality. Jason Lombard had been a smooth talker, and she'd fallen beneath his spell.

Mired in the memory of her mistake with Jason, Dana blotted out everything else. Time ceased to exist as she remembered her one-and-only affair, during her third year at Annapolis. Jason had been an upperclassman, ready to graduate from the prestigious military academy. Her roommates, Molly and Maggie, had warned her about him, but she hadn't listened. Later, after spending Christmas with his parents, Dana had accidentally discovered the awful truth: Jason had bet his buddies that he could lay Dana. They'd called her Ice Woman at the academy. He wanted to see if ice water really did run in her veins. Jason had been the first man Dana had ever slept with. He'd seemed so different from the men she knew; so different from her father. The bitter truth was, they were all alike. They took what they wanted from innocent, trusting women.

No more. The words pounded in her head in sync with her thudding heart. Dana slowly released the pressure from the bridge of her nose and lowered her head. Her nosebleed had stopped. Resting her brow against her drawn-up knees, she felt the shattered emotions still warring within her. She was positive her eye would blacken. My God, she had to report to Whiting Field tomorrow morning as a student pilot!

What would her instructor think? Worse, would her eye swell closed? She needed both eyes to learn to fly.

Women Annapolis graduates were few and far between, and those who passed the rigorous tests to get a chance to earn their wings were even rarer. Dana knew she and her two roommates wouldn't be welcomed with open arms at Whiting. Most of the men saw women as taking flight slots that rightfully belonged to them. Now Dana would be standing at attention tomorrow morning with a black eye—a hell of a welcome to Whiting Field and pilot training.

Dana felt a strong hand settle on her shoulder. She stiffened, jerking her head up. It was him. The man who had helped her. The eagle. His fingers were long and tapered, his grip gentle but firm on her shoulder.

"Are you okay?"

His voice flowed through the chaos of her thoughts. Dana blinked, unable to tear her gaze from his wonderfully warm gray eyes. Her heart opened, receiving his concern. When she didn't answer right away, Dana felt his fingers tighten imperceptibly on her shoulder. He lifted his other hand, and instinctively she winced.

"Take it easy," Griff soothed, barely caressing the woman's mussed black hair. He saw the sudden fear in her eyes. She was jumpy. Managing a slight, one-cornered smile, he added, "My name's Griff. That was a hell of a tackle, lady."

"Dana." He was too close, too overwhelmingly masculine. Her heart was beating even more wildly, his touch dissolving her defenses.

Griff dug into the back pocket of his jeans. "I thought I had a handkerchief," he muttered apologetically. "Oh, here it is." He pressed the clean linen into her hands.

"Th-thank you." A part of Dana wanted desperately to fall into the shelter of his arms. The injured-animal part of her tasted panic, layered with suffocating fear.

"I couldn't believe you did that." Griff gently laid his hand on her forearm, turning it over. The flesh had been scraped away. "The ambulance is on its way. Just hang on."

Dana's black humor always surfaced in a crisis. Her lips curved into a wry twist that could be misconstrued as a grimace. "This isn't the first time I've had a black eye," she offered. "Don't worry about me. What about the old woman? Could you go see how she is? Please?"

Griff wavered. Dana was small and ultrafeminine, but he felt the smooth firmness of muscle beneath the flesh of her arm. The fear shadowing her azure eyes hadn't ebbed. Why? She was safe now. He knew he had a craggy face, with features that were harsh and unforgiving, but she was reacting as if he were threatening rather than helping her.

"Well—"

"Please, she needs help. Go to her. I'll be fine." Did Griff hear the desperation in her tone? Dana wondered as she pulled her arm from his hand. She saw the puzzlement in his eyes. His lips parted to say something, but he changed his mind.

"Okay. But you stay put. Understand? You're in no condition to go anywhere."

A hysterical giggle clawed up Dana's throat as he eased to his feet. If Griff had seen her after her father had gotten done with her, he'd have thought she was dying. A couple of times her mother had taken her to the hospital emergency room. When Griff halted and half turned toward her, Dana muttered, "I won't go anywhere."

Ordinarily she'd have resented a man's order. At Annapolis, especially as a plebe, she'd had to take plenty of stupid, inane orders from upperclassmen bent on driving her out of the academy. Then, as now, she tucked the resentment deep within her. The worry in Griff's eyes was genuine, if she was any judge of the situation. But her track record with men had always been poor, so she feared she could have misread his intent. Still, her heart wanted to accept that Griff was concerned about her welfare.

Griff crouched by the old woman who was shakily putting her glasses back on. Speaking quietly, he placed his hand on her. Dana's face hovered before him. Automatically, he looked over his shoulder. A police officer was kneeling next to Dana, taking a report. She looked disheveled and in need of some care. Internally, Griff chastised himself. He'd gotten out of divorce court only six months ago. Carol, his ex-wife, had appeared strong and capable. But during the five years of their disastrous marriage, Griff had discovered his wife was a clinger, not a woman who could stand on her own two feet as his equal. Carol had fooled him completely. Sensing what he'd wanted, she'd become that for him while they were dating. He was a brash, cocky, fighter pilot who'd earned his wings out of Annapolis. Carol, an only child from a banking family, had fallen in love with his image; he'd fallen in love with her facade.

Disgusted with himself, Griff forced himself to look away from Dana. She had the face of an angel, with eyes the color of the sky he loved to fly in. And that mouth of hers . . . Groaning to himself, Griff wondered if the adrenaline flow was making him unusually responsive to her. Hadn't he learned his lesson about being drawn to women too quickly?

The police officer rose, giving Dana a hand to her feet. She brushed off the seat of her pants. A young woman came up, offering her a Kleenex for her bloody forearm. Quietly thanking her, Dana looked up at the officer.

"May I go now?"

"We've got your address, Ms. Coulter. When and if Mrs. Biddle presses charges against this guy, we'll be in touch."

"Okay." Dana looked past the policeman. Griff was being kept busy by the other officer, who was taking his report.

"Look, you sure you're okay? The ambulance will be here in just a minute. Maybe you ought to go to Emergency and get checked over. That's quite a shiner you've got in the making."

Forcing a slight smile for the officer's benefit, Dana said, "I'll be fine." Then she disappeared into the crowd. Right now, all she wanted was to escape Griff's gray, eagle gaze. Her instincts told her he wanted to be sure she was all right. Dana wavered between disbelief and fear that a man honestly could be concerned about her. She picked up her luggage and hailed a taxi, ignoring the stunned look of the driver. Collapsing in the back seat, she gave the cabbie the address where her roommates, Maggie and Molly, awaited her.

Dana ignored the pain it cost her to sit forward and look across the crowd. Griff stood tall and straight, his shoulders thrown back with natural pride—an eagle among a bunch of chattering blackbirds, Dana thought tiredly. As she sank back again, closing her eyes, his gray eyes haunted her heart. Her tightly coiled emotions begged to explode outward in a sob. Suddenly Dana realized just how tired she was—a kind of bone-deep exhaustion that frightened her more than men did.

She ignored the sunny April weather, the humidity, and the tropical foliage that lined the wide boulevards. Coming to Whiting Field to face her ultimate test had been the culmination of the past four years of her life. Her mother, Ann Coulter, had finally found the courage to divorce her father, Frank. Even her best friends, Maggie and Molly, knew little of her abusive childhood. It was something she was ashamed of; something she wanted no one to know about. Griff's harsh features swam in front of her tired eyes. An eagle with the heart of a dove. Was that possible? Did any man own a heart sensitive to anyone other than himself? Something inside her wanted to believe that Griff might.

Griff... His voice had soothed the pain in her cheek and the ache in her head. How badly Dana wanted simply to sit and talk to him, to find out more about him. But she would never see him again. A terrible sadness overwhelmed Dana. She could have stayed at the airport and waited for him to come back to her. But she'd been frightened by the way he affected her strewn senses. Never would she give her power away to a man again.

"Where is she?" Griff demanded, craning his neck.

"Who?"

"The woman who tackled the thief."

The cop looked around and shrugged. "Dunno, Lieutenant. I told her she was free to go."

Dammit. Throwing his hands on his hips, Griff glared around at the dissipating crowd. The purse snatcher was being put into the cruiser. "I need to see her."

"You know her?"

"No. I need her name and address, Officer."

"Sorry, I can't do that."

Griff glared at him.

"Police policy, Lieutenant. Sorry."

"But—"

"I'm sure she'll show up if there's a hearing, and you'll be there, too." The cop grinned. "Gutsy broad, wasn't she?" He glanced significantly down at Griff's bare left hand. "I'd want her name and phone number, too, if I were in your shoes."

Griff bit back a nasty retort. He didn't like the innuendo in the cop's voice. But he wasn't going to lower himself to the man's locker-room level. "I'll see her in court," he snapped, spinning on his heel and heading in the direction of his dropped bags.

Retrieving the luggage, Griff grimly asked himself why the hell he wanted to see Dana again. She'd taken a nasty punch. Her eye was going to swell shut. Did she have anyone to care for her? To hold her or maybe just listen to her story, her fear?

"You're nuts, Turk. Knock it off and get back to business." Bags in hand, he swung off the curb and made his way to the parking lot where his red Corvette was waiting. This whole situation was crazy. Four days ago his best friend, the brother he'd never had, had been killed, thanks to the incompetence of a woman student-pilot over at Pensacola Naval Air Station. Lieutenant Toby Lammerding had been an instructor pilot at Pensacola, only miles away from Whiting Field, where Griff was also an IP. Toby had taught officer candidates, while at Whiting Field, Griff taught Annapolis grads making a bid to pass the toughest flight tests in the world and become U.S. Navy pilots.

Griff had never believed a woman could meet the tough standards necessary to become a Navy pilot. Women simply weren't physically strong enough—or emotionally prepared—to handle a thirty-million-dollar fighter jet. When Toby had called, excited about his first female student pilot, Griff had felt a cold chill work up his spine. Toby had been ecstatic over the chance to help a woman get her wings. Griff couldn't agree with his friend. In the year Griff had been an IP, or 03 as they were called by the students, he'd never had a woman assigned to his training schedule. He never wanted one.

Unlocking the car door, he threw his luggage into the passenger seat. He'd just returned from Augusta, Georgia, where Toby had been buried that morning. The flight investigation blamed the woman student-pilot for the flight error. The woman had bailed out in time but Toby had valiantly stayed behind to try and save the crippled trainer. The engine had exploded.

After buckling his seat belt, Griff rammed the key into the ignition, his feelings of grief and loss over Toby surfacing. He hadn't cried at the funeral as Toby's family and friends had. No, he'd attended in uniform, stoic and strong for those who weren't. Tears burned in Griff's eyes as the Corvette purred to life. Dana's bruised, battered face swam before his tear-filled eyes. God, but she'd had wide, clear eyes—the kind a man could fall into and feel safe and good about himself.

"Dreamer," Griff growled at himself harshly. That was his Achilles' heel. Though his world required highly complex skills, a mind that worked at the speed of a refined computer and brutal physical demands, Griff recognized his own soft underbelly. He'd dreamed of Carol being more than a "wife." Maybe it was his fault their marriage had fallen apart. Maybe he'd wanted her to be something she never could be. Funny how women touched his wistful-dreamer side, especially when based on his five-year-marriage track record, he was a failure.

Well, tomorrow was a fresh start in so many ways. No more getting together with Toby on weekends to go deep-sea fishing, or Friday-night poker games with the IPs at Pensacola. Griff's apartment would be silent and empty, as usual since his divorce from Carol. When he went to Whiting Field, Monday morning, it would be to meet his next three students for the coming six weeks of daily instruction. He sighed. Very few of his students made it through their time with him. Griff knew he had one hell of a reputation among the student personnel at the base. They called him "the Turk," and he had the highest washout rate of students at Whiting. And for a good reason. He didn't want anyone in the air who couldn't handle the pressures that a naval aviator would experience.

As he guided the red sports car down a palm-lined avenue, Griff acknowledged that his mind and, if he was honest, his heart, still dwelled on Dana. Her trembling words haunted him: "This isn't the first time I've had a black eye...." A hunger to find out more about her ate at him. She was a woman of mystery and of surprisingly heroic proportions. Why had she run from him? The fear he'd seen in Dana's eyes had been real. Fear of him? But why? Pushing his fingers through his short, dark brown hair, Griff muttered a curse. He had to forget Dana. Toby had always counseled him to live one day at a time. Well, starting tomorrow morning, he'd follow his best friend's advice.

Chapter Two

"Dana! What happened to you?" Molly stepped forward between the stacks of boxes that had yet to be unpacked in their airy three-bedroom apartment. Dana stood at the doorway, her face puffy and bruised.

Gratefully, Dana allowed Molly to take her luggage. She shut the screen door. "I had a run-in with a jerk at the airport who wanted to steal an old lady's purse." Tenderly she touched her swollen cheek that ached like fire. "I tackled him."

Molly's eyes widened and she put the luggage down, going back to Dana. "Come and sit down. You look awful! Let me get a cold washcloth and some ice. Come on."

Ordinarily, Dana refused any kind of mothering, but right now, Molly's warmth and care were exactly what she needed. "Okay," she agreed. Crossing to the peach-colored couch, she slowly sat down, holding a hand to her head.

"No. Lie down," Molly told her as she removed two small boxes and placed them on the floor. "It's a good thing

Maggie isn't here. She'd hit the roof! You know how she feels about the elderly in this country, always saying they aren't properly taken care of, and all."

A bit of a laugh escaped Dana as she lay down. The couch felt heavenly. "That's one thing we happen to agree on. Knowing Maggie, she'd go hunt down that bastard and clobber him all over again for the old woman *and* me." Maggie was fiercely loyal to those she loved and cared for.

"She would," Molly agreed. Worriedly she watched Dana for a moment. "You really look terrible."

"Thanks, Mol. You're a fountain of good news."

"Back to your black humor again, I see."

"It's saved my tail every time."

"Stay put. I'll get the ice pack."

Wearily, Dana placed her arm across her forehead, still seeing Molly's blond hair framing her oval face and soft features, her hazel eyes filled with worry. Molly had always been the "mother" of their group, caring for Dana and Maggie when they were down-and-out—which wasn't often. She watched her friend, dressed in a pair of pale green cotton shorts and a white blouse, disappear into another room.

Looking around the quiet apartment, Dana thought how beautiful it was compared to the dorm they'd lived in at Annapolis. They had sent Molly ahead to choose something for the three of them. It was the first time Dana had seen it. The walls were an ivory color to match the carpet. Molly had brought her furniture from Boston and it was bamboo with cushions in pastel peaches, plums and pale greens. Soft, quiet colors, Dana thought, like warmhearted, serene Molly.

Closing her eyes, she released a long, ragged sigh. It felt good to relax, to know she was safe again. In a way, Dana really was glad Maggie wasn't here. The Irishwoman's red hair and quick temper would have created instant passion and emotion—two things she'd had plenty of in the past couple of hours. No, she needed Molly's more tranquil personality.

"Here you go." Molly came back and sat down facing Dana. Gently she placed the ice pack over Dana's eye. "Gosh, that looks awful, Dana. Maybe we ought to get you over to the dispensary of Whiting Field and have a doctor look at it."

Grimacing, Dana held the pack firmly against her eye. "No way, Mol. It's going to be tough enough going there tomorrow with this black eye. If I can't get this swelling down enough, the doc might ground me. I don't want to be grounded for a week waiting for this thing to heal. I'd be a week behind my class. That wouldn't bode well for me or my chances of getting my wings."

"You poor dear." Molly pushed strands of black hair away from Dana's forehead.

"You got any old recipes from your grandma Inez for black eyes?" Molly was close with her rich and influential Boston family, particularly her twin brother, Scott, who was confined to a wheelchair for life. Molly loved to cook, and had used old-time remedies from her beloved granny to help the three of them through the cold-and-flu seasons at Annapolis every year.

"Let's see..." Molly glanced around at the stacks of boxes. The room was filled with them. "Grandma Inez put all her remedies in one book. Where did I pack it?"

"Didn't you number your boxes and what was in them?" Dana smiled to herself, loving Molly fiercely. In some ways, she felt Molly was too soft to have graduated from Annapolis, but she had. Did she have the toughness it would take to get her wings?

Her finger on her chin, Molly scowled. "No..."

"Don't worry about it," Dana whispered. "Look, you go ahead and keep unpacking. I'm just going to lie here and regroup, okay?"

"Are you sure? At least let me clean up that arm of yours. It's awful looking."

Dana grinned, though it hurt to do it. "Is *everything* about me 'awful,' Mol?"

Laughing, Molly stood. "Of course not! How many times have you come in looking beat-up like this?"

"Never," Dana agreed. Not since she'd left home at eighteen for Annapolis, she thought, where her father couldn't reach her.

"I'm allowed to be concerned, then. I just unpacked the bathroom stuff. At least we can clean and bandage your arm."

It felt good simply to rest and let Molly take care of her. Dana knew she trusted very few people to do that, but Molly had earned her trust over four long, harsh years at the academy. Besides, wasn't this what the Sisterhood was all about? Hell of a way to test it out, Dana decided wryly.

As she drifted off, almost asleep, Griff's face suddenly appeared before her. Startled, she woke with a jerk.

Molly turned toward her quickly. "Dana? What's wrong?"

Scowling, Dana relaxed back into the cushions. "Uh...nothing."

"You jumped as if someone were attacking you," Molly chided, sitting back down beside Dana. She arranged the gauze, tape and antiseptic on the floor next to the couch.

"It was nothing. I'm just jumpy after that guy hit me at the airport." It wasn't a lie. Dana didn't like evading her friends, but it simply hurt too much to delve into the reasons behind her defensive, wary nature. They'd accepted her without questions, and she was grateful.

As gently as possible, Molly cleaned the long bloody scrapes on Dana's arm. "You've got to be feeling sore and bruised all over. How about if I draw you a hot bath? I think all you can stand right now is bed and rest. Maggie's out

doing the shopping for us. We can continue unpacking tonight without you, Dana. You really need to rest.''

Tears jammed behind Dana's closed eyes. ''Did anyone
ever tell you that you're Florence Nightingale in this incar-
nation?''

Molly laughed softly, daubing the stinging antiseptic
across Dana's arm. ''Same old Dana: teasing even if you feel
rotten.''

''Humor is the only thing that's saved me,'' she told
Molly seriously.

''Teasing aside, want that bath?''

''Yes. I stink.''

''I wasn't going to put it exactly like that.''

''You wouldn't. You're too kind, Mol.''

Giggling, Molly bandaged her arm. ''Maggie would
wrinkle her nose.''

''And roll those big green eyes of hers.''

''She has great body language,'' Molly agreed.

''I feel better already.'' Dana sighed. With her two
friends, she felt a safety she'd never before been able to
achieve. She felt encroaching exhaustion. ''Listen, I think
after a bath, I'm going to crash and burn. Which bedroom
is mine?''

''The last on the left. It has a lovely dusty-rose carpet.
We've already got the beds put together. While you're getting your bath, I'll put sheets and a blanket on it.''

''Thanks.'' Only Molly would notice such details as carpet color. Dana wasn't as attuned to such subtleties as Molly
or Maggie. No. All her sensory abilities centered on her
survival mechanism. Sometimes Dana wished she could ease
her guard and enjoy the things her friends did with such
relish. Her defensive nature had relaxed some, thanks to
them. Still, Dana knew she had a long way to go. She wondered if she'd ever lose her wary attitude toward all men.

After her bath, Dana went straight to her new bedroom.
Her face was aching again. The ice pack had helped tre-

mendously, and as Dana settled into her double bed, Molly brought her a second pack.

"Listen, you sleep all you want. We won't wake you for dinner. Okay?"

Dana put the pack on the pillow and laid her injured cheek against it. "Fine...."

Molly quietly closed the door.

Outside the open window, Dana could hear the cheerful call of birds. Beyond that, she heard airplanes in the distance. She was sure it was the trainers from Whiting Field and nearby Pensacola Naval Air Station. The spring air was humid, and she could smell the ocean in the breeze from the gulf. Just as she slipped into a deep, healing sleep, Griff's face appeared once again. This time, Dana wasn't jerked awake. She lost herself in his dove-gray eyes, which radiated that incredible warmth. For the first time in her life, she had felt safe with a man—a stranger she'd never meet again.

Dana awakened slowly, realizing it was dark in the room. Her head was throbbing, and she sat up groggily, holding her injured, puffy cheek. It felt as if it had grown in size. Damn the man who'd hit her. She took some small satisfaction in the punch Griff had returned. Maybe there was a little justice in this universe.

The door to her bedroom opened quietly. Dana looked up to see Maggie, her long, lean face shadowed by the light spilling into the room from behind her.

"I'm awake," Dana muttered. "Come on in."

Maggie slipped in, worry showing on her face as she came forward. "I was starting to fret about you. It's 2200. Molly kept saying you were just sleeping, but I thought you might have suffered a concussion from that hit you took."

"I've got too hard a head for that." Dana crossed her legs. It hurt to move her head. Maggie sat down facing her. She was wearing a T-shirt and baggy jeans, her shoulder-length red hair mussed. Dana could only admire the strength and confidence that Maggie radiated. She was first-generation Irish, and the youngest of four redheaded daughters who had all entered the various military services. Dana saw the feisty look in Maggie's glittering green eyes.

"I hope like hell you pulverized that jerk who nailed you."

"I didn't have to. Griff did." Dana began telling her the story.

Maggie shook her head after hearing the full account. "I'd like to hunt that bastard down and let him have it, anyway."

Dana grinned. "Your Celtic warrior side is showing again, Maggie."

Nostrils flaring, Maggie growled, "No man has a right to strike a woman or vice versa."

"Is that an old Celtic law?" She loved teasing Maggie, who was intensely proud of her heritage.

"No, that's Maggie's Law."

"Griff took care of him, believe me. I heard the guy's nose crack."

"At least there's consolation in that," Maggie muttered, reaching out and gently patting her knee. "Listen, Molly tore through every box she owned until she found her granny's remedy journal. She's out there in the kitchen right now concocting some god-awful paste that's stinking up the entire apartment. We'll be lucky if the landlord doesn't throw us out for contaminating the atmosphere. He might even call in the Environmental Protection Agency."

It hurt to laugh, but Dana did anyway. "Mol didn't know which box her journal was in."

"I *told* her to index those boxes!"

"I know. But she was more concerned about getting our houseplants down here uninjured." Molly had driven her sensible station wagon loaded with plants and breakable items to make sure they arrived in good shape. She didn't trust moving vans.

Maggie smiled fondly, looking toward the open door. "If she wins her wings, I think we ought to call her Mom or Mother." Every pilot who graduated came out of flight school with a nickname that stayed with him or her forever.

Dana's smile disappeared. "I worry about her, Maggie. Everything we've heard about flight school being twenty times more demanding than the academy worries me."

Maggie snorted. "I'm worried for myself, too. At the grocery store I bumped into a sixth-week student from Pensacola. He told me ninety percent of his class had already been washed out."

"Wow!" Dana clenched her fist. She had to make it!

"I'm just glad the three of us are going into this together."

"Yeah. Misery loves company."

Grinning, Maggie got up. "You're feeling better, I can tell. You're back to your usual pessimistic sense of humor."

Dana slowly got off the bed, feeling a bit light-headed. Maggie came to her side and slipped her arm around her shoulders.

"I know...you can make it on your own," Maggie chided, leading her toward the door. "But suffer my help, Dana. You look like hell."

"Thanks."

The bright light hurt Dana's good eye. Her other eye was swollen shut. She bowed her head and allowed Maggie's lanky frame to offer partial support. "This hasn't been one of the better days of my life."

"Don't we know it. Come on, let's go out to the kitchen where Dr. Molly is stirring up her brew. I wonder if you have to drink it? The cure may be worse than the black eye."

It hurt to grin, but Dana couldn't help it. The kitchen was huge, with a highly polished light green tile floor. Molly was working furiously over the stove, a white apron wrapped around her tall figure. The apron looked funny with the short shorts she was wearing, but Dana didn't comment, realizing it might hurt Molly's sensitive nature.

"Oh, good, you're up! I found my grandma's journal!"

"Yeah..." Dana sat down very carefully at the table, her legs feeling a bit unstable. Maggie stood at her shoulder, concern on her face. "I'm okay, Maggie. Go sit down."

"Naw, I'm going to get the camera for this one. This goes in our Sisterhood scrapbook: How To Help An Injured Sister."

"Don't you dare!" Dana gave Maggie her best glare.

Grinning, Maggie turned and left the kitchen.

"This won't be so bad," Molly soothed, bringing the pan over to the table. She set it on a hot pad. Wiping her damp brow with the back of her hand, she smiled. "It smells awful, but I'm sure it will help."

Dana eyed the mixture in the bottom of the pan. "Good God, Mol, that stuff smells *horrible!*"

"Well...it's a mixture of horse liniment, crushed comfrey leaves and—"

"Don't tell me any more. It probably contains eye of newt and tail of frog."

"Oh, no! They're just herbs, Dana. Grandma wasn't a witch. She was a healer all her life. You have to smear it all over the swollen part of your face," she explained apologetically. "Grandma said it will reduce swelling in twelve hours or less."

"It better," Dana growled, holding her nose. "I'll put it on myself. Is it hot?"

"No, just warm." Molly sat down, watching eagerly.

Maggie appeared at the entrance to the kitchen, camera in hand. Dana glared at her. Maggie laughed.

"If you *ever* show these pictures to anyone, you're dead meat, Donovan. Got that?"

"Roger, read you loud and clear."

Molly groaned. "You two! You're always threatening each other. Aren't you ever going to stop?"

Dana carefully dipped her fingers into the black mixture. It felt like slimy glue. "Our friendship's based upon mutual irritation," she told Molly.

"Go on," Maggie urged, waiting impatiently to click the camera, "put that stuff on your face, Coulter!"

"Ugh! Molly, this smell's enough to kill a person!"

"I'm sorry, Dana."

Muttering under her breath, Dana spread the ointment across her cheek. The smell was horrendous. "God, I'm going to get better just from the smell alone."

Maggie giggled and the camera flashed.

"By morning, the swelling ought to be down quite a bit, and your eye will be open," Molly said enthusiastically.

"I can't show up for flight school with my eye closed," Dana complained sourly. She applied the mixture liberally. "If this works, I'll kiss your granny's grave, Molly. But if it doesn't, I'll come looking for you."

"Oh, dear...."

Dana instantly felt contrite. Molly's flushed face showed genuine distress. "I didn't mean it," she denied quickly. To prove it, Dana slathered more of the goo across the injured area.

"How's it feel?" Maggie called, taking advantage of another photo opportunity.

Dana shrugged. "Surprisingly, it feels pretty good. There's heat in it."

"That's the horse liniment. My grandma said it was good for everything."

Dana knew the liniment contained a stimulant to increase blood circulation. That in itself should reduce swelling. "I feel better already, Mol. Thanks." A good night's sleep would ready her for tomorrow's first grueling day at Whiting Field. Her stomach clenched with fear. It was a familiar feeling, and Dana didn't respond to it. All three of them had butterflies in their stomachs. What would tomorrow bring? As Dana smeared the last of the paste on her face, she wondered if she would dream about Griff again tonight, when she closed her eyes.

Griff awoke in a foul humor. He'd cut himself shaving, having refused to look into what he knew were bloodshot eyes. Dreams had kept his sleep restless. The first half of the night his mind had run over and over Toby's unexpected death and the funeral Griff had attended yesterday. Near morning, unwilling thoughts of Dana, of all things, had filled his head.

Irritably, Griff turned on the shower. He threw the disposable razor into the wastebasket and stripped off his light blue pajama bottoms. The material pooled around his feet, and he kicked the pajamas aside. *Dana.* The word echoed gently in his heart. Tendrils of warmth flowed through him, and he savored the wonderful feeling her name evoked. Absently, Griff rubbed his chest. Since his divorce, he hadn't felt much of anything except anger, frustration and loneliness. And realizing that the healing process must take place first, he hadn't been much interested in women, either.

As he stepped into the hot, steamy shower, Griff closed his eyes, allowing the water to wash the stench from his body. He'd awakened last night sweating heavily, replaying Toby's crash in his mind. Grabbing the soap, he scrubbed himself savagely, trying to escape the numbness that came with thoughts of Toby.

There would be no familiar phone call from his friend this morning. Griff was an acknowledged grump in the morning, and Toby often called to cheer him up as he drank his first cup of coffee. *No more.* As he shut his eyes and allowed the water to hit his face, Griff saw Dana's face dance before him. Miraculously, the pressure in his chest disappeared and the tightness gripping his heart eased. Shaking his head like a dog coming out of water, Griff turned off the faucets and allowed the water to drip from him.

How could a woman he didn't even know take away his grief? An awful numbness that inhabited him since he'd been notified of the accident, and his recent dislike of women had soared alongside his grief over Toby's loss. Over the past five days, he'd tasted real anger toward women. It was unreasonable, Griff knew, but he couldn't help himself. Maybe it was the divorce, compounded with Toby's death. He wasn't sure of anything anymore. His emotions felt raw and shredded.

After toweling dry, Griff stepped out of the bathroom and pulled a clean one-piece flight suit from his bedroom dresser drawer. Dana came back to his thoughts. She wasn't beautiful. No, she had an arresting face; and her huge blue eyes were her finest feature. Pressing the Velcro closed on his flight suit, Griff sat down on the bed and pulled on his dark blue cotton socks. Next came his highly polished flight boots, shining like mirrors. They weren't patent leather like what a lot of the IPs had. Griff lovingly and carefully shined the leather for hours with polish—the old-fashioned way; the way it was done before patent leather invaded the military.

Sitting on the huge king-size bed, Griff looked around, feeling the awful silence that seemed to sit heavily in his chest. His hands on his long thighs, he stared toward the hall. Funny, even after six months, he missed Carol. Well, maybe not her, but their routine. Griff missed waking up with a woman's warmth beside him and having her make him breakfast before he left for Whiting Field at 0630.

Frowning, he stood, automatically checking to make sure his name tag was in place over his left pocket, his IP badge over his right. Locating a bunch of pens on top of the dresser, he shoved several into the upper-left sleeve pocket of his uniform. His stomach growled, but somehow he wasn't really hungry. When his mother died, the same thing had happened. His father back in Jerome, Arizona, was still alive and healthy. All his other pilot friends were alive—a feat in itself, considering the extreme hazards of fighter-jet duty. Toby had been the first casualty he knew personally.

As he picked up his briefcase and opened the front door to face the apricot sunrise on the horizon, Griff wondered who his next three students would be. Maybe one out of the three would get past his demanding teaching methods. Today, there was no enthusiasm in his stride down the concrete walk. Griff barely saw the pink-and-white oleander bushes that hid his tan bungalow from the quiet street of homes that surrounded him. He felt only a terrible heaviness in his heart, and he had no desire even to get to Whiting Field in time for the 0700 IP meeting. The only thing that told him he was still alive, still capable of feeling, was thinking of Dana.

As he unlocked his car door and got in, Griff allowed her face to remain with him—her short pixie-style black hair, the small earlobes graced with tiny pearls. Everything about her shouted exquisite refinement. How could someone who appeared fragile be so damned bold, stepping into the path of a crazed thief? he wondered. Shaking his head, Griff started up the Corvette. Somehow, he had to see Dana again. It was a crazy thought. Crazy! Anger welled within him at the thought of women—yet her face, her presence, had given him an island of peace within his shattered world. How could that be?

Nervously, Dana stood with Maggie and Molly among twenty-five other students. They had been processed and taken to the ready room at Whiting Field. Accustomed to the often hostile stares of the male students, Dana internalized her dread. They had all been assigned to VT2 upon arrival, and Maggie had discovered that VT2 had the highest washout rate of the three student squadrons. Molly had ferreted out that an 03, Lieutenant D. G. Turcotte, had the highest washout rate of the seven VT2 instructors. He was called the Turk, Molly had told them in a tense voice.

God, let me have a good instructor, Dana thought. She sat with Maggie on her right, Molly on her left. Because Dana was so small, her olive-green flight suit fit sloppily. It would have to be taken in, the sleeves and pant legs shortened considerably. For now, Dana had rolled them into thick wads at her wrists and ankles. With her clownlike garb and glorious black eye, she was painfully aware of being the center of attention. Thanks to Molly's grandmother's recipe, though, her eye was opening this morning, and the swelling somewhat reduced from the night before.

"Here he comes!" Maggie whispered, nodding to the left. A door on the stage opened.

Dana's heart began a slow pound. She swallowed convulsively. There were twenty-eight students. Each instructor would be given three to teach for the first six weeks. *If* a student managed a passing grade of 2.0, then he or she would have different flight instructors for the remaining nine weeks of training. Word was out that these six-week IPs made or broke the student. Only one out of ten students went on to become a Navy pilot. Dana felt dampness in her armpits as she watched Commander Hager walk confidently toward the podium at the center of the stage. He was dressed in his tan uniform, the gold wings glinting above his left breast pocket proclaiming that he was a naval aviator.

"Good morning. Here are the flight-student and instructor-pilot assignments. Ensigns Wilson, Dunlop and Coulter to Lieutenant D. G. Turcotte."

Dana gasped softly. Molly gripped her hand, giving her a sad-eyed look. Maggie's full mouth pursed.

"Lieutenant Turcotte's students will report to him in room 303 at the administration building in the following order and time. Ensign Coulter, 0900. You will fly at 0700 every other day, Monday through Friday."

Trying to still her panic, Dana wrote down the information. She had the Turk, the 03 with the highest washout rate at Whiting. What had she done to deserve this? It was 0800. There would be an hour's briefing, and then all students would be dismissed to go about their respective duties. Her mind whirled with questions and haunting fear. Was Turcotte a woman hater? Was he like a lot of the Annapolis grads who thought women couldn't hack it, or make good military officers?

Molly's hazel eyes were wide with silent sympathy. She leaned over to Dana. "Hang in there. Maybe he'll consider you something special."

Dana shook her head. "I'll just bet he will," she whispered back. What would Turcotte think? Dana had to care, because suddenly her dream of a flight career hung precariously upon this stranger's thoughts and feelings.

Griff stared disbelievingly at the assigned student list that had been given to him by Sergeant Johnson. "Danielle Marie Coulter, Ensign" stared back at him. He dropped the paper on his desk.

"Ray!" he roared from his office. The black yeoman third-class appeared at the doorway.

"Yes, sir?"

"What the hell is going on here?"

"Sir?"

"You've made a typing error. There's no way I'm taking on one of those women student pilots."

Johnson shrugged apologetically. "Sir, Chief Yeoman Tracer gave me the list earlier. I know how you feel about it, and when I saw the assignment I asked the chief if it wasn't a mistake. She said no."

Griff got to his feet, grabbed the paper and shouldered past the yeoman. There had to be a mistake! Striding down the long, narrow hall toward Captain Ramsey's office, Griff had to control his raging feelings. Ramsey knew he had no use for women in the military world. Over the years, Griff had softened his view somewhat, but had remained adamant that flying a military aircraft was a man's job. Besides, how he felt about women right now made him rabid about not accepting Coulter.

Captain Burt Ramsey was leaning over his yeoman's desk, giving her instructions, when Griff stepped into the outer office.

"Morning, Griff," Ramsey said.

"Sir. May I have a few words in private with you?" Griff remained stiffly at attention. He was shaking inside.

"Certainly. Come on in."

Making sure the door was closed so the yeoman couldn't overhear, Griff stood at parade rest in front of the captain's highly polished maple desk. Ramsey, a fifty-five-year-old officer, sat down. Folding his hands on the desk, he looked up at Griff.

"What's on your mind?"

Trying to steady his hand, Griff thrust the assignment paper toward him. "This, sir."

"Those are your assignments for the next six weeks."

"I know, sir. But—there's a woman in there."

"I'm aware of that," Ramsey replied coolly.

Struggling for self-control, Griff bit out, "Sir, I respectfully request that Ensign Coulter be reassigned. I don't believe a woman can be a good pilot of a military aircraft. My best friend was just killed by a woman student pilot over at Pensacola. I—"

"Lieutenant, I feel Ensign Coulter has what it takes to be with the best instructor at Whiting. That's you. You're tough and exacting. Her grade point at Annapolis was a straight 4.0. That's a rarity in itself. Take a look at her file, and I think you'll agree, she's fine material to work with. The Secretary of Defense is getting pressured to put more women in flight slots. We need P3 pilots badly. If she can handle your instruction, then I feel we have a candidate for the antisubmarine-warfare squadrons that are low in pilot manpower—er, person power."

Despair ripped through Griff. "But, sir—"

"Ensign Coulter is your student, Lieutenant. And despite your personal prejudice, which needs work anyway, you are to treat her just like any male student assigned to you. Is that understood?"

Griff tensed. A lot of responses went through his head, but the only wise answer was "Yes, sir."

"I don't want to hear Coulter smacking us with a sexual-prejudice lawsuit, either."

His heart sank. Ramsey expected him to railroad her out of flight school. Well, wasn't that what he'd planned to do if forced to take her? "I'll treat her like any student assigned to me, sir."

Ramsey nodded. "Good. Dismissed, Lieutenant."

"Yes, sir." Wearily Griff turned on his heel and left the office. Outside in the hall, he slowed his pace, wrestling with an incredible avalanche of feelings. A woman had killed Toby. Coulter could kill him. Women didn't have good judgment in times of emergency. Carol fell apart under the most trivial circumstances. She had always cried and clung to him.

Rubbing his brow, Griff headed back to his small office. Glancing at his watch, he saw he had exactly half an hour before Coulter reported to him. It would give him the necessary time to bone up on her file. No doubt she'd be a lot like Carol: appearing strong on the surface, but internally flawed and weak, needing a man to tell her how to run things or make decisions.

Yeoman Johnson already had placed Coulter's file on his desk. Reluctantly, Griff opened the thick folder. He nearly came unhinged at her physical statistics: five foot two, one hundred pounds and only twenty-two years old. She was too small to wrestle the weight of a screaming, out-of-control jet! His anger mounted as he continued to peruse Coulter's file. In her plebe year—the first year as an underclassman—Coulter had won the right to carry the company colors. Who had she twisted around her finger to get that plum?

Academically, Coulter appeared to be brilliant. She excelled at mathematics and computers and earned a degree in aeronautical engineering. On the Annapolis swim team, she'd been first in freestyle and butterfly. She'd been appointed team captain in her third year at Annapolis, and under her guidance, the team had tacked up impressive wins over the next two years.

Griff wasn't impressed. He slammed the folder shut, shoving it away. "That doesn't mean you have hands, sweetheart. You might be good in the water, but air is an entirely different matter." "Hands" was the term used for an individual's feel for a plane. To have good flight hands meant possessing a natural knack with the aircraft and flying. Griff raised his head when Johnson gave a brief knock and stuck his head inside the office door.

"Ensign Coulter's here to see you, sir."

Girding himself, Griff growled, "Send her in, Johnson."

"Yes, sir."

Dana sat on a long wooden bench in the hall with several other student pilots. They were all nervous. The man nearest her, Ensign Manning, a fellow Annapolis grad, shook his head.

"I hear you got a screamer, Coulter."

Dana frowned. "A screamer?"

"Yeah. Word's gone 'round that the Turk's a screamer. You know, he yells at you constantly in the cockpit."

Dana's throat got a little tighter. "I'll take it one day at a time." One hour at a time. First, she had to get past this initial interview. Ever since high school when she'd found out that the Navy pilots were considered the best in the world, Dana had dreamed of becoming one of them. Flying, for her, meant having the unshackled freedom of an eagle.

To sail above the earth meant to sail over the misery that would meet her once she landed. No. Getting her wings was the most important goal she'd ever set for herself. And she'd win those wings—with or without the Turk's help.

Manning shrugged. "Sorry you got such rotten luck. I wouldn't wish the Turk on my best enemy."

Dana managed a laugh, although it still hurt to smile. Her eye had nearly swollen closed again. "I'm known for my rotten luck, Manny. I'll just persevere like I always do." When they'd first met Manny at Annapolis, he'd hated the three women; but later, as part of Dana's freestyle swim team, he'd been won over by her physical abilities. In the last year, Manny had become their staunch supporter.

"What do you think will happen when he sees that black eye?"

"He'll probably think I started a barroom brawl somewhere and had it coming," Dana muttered.

Manny shook his head. "You're something else, Coulter. A sense of humor even as you walk into the jaws of death."

Dana saw Sergeant Johnson crook his finger in her direction. Time to meet the dreaded Turk. She grinned as she rose, smoothing at the wrinkles in her too-large flight suit. "My black humor has gotten me this far, Manny." If only it could get her successfully past this interview.

"Break a leg," he whispered.

As Dana walked down the long, polished passageway, she wondered if the Turk would try to break her spirit as a way of washing her out. Nervously she wiped her damp palms against her thighs. Johnson opened the door, giving her a slight smile that she read as encouragement.

"Go right on in, Ms. Coulter. Lieutenant Turcotte is waiting."

"Thanks," she said. Dana moved around the door and closed it quietly. The small office was filled with bookshelves. Behind the massive oak desk sat a man, his head bent, studying what might be her file. Sweat popped out on her upper lip. Dana faced him and prepared to snap to attention. But before she could, he raised his head. A gasp escaped her.

"You!" she croaked. *Griff.* Dana saw the shock in his eyes. He was no less stunned than she. Her defenses shattered as his gray eyes momentarily thawed from ice to smoldering heat. Then, just as quickly, they hardened again. Off balance, Dana stood, her lips parted, words deserting her. How could Griff be the dreaded Turk? This man, his words, his incredibly gentle touch on her shoulder, had been anything but threatening at the airport.

Griff stared up at her in utter disbelief. She stood helplessly, her hands open in a gesture of peace toward him. "Dana?"

"I—yes, it's me. But—you said your name was Griff."

He stared down at the file, a gamut of emotions colliding within his heart. "Griff is my middle name. Your file said Danielle Coulter."

"Yes," she choked out. "But I've always been called Dana. No one calls me Danielle."

Angrily, Griff noticed his hand tremble slightly over the file. Of all the tricks to be played on him! Her left eye was nearly swollen shut, her entire cheek black-and-blue. A huge part of him wanted simply to get up and hold her. She had to be in constant pain from that injury. Her eyes were huge, and he could read the shock in them. He was sure his IP reputation was foremost in her mind. She was probably trying to reconcile it with the man who'd helped her capture the thief at the airport.

Dana watched as the care that had again surfaced in his dove-gray eyes dissolved. Automatically she snapped to attention, tucking her chin against her chest. "Ensign Coulter reporting as ordered, sir."

Griff wanted to curse so badly he could taste it. Life was one lousy joke after another. Dana's face, once open and readable, was now closed, showing no expression at all. Griff reminded himself that she was a ring knocker, an Annapolis grad, one of the elite few. She was tougher than most women, he told himself, but still a cream puff underneath it all.

Slowly rising, Griff glowered at her. As much as he wanted to stop himself, stop the anger from boiling up and out of him, he couldn't. "Remain at attention, Miss Coulter!" he snapped at her, and rounded the desk. His nostrils flared as he approached her. Griff waited to see her melt, but she remained unwavering beneath his towering scrutiny. She was such a small, helpless thing! He was six foot three, casting an ominous shadow across her.

"All right," he rasped, watching as her eyes remained fixed straight ahead. "This is the end of the line for you or any other woman who thinks she can take it to become a Navy pilot." Griff stalked around her, his hands behind his back. "You might be real special back in Annapolis, Miss Coulter, but here, you're nothing more than a plebe. I break men who think they've got what it takes to fly a Navy jet. They come in here cocky and full of confidence. After two or three weeks with me, they wash out."

Dana froze inside. Griff's deep voice was like a chain saw cutting into her heart and her barricaded soul. If only she hadn't seen his human side! He threw his words at her like a glove in a duel. The hatred in his voice was real, further eating away at her normal defensive array. Anguish soared within Dana. She had to forget the human named Griff. This was the Turk, the IP who wanted her washed out. He circled her like an eagle ready to strike at her, the quarry. Her mouth flattening, Dana rapped out, "Sir, I'll do my best to earn your respect behind the stick."

Turcotte glared at her. Her voice was firm, but lined with grating resolve. "These next six weeks are a survival school, Coulter."

"Survival is one thing I'm very good at, sir."

Taken aback, Griff moved around the desk, putting it between them. He'd had students cower like whipped dogs by the time he'd finished his initial briefing, but Dana showed absolutely no fear of him. She seemed to gather strength from his assault on her confidence. Opening his mouth to retort, Griff suddenly remembered her sitting on the concrete sidewalk at the airport, a rueful, almost painful smile on her mouth as she'd told him it wasn't the first time she'd had a black eye. God, what a mess!

"I don't tolerate tardiness, Coulter."

"I'd be late for a flight only if I were dead, sir."

"Women can't take the punishment of flying."

"I don't accept that, sir."

"You will," he ground out softly.

Dana pinned him with an equally frosty gaze. "I know what prejudice is all about, Lieutenant. You don't like me because I'm a woman. Fine. You've drawn the battle lines."

Griff stared at her, nonplussed. What a hellion. "If you were a man, I might be impressed with your guts in standing up to me."

"If I were a man, you wouldn't be giving me this speech," Dana retorted coldly. His gray eyes turned black as a thunderstorm. A part of her cried inside at the loss of the Griff who had been so gentle with her and the old woman at the airport.

"You're wrong, Ensign. Every student that enters that door leaves knowing I'm intent on only one thing: failing you. You either have what it takes to stay in the kitchen and take the heat I'll turn up on you, or you get out. I don't want to be flying with any student of mine someday, unsure if he's got what it takes when the chips are down in combat."

"I'd say this is combat right now," Dana whispered.

"As close as you'll ever get to it, Ensign."

The gauntlet had been flung. A sharp pain shot through Dana. Griff was turning out like so many other military officers she'd run into during her four years in the Navy. It would do no good to continue lobbing verbal grenades at each other. What was going to count was her performance in the cockpit of the single-engine trainer.

As always, Dana knew she would retreat to that safe place deep within herself when things got unbearable. It was a survival tool learned through years of painful experience. To everyone else, she would appear calm, cool and collected. Like swimming, retreating deep within herself meant safety.

"What time do I report for flight duty, sir?"

Griff stood, his hands on his hips, and watched her. With that swollen left eye she'd have trouble seeing. If she were a man, he'd send her to sick bay to get a chit until the eye was properly healed. Making her start in this condition didn't give her a fair chance. Even as he thought it, though, his anger at women—and this no-win situation—surfaced. "Be at the ready room at 0800 tomorrow morning, Coulter. And be ready to fly."

"Yes, sir." Dana made an about-face and marched to the door. She opened it and stepped out into the passageway. After shutting the door behind her, she leaned against it momentarily. Fortunately no one was around to see her lapse of military protocol. Straightening, she absently touched her throbbing cheek, then placed the garrison cap on her head. Next stop was the bookstore where she'd pick up an armload of texts. When she wasn't flying during the next fourteen weeks, she would be taking part in grueling academic sessions, learning about aerodynamics and meteorology.

As she left the administration building and walked the palm-tree-lined route to the bookstore, Dana couldn't ignore her emotions. Somehow, she had to get Griff out of her mind and heart! The man at the airport had been a sham. The Turk was the real man—the bastard out to make her fail at any cost. He hated women encroaching on his male-dominated world. Fine. She'd withstood the men at the academy who'd wanted her to fail. But there was a difference here: her flight grades for the next six weeks rested entirely in Griff's hands. She knew if she dropped below a 2.0 grade, a Board of Inquiry would be called. Rumor had it that any student with two "Boards" was washed out automatically—whatever the reasons.

Dana ignored the other students hurrying to the bookstore or to flight interviews with their new instructors. If Griff chose to wield his prejudice against her even if she was flying adequately, Dana would be in trouble. And it would be so easy for him to do—his word against hers. He was an 03, a first lieutenant, while she was an 01, an ensign, the bottom rung on the officers' ladder. No one would take her word for anything. And if she cried prejudice or sexual discrimination, they'd laugh her out of school.

Grimly Dana swung into the bookstore and pulled a list from the thigh pocket of her flight suit. Griff seemed very sure she wouldn't make the grade. Well, she would do everything in her power to fly—and fly well. Still, Dana couldn't erase the memory of Griff's soft gray eyes filled with concern. If she could forget that episode, she could easily bring up her defenses and weather his hatred of her. Maybe Molly or Maggie would have some sage advice; both of them seemed to have more understanding of men than Dana did. After all, her one relationship had been built on lies and was a proven disaster.

"So," Dana ended tiredly, "that's the whole story on Turcotte."

Maggie leaned back in the cushioned, bamboo chair, putting her feet up on the small stool. "You can tell you don't have any Irish blood in you to give you some luck."

"Worse, she saw his good side," added Molly, sitting cross-legged on the floor next to Maggie's chair.

Dana studied Molly. Her blond hair was shoulder length, the ends softly curling around her oval features. Molly had always worn her heart on her sleeve and was tremendously sensitive to others. Dana held her understanding gaze. "That's the worst part of this. If I hadn't seen Griff in action at the airport, I could handle how he sees me now."

"Jekyll and Hyde," Maggie muttered defiantly, brushing some auburn strands off her brow. "He obviously hates women."

"I don't think so," Molly objected. "He didn't treat Dana like that at the airport."

"No, he was solicitous and—" Dana chewed on her lower lip for a moment, almost unable to say the word.

"What?" Molly prodded.

"Gentle."

Maggie smiled. "There *are* a few men who have that quality, Dana. I know you don't believe it, but there are."

"That's why I need your advice. You've both had positive relationships with men." Maggie's father adored her and his three other daughters. He was a warm, caring man, as Dana had discovered firsthand on a trip home with Maggie one time. Molly's father was cooler and more aloof, favoring Scott, his son, over her. Nevertheless, Molly's father was a vast improvement over Frank Coulter, as far as Dana was concerned.

Dressed in comfortable jeans and a lavender tank top, Maggie balanced a book on aeronautics on her lap, and held a glass of lemonade in one hand. It was six in the evening—their second evening together at the new apartment. "They aren't all ogres," Maggie said. "If the Turk was nice at the airport and a bastard at base, something isn't jibing."

"I think he hates all women," Dana muttered.

"No," Molly protested. "Maybe just women in the military. You know: the same old male prejudice about us bringing down their last bastion or some such crock."

"That's another thing," Maggie added. "Why didn't he send you to sick bay to get a chit until your eye heals properly?"

"Because he wants me to wash out fast." Dana touched her eye gingerly. Molly had made up a new batch of her granny's recipe and it still coated the injury, somewhat reducing the swelling.

"After all," Molly said thoughtfully, "the guy didn't have to get involved with that thief...."

Dana gave Molly a sour look. "*You* be his student, then."

Grinning, Molly stood and leaned over Dana, putting her arm around her. "Maybe, with time, Turcotte will soften up about you. We know you have what it takes to get your wings. Look at your academy record!"

"You're such an idealist," Maggie drawled. "My mother would swear you were bucking for sainthood."

With a laugh, Molly hugged and released Dana. "I know, but you gals tolerate me anyway."

"Well," Dana said glumly, giving her best friends a warm look, "at least you two have decent instructors."

Maggie nodded. "Let's take this one day at a time with Turcotte. I think the first thing you ought to do is get over to the doctor and have him evaluate whether you're up to a first flight or not with that eye."

It was sound advice. Dana knew she'd need every advantage, and her eyesight was precious. "I'll do it tomorrow morning before I report to the ready room. I'm not going to let Griff sandbag me."

"Good girl!" Maggie crowed. "Fight back! It's the only thing Turcotte understands or respects."

Chapter Three

Griff was in his office the next morning at 0600. His conscience had kept him awake most of the night. Yeoman Johnson had wisely made coffee early when he saw Griff stalk into the building, and had it on Griff's desk ten minutes later. After taking a gulp of the scalding hot brew, Griff ordered Johnson to call sick bay.

"You want to talk to Dr. Collins?"

Griff refused to look up from his paperwork. Collins was the flight surgeon. "Yes."

"To look at Ensign Coulter's eye?"

Frowning, Griff nodded. It was amazing how Johnson seemed able to read his mind. "When Coulter arrives at the station, have her report to Dr. Collins. Tell him I want to know whether she can be put on flight status."

"Yes, sir."

Griff looked up at the smile he could swear he heard in Johnson's voice. The yeoman had already turned and was heading out the door. At least his conscience had stopped needling him, Griff thought. Collins would probably put Dana on flight waivers for at least three or four days. Her black eye was serious, and he knew it would interfere with her flying.

Angry at himself, he slammed the pen down on the papers and glared around his small office. *Dana.* Why couldn't he think of her as Coulter? Last names were generic, less intimate. She was a woman. And women meant nothing but trouble in his book. And he sure as hell wasn't going to wind up like Toby—dying in the rear seat of a cockpit because a woman screwed up on a flight. No way.

Dana couldn't contain her surprise when the corps Wave at the dispensary picked up an order with her name already on it.

"Lieutenant Turcotte has ordered you to see Dr. Collins, the flight surgeon. He has concern that your left eye will interfere with your ability to fly, ma'am."

Nodding, Dana took a seat in the crowded dispensary, waiting her turn. So Griff had ordered her to see Collins. As she sat, hands clasped in her lap, she wrestled with her feelings. Why hadn't he sent her over here yesterday? With a sigh, Dana realized that even if Griff had an impersonal hatred of her because she was a woman, he had a streak of decency, too. Another part of her worried that being put on flight waivers upon her arrival at Whiting might look bad on her record.

Looking around, she studied the other waiting student pilots. They all looked frightened. Some moved around nervously, crossing and uncrossing their legs. Others wiped sweat from their faces. Others sat stoically, their eyes dark with fear. Fear, Dana wondered, of what? Flying? Possibly failing? Maggie had told her last night that the big illness going around Whiting Field was gastroenteritis—a stomachache. She'd heard from a tenth-week student that the dispensary was always filled to capacity early in the morning with students who were afraid to face their instructors or a grueling flight test.

Well, it wasn't going to happen to her, Dana decided. As soon as she saw Dr. Collins, she'd be sitting on the Turk's doorstep, letting him know she wasn't afraid of him, of that trainer or of flying with him. This was only the first skirmish in a long six-week war, as far as Dana was concerned. And she wasn't going to let him win round one.

Griff heard a firm knock at his office door. He'd just gotten off the phone with Dr. Collins, who had put Dana on flight waivers for an entire week. Part of him was relieved. He had to admit that another part of him wanted to see her; but that was a stupid and immature reaction.

"Enter," he growled. His next student, Ted Dunlop, wasn't scheduled until 1030. He had the whole morning to catch up on the unending paper chase that crossed his desk daily.

Dana stepped into Griff's office and came to attention in front of his desk. She didn't dare look at him. "Ensign Coulter reporting for duty, sir."

Griff sat back, stunned. This morning her flight uniform fit her a little better. It was obvious she'd trimmed the sleeves and pant legs and done quite a bit of sewing last night, but she still looked small and vulnerable in the olive-green uniform. He shoved back his response.

"What the hell are you doing here? Dr. Collins put you on flight waivers, Coulter."

"I may be on flight waivers, sir, but that doesn't stop me from learning what I can on the ground. I don't like missing a week of flying."

"This just goes to prove my previous point. Women can't take it. You're weak, Coulter, and that's why you were placed on waivers."

Dana glared down at him. Ordinarily, Griff should have told her to move to parade rest, but he hadn't. Standing at attention for a long time was tiring, but she wasn't going to say anything. "Women *aren't* weak, *sir*."

Griff reared back in his chair and held her blazing blue gaze. "The hell they aren't."

"The injury to my eye prevents me from flying only," Dana hurled back at him.

"I wonder what it will be next, Coulter?"

"There won't be anything else."

Griff managed a twisted smile. "Bet me."

"Any amount you want, *sir*."

He measured her for a long moment, the silence growing brittle. "Women, by nature are weak, Ensign."

"Where I come from, they're strong and capable, sir. I guess you just haven't run into any of my kind."

With a snort, Griff got to his feet. How he wanted to throw down the red flag of war and surrender to those defiant blue eyes. Dana's mouth... Sweet heaven, Griff thought. What would it be like to mold those lips to his and taste her fiery response? And then he remembered Carol, who had appeared so capable and independent, too—at first.

"Ensign, you've got nothing to do but get well. Now get out of here."

Dana stubbornly remained. "It's 0800, Lieutenant. Can't you at least walk me around and introduce me to the trainer? I can read up on the manuals while I'm recuperating. I'm not an invalid, you know."

Pleased with her response, Griff shrugged. "A walk-around? You're picking up the lingo fast, Coulter."

Moving into a parade-rest position, hands behind her back, Dana continued to meet his stormy gray gaze. "Give me half a chance to prove myself, Mr. Turcotte, and I'll earn my wings."

For a moment Griff almost believed her. "Come with me, Dana—er, Coulter. If you want to play at learning how to fly, I'll go along with your game."

Throttling her anger, Dana followed him out of the office. As they left admin, she noticed the pink dawn on the horizon for the first time. Whiting Field was small, she had heard, in comparison to the Pensacola air station where most of the student flying was conducted. Both sat on the Gulf of Mexico, in Florida's panhandle. Still, the airport had six runways, a large, glass-enclosed control tower and a number of barracks that housed students and personnel alike. She was glad that she and Maggie and Molly had an apartment off station.

"Why do you use the word *play,* Lieutenant?" Dana lengthened her short stride to keep up with Griff. He towered over her, his shoulders thrown back with pride. Despite his arrogance, she would never forget his actions at the airport.

"Women play at everything. Life's a game with them, Coulter. I'm sure you know that."

"No, sir, I don't know that. I take my commitment to the Navy seriously."

"Yeah, a six-year commitment. You'll probably snag a higher-grade officer, get married and end up with a brood of kids and quit."

"Barefoot and pregnant?"

Griff heard the steel in her lowered tone. "Isn't that the goal of every woman, Coulter? A husband with a big fat paycheck? Security?" That had been Carol's aim, she had confided timidly the day she'd asked for a divorce.

"I wouldn't be here if that were my goal, Lieutenant."

With a harsh laugh, Griff headed onto the tarmac after flashing his security badge at the gate guard. In front of them were five neat lines of parked aircraft, six to each row. The trainers had been serviced and checked the night before by teams of hardworking enlisted mechanics, and now were ready for their demanding flight schedule for the coming day.

Griff looked for tail number 13115, his trainer. It sat at the end of row three. Glancing down, he noticed Dana's alertness. Her eyes roved restlessly, and she didn't seem to miss much. It was one thing he looked for in a prospective student. Alertness could save a student's life—and his, too.

Halting, Griff stood in front of the trainer. "This is 13115, Coulter. My plane. A walk-around consists of checking out the external surfaces of the aircraft. You're to look for possible hydraulic leaks under the wings, check the ailerons, rudders and elevators to make sure they work properly." Griff moved in a counterclockwise circle around the trainer, pointing here and there. "The student is responsible for the walk-around. The crew chief on this plane is AVM Parker, and he'll present you with the discrepancy book on it. You're to look at it, see if everything's been repaired and sign it off after the visual inspection." Griff pinned her with a dark look. "Failure to do so leads to an automatic Board."

"You don't have to look so happy about it, Mr. Turcotte. I'm not going to fail to sign off the discrepancy log."

With a grimace, he muttered, "I'll believe that when I see it. But then, you won't be making it past six weeks with me, anyway. I'll bet you fall apart on me within the first week, Coulter."

Dana held his glare. "You really believe that, don't you?" What made Griff feel so strongly about women? It was on the tip of her tongue to ask, but she decided not to—at least, not right now. Some of Griff's surliness had disappeared as he'd gotten out on the flight line. Even now, a new eagerness and excitement in his eyes had replaced the brooding glare he normally had around her.

"In my experience, Coulter, women pretend they're strong until the chips are down. Then they fall apart, expecting a man to pick up the pieces." He halted at the tail of the plane, placing his hands on his hips. "Well, I'm going to let you prove it to me all over again."

It hurt to grin, but Dana did anyway. "Obviously your experience is limited, Lieutenant. I'll show you differently."

"No way."

Dana didn't respond, instead allowing Griff to teach her all he could from the ground. If she didn't know better, she'd think he seemed perversely pleased by her incessant questions after the walk-around. She took notes, opened her walk-around manual, and asked more questions.

With a pang, Dana wished that she could climb into the cockpit, as other students and instructors were doing right now.

Griff saw the longing on Dana's face. He wanted to tell her to sit in the cockpit and run through the start-up and shutdown routine, but he squelched the urge. He was damned if he would give her an edge. A smart student would make a cardboard mock-up of the cockpit at home and spend nights memorizing where the dials and gauges were located. But he wasn't about to suggest that, either.

As they walked down the flight back toward Operations, or Ops, Dana risked everything: "Where do you come from, Lieutenant?"

Disgruntled, Griff gave her a sidelong look. "Jerome, Arizona."

"Hot country?"

"Yeah, and if you're stupid, it can kill you."

Delighted that he was at least talking to her, Dana eagerly took the lead. Knowing something about Griff might help her anticipate what he would be like in the cockpit. She had no idea what a "screamer" was, but her survival reflex told her that any bit of information that might help turn a negative situation into a positive one was worth pursuing.

"Why is that?"

"Jerome sits on the side of Mingus Mountain. Below is a desert valley. I was taught from the time I was old enough to walk, always to carry a canteen of water and a hat with me.''

"So if the car broke down, you weren't caught without water in the desert?'' Dana saw his surprised look. For an instant, she thought she saw admiration in his gray eyes at her quick grasp of the situation. Just as quickly, his eyes became hooded again.

"Yeah.''

"So, how big is Jerome?''

"Small. Maybe a thousand people live up there.''

"You're a country boy, then. And you like your privacy.''

Uncomfortable at Dana's insight, he ignored her remark. "Jerome was a copper-mining town. My dad was a miner until the shafts closed down.''

"And your mother?'' Dana hoped to find out more about Griff's negative attitude toward women. She held her breath, hoping he'd respond.

"She was an invalid. While she was in labor having me, she suffered a stroke.''

A lump formed in Dana's throat. She heard the regret—and maybe guilt?—in Griff's icy tone. Softly, she offered, "I imagine it was hard on you growing up thinking you'd caused your mother's illness.''

Griff slowed his walk, remembering the times he'd sat with his bedridden mother. Her entire right side had been paralyzed, making it tough for her to get anywhere without help. "I spent a lot of time with her when I was young. She taught me to read at an early age. I was reading Erle Stanley Gardner mysteries to her when I was twelve.''

A tremor passed through Dana—of understanding, of sympathy for Griff. "She must have loved your sensitivity and thoughtfulness.''

Catching himself, Griff gave her a strange look. Just what was Dana up to? He halted at the guard gate. "Ensign, I've got work to do. Dr. Collins has ordered you to report for flight training next Monday." Abruptly, he swung away, heading back to his office. Dammit, how had he let Dana into his personal life? The soft blue of her eyes had touched him deeply, the compassion in them bringing up a wealth of wonderful old memories. His mother had died when he was fifteen. Until that time, he'd faithfully come in and read to her from her favorite authors every night. It had been his way of showing his love.

Griff mulled over Dana, Carol and his mother as he walked toward admin. Carol had never really asked him about his childhood. She'd been more interested in his career as a fighter pilot. He'd been the one to bring up his mother, and Carol had made the appropriate sympathetic sounds and comments. But Dana's eyes mirrored the tragedy he'd felt as a child growing up. She understood. Shaken, Griff tried to ignore that discovery about Dana. How had he let himself fall under her spell?

When Maggie and Molly returned to the apartment that evening, Dana proudly showed them the cardboard cockpit she'd drawn and set up on a kitchen chair. Bringing up another chair, Dana sat down.

"We can all practice with this mock-up," she told them excitedly. "I used the trainer manual and drew in all the dials and gauges." With a grin, Dana looked up at her friends. "I figure if one of us calls off the preflight checklist and emergency maneuvers, the person sitting here can go through it."

"Smart move," Maggie congratulated enthusiastically, eyeing the mock-up.

"It's perfect!" Molly said. "And you've done such a good job, Dana."

"I had to do something," she explained wryly. "Turcotte wasn't about to let me sit in the cockpit. He knew I wanted to, but walked away from the opportunity to let me do it."

"How about your eye?" Molly asked, setting her books down on the kitchen counter.

Dana told them the whole story. Maggie grinned devilishly.

"So, the Turk has some redeeming qualities, after all."

"Maybe," Dana hedged. And she told them about his family situation.

"Weak mother," Maggie murmured, opening the refrigerator and pouring them all some iced tea. She handed the glasses around and sat down at the Formica-topped table. "Maybe that's why he thinks all women are weak."

Dana squeezed fresh lemon into her tea and sat down with Maggie. Her friends were both still in flight suits. She was glad she'd changed into a pair of yellow shorts and a sleeveless white blouse earlier. "It's a start."

Molly was sitting at the mock-up. She looked toward them. "Is Turcotte married?"

Dana shrugged. "I don't know...."

"Intriguing question," Maggie said. "You know Manny's a real gossip. I'll ask him to do some snooping around for us." She jabbed a finger at Dana. "I asked my IP today about Turcotte and he got real tight-lipped. All he'd say was that he was tough as hell. I think if we give you our experiences this week in the cockpit, we can help you prepare to start flying with Turcotte next week."

"Not only that," Molly added excitedly, "but you're going to blow him away when you have cockpit start-up and shutdown procedure down pat. He won't expect you to know that, Dana."

"Probably thinks I'm out getting a tan, partying and playing around," she agreed.

Maggie got up. "Well, it's my turn to cook, ladies. How about Swanson Hungry Man frozen dinners?"

With a groan, Dana laughed. "At the academy, we had three squares a day over at the chow hall. Here, we've got to get into the routine of fixing our own meals. What a drag. Are we spoiled?"

The laughter lightened the kitchen, and Dana got up and out of Maggie's way. They had set up a roster of duties. Each woman had her own particular chore to complete each day. The camaraderie was binding, just as it had been at Annapolis. They were a family, believing deeply in one another and relying on each other's abilities.

Moving to her bedroom, Dana changed into her swimsuit, and pulled on jeans and a blouse over it.

"Going to swim in the gulf?" Molly asked, poking her head around the open door.

"Yes. It's the only way to get rid of tension, as far as I'm concerned."

Frowning, Molly leaned against the doorjamb, her arms crossed on her chest. "It's really tough luck drawing the Turk. I'm sorry, Dana. Maggie and I have super instructors. Neither one is a screamer. Our first flights were nerve-racking but exciting. I got a 2.1 and Maggie got a 2.2."

"Somehow, I don't think it will be wonderful for me next Monday. Griff's not interested in teaching me how to fly. He only wants to see me fail." Grimly she pressed her lips together as she picked up her colorful towel. "I'm going down to the beach for at least an hour."

"Okay. Be careful. I hear there are a lot of sharks and jellyfish in the water around here."

With a laugh, Dana slipped past Molly. "I grew up on the Pacific Ocean, remember? I've had my brushes with sharks and been stung by enough jellyfish to become one. I'll be okay. See you in an hour or so...."

Griff walked the lonely beach on Santa Rosa Island, hands deep in the pockets of his ragged cutoffs, his bare feet sinking deeply into the sand. The gulf was glassy smooth at this time of the evening, with the tide moving out. Hunter's Point was his favorite getaway spot, a place where he could think without being distracted by a lot of tourists crowding the long sandbarlike island that stretched endlessly in a slight crescent, parallel to the Florida coast. The white sand met the blue-green water, the waves small and frothy. His shoulders fell and relaxed as he allowed the lap of the water and the cry of the sea gulls to take away his tension. It had been one hell of a day.

Scuffing his toes into the damp sand, Griff watched as the sun, low on the horizon, dipped behind towering cumulus clouds. His mother would have commented on what looked like the face of a dog in the clouds. Carol wouldn't even have noticed it. What would Dana have said? Disgusted with his meandering train of thought, Griff spun around, allowing his chin to drop toward his chest, introspective.

Dana. What was he going to do about her? This morning, she'd displayed the kind of eagerness that he liked to see in a student, but didn't often get. Her melting blue eyes haunted him. He knew she was in pain from the black eye. Having collected a few shiners in his seven-year naval career, Griff knew they ached like a son of a bitch for at least a week. It hurt to talk, to chew food and to smile. Dana wasn't a complainer as Carol had been. If Carol cut her finger slicing a tomato, she acted as if he should take her to an emergency room.

Mulling over the comparison, Griff stopped and turned, facing the ocean. The horizon was turning a peach color, the sun behind the clouds lining it with blazing gold edges. He'd seen gold flecks in Dana's eyes when he'd begun teaching her about the walk-around. Did gold mean she was happy? With a groan, Griff rubbed his face and tried to erase Dana from his mind and heart.

A movement caught his attention. Squinting, he saw a lone woman about half a mile up the deserted beach. His heart thudded. It was Dana. Wading into the ocean in a dark blue one-piece bathing suit, she didn't seem aware of his presence. Hunkering down, Griff rocked back on his heels and watched her. He was sure she hadn't seen him. She had left a bright, flowery print towel on the beach and was moving her arms in warm-up motions. That's right, she'd been the captain of the Annapolis swim team, he remembered. Quirking his mouth, Griff hated the thought that his brain had retained everything in Dana's file.

She was incredibly slender, Griff observed almost with alarm. So small and graceful as she leaned down, cupping the water and sluicing it across her body. Her thighs were curved and firm, the calves tightly muscled and slim. His gaze ranged higher, to her small waist and breasts. Women would probably die of envy for her waist, Griff thought. It couldn't be more than eighteen inches. He sat down in the sand, enjoying the sight of her economical movements. Warming up before swimming was to be applauded.

When Dana dived into the water, Griff's breath lodged in his throat. She reminded him of a sleek, shining dolphin. When Dana resurfaced, she was nearly a quarter of a mile out to sea. She had incredible lungs to swim that far without air. Griff kept forgetting she had captained the swim team. With each stroke, she moved farther and farther out across the rose-colored mirror of the gulf, tiny ripples forming around her with each clean, slicing stroke. Shading his eyes even though he wore aviator sunglasses, Griff could barely keep Dana in sight. Worry nagged at him. She was a good mile out from the coast.

Standing, he cupped his hands around his eyes. The little fool! There were sharks out there. In a calm sea like this, her swimming motion would draw them. She might be a big-time swimmer in a pool, but it was obvious she had no inkling of safe conduct in an ocean.

"Damn her," he growled, jerking off his polo shirt and throwing it down. Dropping his threadbare tennis shoes, Griff stuffed his dark glasses into one of them. Without hesitation, he jogged down to the shore and into the warm water.

"Dana!" he hollered, his voice carrying strongly. She hadn't heard him. Worried, Griff lunged through the shallow water. When it was waist deep, he dove in. He might not be a champion swimmer, but he'd been in Florida for two years, and he knew plenty about the gulf from his weekly swims. Taking large, clean strokes, he aimed toward her. Yelling at Dana would be futile. He'd have to get her attention another way. Anger fueled his strength, the water exploding around him as he swam in her direction.

Dana languished in the salty water, slowly turning over on her back for a moment. The freestyle swim had taken the edge off her worry about her potential flying skills. The water was like a mother, cradling her protectively in a safe and loving embrace. Laughing, Dana rolled again, feeling like a porpoise, then dove downward, enjoying the rush of water surrounding her like a friendly welcome. The goggles she wore to protect her eyes from the salt water hung around her neck, and she dove blind, her eyes tightly shut, feeling the pressure build around her as she went deeper and deeper. She could hold her breath for nearly four minutes without having to resurface. The reassuring pressure against her body was something she gloried in. Mother Ocean, as she had always called the sea, would never harm her. Here, she was safe. Safe.

A viselike grip encircled her waist. Startled, Dana released the last of her air, twisting around. Her eyes flew open. At first she thought it was a shark, pain rearing up through her lower ribs as she was hauled surfaceward. And then, to her surprise, she realized it was a man. The salt water stung her eyes. Out of air, Dana had no resource, unable to fight his powerful grip.

They erupted from the water simultaneously. Blinded by the salt water, she struck out at her unknown male assailant, trying to jerk free. Her fist gave him a glancing blow alongside his head. She gulped water and choked, lifting her feet and shoving them hard against his chest. In seconds, she was free.

"Dana!" Griff croaked, flailing, shocked by her attack. "It's me, Turcotte! Hold still!" He lunged for her arm, but she slithered free.

Coughing up seawater, Dana rubbed her eyes, clearing them. Griff Turcotte trod water a few feet away, his face a thundercloud of anger. "What," she choked, "are you doing out here?"

Angrily, Griff jabbed a finger at her. "Trying to save your neck, that's what!" he roared back. "What the hell do you think you're doing? The ocean's flat and calm. Swimming out this far under those conditions can attract sharks. I came out to bring you back before you became dinner for one of our great whites, you idiot!"

Gasping, Dana laughed. "*You* came to save *me?* Oh, brother, Lieutenant, that's a real laugh."

Stung by her ungratefulness, Griff glowered at her and swam closer. "Okay, so you're a feminist and I'm still back in the caveman era. But I'll be damned if you're going to become a steak for some patrolling shark on my beach."

He was serious! Dana blinked, shoving the hair off her brow. "Your beach? For your information, this is a public beach, Turcotte! I came down here to swim! You had no right scaring the hell out of me! Just who do you think *you* are?"

Griff clenched his teeth, impressed in spite of himself at her spunk under the circumstances. "Just because you were swim captain at Annapolis, Coulter, doesn't mean you have an ounce of brains about swimming in the ocean. Did it ever occur to you that sharks are drawn to flailing sounds on top of the water? They signal a meal waiting to be eaten."

Dana began to laugh. She couldn't help herself. It was all so ridiculous! "You're something else, Turcotte. I was on this beach minding my own damn business. Did it ever occur to you I know what I'm doing?"

Griff momentarily lost his anger. When Dana smiled, he felt some old, heavy burden buried in his heart dissolve. Her laughter was rolling and contralto, like a song of a beautiful bird. And her eyes... Sweet heaven, but he wanted to capture that smiling mouth and feel her move sensually against him. The water glinted off her neck and arms like jeweled sunlight. The gold flecks were back in her eyes, and he knew now, without a doubt, she was happy. Just the graceful way she moved in the water told him she was ultimately at home within its grasp. Her incredible beauty nullified his anger.

"I was worried, that was all."

Her eyes crinkled. "I wouldn't think you'd care if I did get eaten by a shark. After all, you don't want me as a student."

Griff ignored her comment.

"Besides," Dana added lightly, stretching out on her back on the water's surface, "I was born by the ocean, Lieutenant. When I was three, I was swimming with my mother in it." She twisted her head in his direction, noticing his straight brows drawing into a frown. "I've had plenty of head-ons with sharks, jellyfish and other denizens of the deep. Once, a six-hundred-pound grouper attacked me. I just hit him with the hammer I carried in my diving belt. I was looking for abalone off the coast of San Diego when it happened. He got the worst of the deal."

"You're qualified for scuba diving, too?"

"Up to two hundred feet. I've had diving certification since I was fourteen years old."

Griff felt heat crawling into his face. He got the message: Dana was extremely capable of taking care of herself in any ocean situation. Embarrassed, he rubbed his jaw where she'd struck him earlier. When he'd seen her dive suddenly, he'd thought she was drowning and had gone in to rescue her. Griff knew better than to own up to that admission.

When he looked over at Dana, he expected her to be laughing at him, but she wasn't.

Dana relented, touched that Griff had cared enough to come after her. "Did you come to my rescue because you thought I was too weak to swim back to shore?" she teased lightly. The water cascading down the hard planes of his face increased his rugged intensity. The color of his eaglelike eyes grew charcoal. She wasn't sure if it meant he was angry or pleased.

"It's obvious you don't need any help at sea," Griff bit back. "But the air's my domain, Coulter. Not yours."

She shrugged, silently wishing he'd lose the chip on his shoulder toward her. "The air belongs to everyone, Lieutenant, just like the ocean." She spread her arm out in front of her, fingers lightly skipping across the surface.

"You made a mistake coming to Whiting, Coulter."

"Oh?"

"You'd have been better off staying in the ship part of the Navy—it's obvious you like the water."

Smiling, Dana rolled gracefully in a complete circle, surfacing on her back and floating. "It's not my nature to do what's easy. I like a challenge."

Grudgingly, Griff prepared to swim back to shore—by himself. "Come next Monday, you're going to face the biggest challenge in your life, Coulter."

Her smile disappeared and she held his dark eyes. "Lieutenant, nothing you can throw at me will ever equal what I've already survived. Nothing."

Dana lunged past him, swimming strongly toward shore. Griff stared at her, assimilating the low tremble in her voice and the rebellion in her azure eyes. He trod water, wondering what she was talking about. Bothered, he began a leisurely swim back to shore. His threats rolled off her like water off an otter's back. Dana was no more afraid of him than she was of this ocean. She didn't scare easily. It had to be a facade. There was no other explanation. Underneath, Dana was just as weak and brittle as Carol had been.

The water sloughed away the rest of his anger. By the time his feet touched the sandy bottom, Dana had already retrieved her towel and was walking toward the parking lot. Flinging his head from side to side, Griff went in the opposite direction to retrieve his shirt, shoes and sunglasses. Running his long fingers through his hair, he got rid of most of the water.

He turned and looked over his shoulder. Dana had disappeared, and the beach once more was deserted. What had she survived? Needled, Griff shrugged on the black polo shirt and slipped on the sunglasses. He sat down, brushing the wet sand off his feet, struggling to put his tennis shoes back on. Dana's words echoed in his head: *"Nothing you can throw at me will ever equal what I've already survived. Nothing."*

Was she referring to the rigors of Annapolis? God knew, it was a hellish place for a man, much less a woman. Ring knockers were a brotherhood, and didn't take lightly to newcomers in their ranks. The first two years at Annapolis were the most grueling challenge Griff had ever faced.

Jerking his shoes onto his feet, he got up, dusting the sand from his wet shorts. Griff mulled over Dana's low, trembling voice. Something told him she wasn't talking about Annapolis. But what? A marriage and then a divorce, possibly? Her file said she was single, but it didn't say if she'd been married previously. And what about her comment that this wasn't her first black eye?

Stymied, Griff headed across the dunes to the parking lot. Dana Coulter was an enigma; a mystery of the first order. His forte was solving mysteries. Irritated by his own curiosity, Griff consoled himself with the thought that come next Monday, more would be revealed about Dana. His method of instructing was sure to garner a host of reactions that would reveal a great deal more about her. And when he had her figured out, he'd make sure she'd never graduate as a pilot. Toby was dead, and he was damned sure he wasn't going to be some woman's next victim.

Chapter Four

Dana was in the ready room where all the students who were going to fly met their IPs. It was 0700, and she wiped her damp palms against her thighs just as Griff entered. A number of the other students gave her sympathetic glances as her instructor appeared. If Dana read their looks accurately, she was seen as a lamb going to slaughter. Despite the fear sitting in the pit of her stomach, her heart responded strongly to Griff. There was something different about him from any other man in the room.

Dana stood as he walked toward her. She searched his clear gray eyes and found them icy, without emotion. His mouth, always an intriguing part of his face, was grim. The dark blue garrison cap sat at a cocky angle on his head. She noticed the way the olive-green flight uniform fit his tall, tightly muscled body.

Dana shook her head, wondering if the nervousness over her first flight was making her crazy. Ordinarily, she never looked at men this way. The fear of how they could harm her always came first. With Griff, it was different. In some part of her, she instinctively knew he'd never raise a hand to physically hurt her—even if he was bound and determined to wash her out of flight school.

I'm crazy, Dana decided, unable to explain logically her reactions to him. Maybe the four years of grueling strain at Annapolis were catching up with her. Rising from the table, holding her new flight log, Dana held Griff's eaglelike gaze.

"Ready, Coulter?"

He couldn't even say "Good morning." Dana fought to regain that familiar sense of control, to protect herself from the inevitable pain of opening herself to caring what he did or thought. "Yes, sir, I am," she replied coolly.

Griff frowned. She'd been smart enough to get a flight logbook. He'd planned on berating her for little things right off the bat—things she was responsible to get and have ready when he arrived. It had been six days since he'd last seen Dana. For the most part, her black eye had disappeared. Her cheekbone was back to normal, and only a slight yellowish color beneath the left eye still showed. Her black hair was thick, glinting with bluish highlights beneath the fluorescent lights. Drawn to her azure eyes, thickly fringed with black lashes, Griff felt a hypnotic pull to simply lose himself in them.

With a growl he spun around, muttering, "Follow me."

Walking helped take the edge off Dana's nervousness. The late-April morning was clear and the winds were calm, the meteorologist at the weather desk had told her. Griff had frowned when he'd taken her to the weather station to get the forecast. A well-prepared student, Dana had pulled the slip of paper from her flight log, handed it to him and repeated the information on it. Griff's gray eyes flashed with grudging admiration laced with anger. Dana curbed a smile. She had spent the week learning flight routine from Maggie and Molly. Plus, she'd spent ten-to-twelve hours a day studying the textbooks, cramming every conceivable bit of information into her head so that it would be at her disposal, should Griff require it. And every evening, when her friends returned from the station, they would sit in the kitchen with the trainer mock-up and each spend at least an hour going through different flight procedures, burning them into their brains until the moves became second nature. In the cockpit they wouldn't have to stop and think; they would simply respond.

Griff stood openmouthed as Dana flawlessly performed the walk-around inspection of his trainer. She missed nothing. Nothing! The crew chief, Aviation Machinist Mate Parker, handed her the discrepancy log, and she noted and signed it off, giving him a warm smile of thanks. Griff bridled. Dana's smile had been genuine, and he found himself wondering if she'd ever bestow one on him. Her blue eyes were intense and focused. But the moment Parker came up with the log, her business facade melted. In its place were her dancing blue eyes and a smile that could melt the hardest of hearts. Even his.

As Dana turned toward Griff, she saw him scowling at her. Automatically, she became all business again.

"Ground inspection completed, sir." At every other trainer on the flight line, the same procedure was going on between IP and student. Voices were low and strained. Dana felt the tension and tried to keep her shoulders relaxed, her voice unruffled. Griff looked positively beside himself; like a mad dog wanting to bite someone, but unable to decide whom. She knew he hadn't expected her to move through the routine without a hitch. But she had. Now came the next test: the cockpit.

"Climb in the first cockpit, Coulter."

The first seat located behind the prop of the plane was hers. Dana placed her flight log in a leg pocket, pressing the Velcro closed to keep it there. Her heart raced with excitement and nervousness as she climbed on board. To her dismay, her legs were too short to reach the rudder pedals. She felt Griff next to her, and she automatically lifted her chin.

"Just another reason why women shouldn't fly. You're so damned small, you can't even reach the controls."

"I'm sure this seat's adjustable." Dana forced herself to remember where the lever was to move it forward.

Their hands met and collided.

Dana jerked hers back. He glowered at her, growling, "Move forward."

Her hand tingling from his strong, firm touch, Dana tried to rise above her physical reactions to Griff. It was impossible. Once the seat was repositioned, her feet rested comfortably against the rudders. Griff leaned against the fuselage, beginning to explain the cockpit panel, the controls, levers and various other instruments. She sat, nodding from time to time, valiantly trying to ignore his male energy, that tightly wound sensation that inevitably tugged at her concentration.

At the ocean a week ago, Dana had been wildly aware of Griff's unavoidable magnetism. She might be poorly experienced in relationships, but Dana knew she was powerfully drawn to Griff as a man. It was the most illogical thing in the world. This man wanted to end her flight career before it even began. He had no personal interest in her—but try to tell that to her heart.

For the next hour, Griff droned on in a bored voice about everything Dana should know about escape procedures from the trainer, should something go wrong and they had to bail out. Ordinarily, he was excited about taking on a new student. With Dana, it was hell to keep his hands off her and his reactions to her to himself, instead of hungrily staring at her like a starved wolf looking for a mate. It was the most miserable hour of his life.

As Griff leaned over, he could smell her sweet fragrance, a whiff of some light, flowery perfume. Although Dana wore absolutely no makeup, she didn't need any in his opinion. The urge to thread his fingers through her thick, ebony hair was very real. Disgruntled by his reactions, he heard the anger reflected in his voice. If Dana was bothered by it, she didn't show it.

Demonstrating how to put the helmet with the double visor on, Griff climbed into the rear cockpit, divided from the front one by a panel. As he settled into his seat and strapped in, his gaze automatically swept the controls and instruments. He had an identical set of controls so he could take over in case a student froze or couldn't respond to an in-flight emergency. They were ready to fly.

For Dana, it was a thrilling moment when she pressed the button and the prop began to whirl sluggishly in front of her. In a moment, the prop caught, and the engine roared to life. The entire plane shook and trembled around her. A smile pulled at her mouth as she sat absorbing the sensation, her heart racing with incredible happiness. *This* was what she had been waiting for all her life: to fly! It was true, the water was her friend. But the air would be her lover. The moments of discovery were sweet. Then Griff's growling voice came over the headset in her helmet, and bitterness coated her initial reaction.

Dana wanted badly to show Griff she could take his instructions and do it right. She taxied the plane to the end of the airstrip, learning how to converse with the tower and give the appropriate responses to the controller. The silence over her headset was ominous; she could almost feel Griff ready to pounce on her, waiting for her to make the smallest error.

"I'll take this bird up," he told her. "You just put your hand on the throttle and the other on the stick and follow through with me. Understand?"

"Yes, sir." Dana wrapped her gloved hands lightly around the proper controls, her heart accelerating as Griff eased the throttle forward, the plane's engine deepening with power. It shook like a shackled eagle wanting to take off.

Her gaze swept the instruments, left to right. Everything looked fine. Dana was anxious to take off, to feel the plane lift from the earth. It was her duty to look in all directions, making sure no other student pilot was in their takeoff pattern. Sometimes, Griff grimly informed her, students screwed up, flying through the designated flight patterns.

"Call the tower and request takeoff, Coulter."

Excitedly, Dana pressed the button on the stick that would link her with the controller. She tried to keep her voice businesslike, hoping her thrill over flying wouldn't show. In moments, she got permission.

"Release rudders," Griff ordered her.

Dana eased up on the rudders, which also acted as the brakes. The trainer lunged forward, speeding down the gray concrete runway. Her breath caught as she became lost in the sensations of tires spinning against the surface, the shaking and shuddering going on around her, and the smell of engine heat entering the cockpit. Dials and gauges jumped to life, their hands waving like wheat in a field. The instant Griff pulled back the stick, the plane leaped skyward—and Dana's stomach grew alarmingly queasy.

Panicky, Dana spotted the plastic-lined "burp bags" that were installed in the cockpit. Her eyes rounded as Griff took the plane up to fifteen-hundred feet and out of the flight pattern to find some clear airspace above the gulf. Although it was early morning and the air was supposed to be calm, the trainer bumped along, continuously hitting small air pockets. With each bump, Dana's stomach became more upset.

"Are you listening to me, Coulter?" Griff snapped. He'd ordered her to take the controls and she hadn't. He heard a very familiar sound through the headset. She was airsick! His mouth flattening, Griff gripped the controls.

"Dammit, Coulter, throw up and get it over with! Stow the burp bag and grab these controls!"

Gasping, Dana rubbed her watering eyes, distraught. Airsick! She was desperately airsick! How could that be? Oh, God, she hadn't counted on this. Hadn't her body always responded beautifully to anything she'd ever asked of it? The trainer hit a large air pocket and dropped a good twenty feet before Griff steadied it back to smooth, even flight.

"I—I'm going to be sick again," Dana rasped, reaching for a second bag with shaking hands. In moments, the rest of her small breakfast had come up.

Cursing, Griff hissed, "This just proves my point, Coulter: Women can't take flying. You're weak. You're weak and you can't handle a little morning-air turbulence. What makes you think you can handle a jet or four-engine turboprop in severe turbulence? The men in your crew are in your hands. Their lives are on the line while you're heaving out your guts because you can't take it! Just what the hell kind of pilot would *you* be? One that gets her crew killed!"

Sweat rolled down into Dana's narrowed eyes. Miserably, she tucked the second bag away, gripping the controls. "I've got the controls," she rasped. Griff's anger was like hot needles in her already pulverized emotions. It was impossible to respond to his litany of anger, because now she had to fly the plane. Her stomach rolled warningly. She couldn't get sick a third time! Griff's voice droned in her ears.

"Get those wings level, Coulter, and keep them that way. You have twenty-five feet of altitude variance. The moment you go above or below that, I'll be all over you. The port wing's down. Get it up!"

Instantly, Dana corrected. But she overcorrected. The trainer was highly responsive. It tipped starboard.

"Dammit, Coulter! Level out!"

Her stomach queasy, panicking because she couldn't seem to do anything right, Dana fought the plane for the next two hours.

Wrung out, her flight suit wet with perspiration, Dana suffered the ultimate disgrace: Griff had to land the plane because she had become completely uncoordinated in the cockpit. To add to her misery and embarrassment, she'd thrown up three more times. Worse, Dana was starting to realize she couldn't keep her feelings under control where Griff was concerned. Terror, more powerful than she'd ever experienced, deluged her. There was no safe place to hide from him. Emotionally, she'd be exposed and completely vulnerable to every attack he launched at her.

Pushing back the canopy, Dana began to unharness herself with shaking hands. She felt Griff's ominous presence before she saw him. His shadow loomed across her cockpit. Tucking her lower lip between her teeth, Dana refused to look at him.

"You're weak, Coulter," he ground out, glaring down at her. "And for your sake, you'd better not have messed up Parker's cockpit. My crew chief doesn't clean up after squeamish students. You ever miss the burp bag, *you*'ll be out here scrubbing that instrument panel, not him. Got that?"

"Y-yes, sir." The harness released, and Dana felt like crawling into a hole. All six bags were neatly stowed around her seat. There was no pride in having to carry them back to the ready room, either. She'd failed—completely.

"Climb out of there."

Griff stood back on the tarmac and watched Dana leave the trainer. He saw dark rings of sweat beneath her armpits. Her face was waxen, her eyes dark with misery. When her lower lip trembled, Griff had to stop himself from walking over and helping her out of the plane. She was weak and trembling. A huge part of him felt like hell for yelling at her. Airsickness was not uncommon among students. The movement of the plane was something most people, with time, adjusted to. A few didn't. He watched as Dana straightened and, miraculously, found a deep well of strength somewhere within her to throw back her shoulders and lift her chin.

"You're off to a lousy start, Coulter," he said as she walked up to him. "You couldn't keep the wings level, and you kept losing altitude. Not only that, you were incapable of landing the aircraft." Blackly, Griff wrote the grade down at the bottom of the paper and scribbled his name on the bottom line. "Here," he directed. "Take a look. If you've got a problem with the grade, we hash it out here and now. Once you've seen it and signed your name, that's it. If you disagree with my grade and don't sign it, it's an automatic Board. There you'll be given an opportunity to tell three of your peers why you felt you didn't warrant the grade I've given you. If you sign this, I send it up to the Ops office. Your grade will be posted that day on the bulletin board. Questions?"

Dana's gaze flew to the bottom line. He'd given her a 2.0, the lowest possible grade just this side of failing. A 1.9 would mean an automatic Board, anyway. She knew to disagree with the grade would be foolish. Gulping, having expected a 1.9 because of her constant mistakes, Dana shakily took the clipboard and signed her name next to Griff's. "No," she whispered. "No questions." She was surprised and grateful he'd given her a 2.0 under the circumstances.

Griff gave her a hard look. "Be here at 0700 Wednesday morning, Coulter. And for your sake, you'd better go over all the mistakes you made in the air this morning and have them straightened out by then. You screw up like this again, and I'll give you a 1.9 so fast your head will spin."

She saw triumph in his eyes just before he swung around and left her standing alone on the ramp. Dana stood in abject misery. Part of her breathed a sigh of relief. At least Griff hadn't given her a 1.9 on her very first flight. There was no mistake he'd give it to her next time. Rubbing her sweaty brow, Dana settled the garrison cap on her head and picked up her helmet and burp bags. She walked back to the ready room on unsteady legs.

In the small locker room reserved for women students, Dana got out of her smelly flight suit, took a scaldingly hot shower and changed into her light blue jacket-and-skirt uniform. Low black pumps were the last to be put on. Dana listlessly combed her black hair. Avoiding looking in the mirror, Dana went back to her locker to pick up her books and mentally tried to prepare herself for the 1100 class. Griff was also her meteorology instructor. Just thinking about the flight made her stomach upset again. Always before, flying had been her answer, her ultimate escape from the pain of her earthbound life. Dana had counted on flying as a means of having control over her life—not having someone else jerk her strings as if she were a puppet, as her father had. Her love of flying was overwhelming. Somehow, she would persevere. She had to.

Arriving at the admin building where all the classrooms were located, Dana met her friends, and they sat together.

"You look like death warmed-over," Maggie commented worriedly. "How'd it go?"

"I screwed up on the flight. I got airsick six times."

"Oh, no!" Molly whispered, and watched the door in case the instructor arrived a few minutes early. Talking once the teacher was in the room could mean demerits. "What happened?"

In a low voice, Dana told them everything.

"That rotten bastard!" Maggie grated fiercely. "Just who does he think he is? Yelling at you constantly in the cockpit isn't going to give you flight confidence! It's designed to destroy you, Dana."

"Point well made," Dana said hollowly. She took a deep, ragged breath and stared at the blackboard. The lecture podium would soon be Griff's domain—again. "Somehow..."

somehow, I've got to get a hold of my emotions. And this airsickness—I can't believe it! I never expected it! Never! How long does it last?''

Both women shrugged.

Molly added sympathetically, ''Maybe it will go away in a week or two, Dana.''

''But you two don't have it.''

''No,'' Maggie said archly. ''But neither of us have a screamer sitting in the cockpit behind us, either.''

Dana hung her head. Was her airsickness a nervous response to the fact that Griff wanted to fail her? Clenching the pen in her fingers, she desperately wanted to escape to the ocean to swim, to release her fear and anxiety in the soothing water. Classes didn't end until 1500. By 1600 she would be on that beach, back in the arms of her mother—it was the only place she could turn for comfort when things went bad. And things were even worse than Dana could ever have imagined.

Griff needed to be alone. He parked his Corvette at the far end of Hunter's Beach, hoping no one would be there. If only Toby were here to talk to him. He needed to unload his guilt about Dana. Toby would understand why he'd reacted the way he had in the cockpit with her this morning.

Dana . . . The name riffled softly through him, and he lifted his chin to stare across the moody, choppy sea. The wind was up, the waves reaching two or three feet in height. They mirrored the chaos he felt inside. Dammit! Why had he rubbed her face in the fact she'd gotten airsick? My God! Most students would have called it quits if they'd gotten ill six times in a row. But Dana hadn't. She'd doggedly gripped the controls and flown that trainer. And for a first time at the stick, Griff grudgingly admitted as he ambled down the dunes to the beach below, Dana had flown damn well under some hellish circumstances.

Had she gotten sick because she'd been tied in knots knowing he was going to try to fail her? Guiltily, Griff shoved his hands into his pockets "Damn you, Carol," he whispered. "Damn you for being weak."

Dana hadn't been weak. She'd been anything but that. Griff couldn't ever recall a student rallying as she had, despite her physical debility. It hurt to think he'd cruelly goaded her, called her weak when, really, she hadn't been at all.

"Damn..." Griff halted, running his fingers through his hair. Inside, he felt dirty and uneasy. Dana didn't deserve this. He saw by the defiance in her dark cobalt eyes after the flight that she wasn't a quitter. She should have received a better grade. She'd had at least a 2.1 coming. His mouth compressed, Griff continued to walk listlessly, his shoulders slumped under the load he'd brought on himself.

Fifteen minutes later, he came across a flowery print beach towel on the sand not far from the water. Scowling, he picked it up. It was Dana's. Looking up, Griff scanned the ocean beyond the breakers. He hadn't seen her car in the parking lot. Worriedly he squinted against the glare of the sun on the water. Was she out there somewhere? Was she all right?

Not about to make the same mistake twice, Griff stood for another fifteen minutes before he spotted Dana swimming strongly back toward shore. Wavering, wanting to stay and knowing it would be the wrong thing to do, he waged an internal battle with himself. He wanted to apologize to her. It wasn't in his makeup to be the kind of bastard he'd been to her. There was a fine line between instructing and badgering a student. He'd badgered her. Kicking at the loose sand, Griff backed about twenty feet away from her towel and waited for her to come ashore. Somehow, he was going to have to make amends and try to start over with Dana. She deserved his apology.

Dana's eyes narrowed when she realized it was Griff standing, waiting for her. As she came out of the surf, she allowed the warm salt water to wash off her arms and fingers. Pushing her hair out of her face, she tried to gird herself. Had the bastard come here, knowing she'd be here, to rub in her performance today? Was he going to ask if she got seasick, too? Anger overwhelmed other, more fragile feelings. Still, her pounding heart told her that, in his slacks and dark blue short-sleeved shirt, he was devastatingly handsome.

As she approached, she saw him pick up her towel and hold it out toward her. The uncertainty in his eyes threw her off guard. Halting a good ten feet from him, Dana clenched her fists against her legs.

"Just what the hell are you doing here?" she rattled tensely. "Didn't you rub my nose in it enough this morning, Turcotte? I've heard of instructors badgering a student, but this is going beyond the call of duty. Or do you hate me so much that your battle lines have no parameters and I'm fair game twenty-four hours a day?"

Griff blinked and opened his mouth, taken aback by her fury. Her blue eyes blazed with a terrible light. "I didn't know you were out here," he began defensively.

Dana walked forward, grabbing the towel from his hand. She moved away, rubbing her hair, then placed the towel across her shoulders. It hurt to breathe as the anger bubbled up through her. "I'll be coming here every day, Turcotte. And I don't appreciate your presence. I may be stuck with you back on Whiting, but I don't have to put up with you after hours. Now just leave me alone!"

Her voice cracked, and Griff saw tears in her eyes. "But, I—"

"You really are a bastard, you know that? You haunt your students to death! No wonder you have the highest washout rate, if this is what you do to get them to quit!"

"You don't understand, Dana, I—"

With a cry, Dana whirled away, running down the beach toward a second lot half a mile away where her car was parked.

Griff stood stunned. He watched Dana run with the born ease of a consummate athlete. Well, what had he expected? A welcome wagon after he'd raked her over the coals this morning? Bitterness coated his mouth as he assimilated her anger. He deserved it. She'd called him a bastard. So had Carol. But circumstances were far different. Unhappy with himself, Griff turned away and moved down the deserted beach, alone. Wednesday would bring another skirmish between them. Dana hated him now, and it was the last thing he'd wanted. But he'd been unable to stop his own feelings of the past from interfering with the present.

Dana sat tensely in the ready room. It was 0658. Griff would come through the door in two minutes. She placed her hand against her knotted stomach. Would she get airsick again? *Oh, please, don't let it happen. Don't—*

"Hey!" Manny sidled up to her and gave her a sunny smile. "I got the scoop on your IP."

Vaguely, Dana recalled Maggie asking him to snoop around for personal information on Griff. "What did you find out, Manny?"

"Get this. Turcotte just got a divorce from his wife, Carol, six months ago. They were married five years and have no kids. She was a banker's daughter and came from a pretty wealthy family. An only child, from what I hear."

"A messy divorce?" Dana asked, thinking that Griff's hatred of women could stem directly from that.

"Very messy. It was smeared all over the local newspapers, and even hit the society column in Palm Beach where her father has an estate."

Griff wouldn't be the type to enjoy any kind of press, Dana thought. Nor would she. "What about his wife? Did you find anything out about her?"

Manny watched the door, and kept his voice low so that no one else could overhear their conversation. "Carol Turcotte was what I'd call a clinger. You know: one of those women who comes from the double-standard society."

"Helpless without a man around?" Dana guessed grimly.

"Yeah, that type. I guess she was a spoiled only child, used to having everything done for her. She had a record of nervous breakdowns. According to my source, she was hospitalized twice a year with different complaints. She tried to commit suicide once the last year she was married to Turcotte." Manny shrugged. "Maybe he drove her to it."

Dana wouldn't be surprised. Still, her heart twisted in her chest. She mulled over the fact Griff had accused her of being weak. Carol obviously had had problems. Did he project that image on all women as a result? And then she made the connection. Griff's mother had been an invalid since the day he'd been born. No wonder he thought all women were weak and incapable of standing on their own two feet!

Gripping Manny's hand, she squeezed it. "Thanks for telling me this."

"You owe me."

She grinned slightly. "I'll buy you an ice-cream cone over at the exchange. I know your downfall."

With a laugh, Manny got up. He was married and already the father of two young daughters. "Bingo, Dana. Okay. A triple-decker Rocky Road after classes today at 1500. Deal?"

She laughed with him, her fear lightening beneath his teasing demeanor. "Deal, Manny. Thanks."

As Dana turned, she saw Griff come through the door. Dark circles showed under his eyes, and if possible, he looked even more grim. Automatically her stomach clenched. His eyes never left hers. Her mouth dry, Dana stood, trying to find the strength to withstand his silent appraisal. What would today's flight bring? She broke into a sweat, afraid as never before as he stood waiting for her.

Chapter Five

The airsickness pill that Dana had taken earlier was making her feel woozy, as if she were in a dreamworld, floating half out of her body. It was the only nonprescription drug she could find that might ward off sickness on the Wednesday-morning flight. Shaking her head in an attempt to clear it, she moved around the trainer under Griff's critical gray gaze. His entire demeanor spoke of icy reserve. Dana was sure he was remembering their confrontation at the beach Monday evening. Tough. Who did he think he was, coming out to continue harassing her on off-hours?

As she leaned beneath that port wing to check for leaks, Dana considered lodging a protest with Captain Ramsey. In her experience at Annapolis, women were tolerated, and if they proved themselves, they were grudgingly respected. But if it came down to a woman's word against a man's, the man always won. Placing a sexual-harassment protest against Griff would more than likely cost her her Navy wings and a career in aviation. No, she'd have to keep her act together, rely on her internal strength and outlast Griff's hatred of her.

Griff watched Dana moodily from a distance. Her face was unreadable, her blue eyes insolent. This morning he'd considered trying to explain why he'd been out at the beach Monday evening, but at her frosty look when he'd entered the ready room, his own anger resurfaced. Other instructors had told him they'd heard of Dana's prestigious academy record, and envied him. Even Captain Ramsey was making an effort to note her flight grades because of her 4.0 average at Annapolis. Everyone seemed to like her except him.

Well, that wasn't quite accurate. He didn't dislike Dana. In fact, he found himself alarmingly drawn to her. There was undeniable attraction between them, Griff sourly admitted. If only she wasn't his student. If only she wasn't a woman vying for a pilot's slot, he could easily chase her until he caught her. Every damned night he dreamed about her, about that sweet athletic body of hers. Griff wondered about her passion—if the gold fire in her eyes was a telltale sign of her carefully hidden expression as a woman. And her mouth... Sighing, Griff forced himself back to the present. Dana had completed the walk-around, signed off the discrepancy log to Parker and was climbing into the front cockpit. Griff wondered if she was going to be airsick again.

This time, he ordered Dana to take off. He sat in the rear seat, his hands and feet hovering close to the controls in case she screwed up. He wasn't about to become a fatality like Toby. To his surprise, Dana brought the responsive trainer off the runway at exactly ninety-five miles per hour. At one thousand feet, wings still level, she requested a left-hand turn from the control tower and got it. Ordinarily, at 0700, the air was dead calm. But today, cumulus clouds were already building over the gulf, and the air was filled with bumpy pockets. The trainer began to drop and rise twenty or thirty feet at a time.

"Steady her out, Coulter," Griff snapped. "Get the wings level! Ride those rudders."

Dana broke out in a heavy sweat, feeling her stomach react instantly to the rough air. She choked down the bile, frantically trying to keep the wings level. It was impossible. The air seemed uncooperative and unrelenting.

"Dammit, Coulter, steady! What the hell are you going to do when you're in the jet wash of a refueling tanker? You've got to be stable no matter how rough it is!"

Compressing her lips, Dana worked hard to get the trainer under control.

Griff was about to deliver another tongue-lashing when he heard her retch violently. Dana was airsick—again. He swallowed his tirade. "I've got the controls," he gritted out.

Miserably, Dana wiped her mouth with the back of her gloved hand. She took back the controls minutes later.

"Get out of the traffic pattern. Make a ninety-degree right-hand turn," Griff snarled.

The air smoothed out a bit. Dana gulped, and wished mightily for something to wash the terrible taste out of her mouth. This time, she hadn't eaten any breakfast, thinking it might have contributed to her airsickness before. But evidently it hadn't, and the airsickness pill had failed her—although it was making her dry-mouthed and dazed.

For the next thirty minutes, Griff drilled Dana on making smooth, banking turns while keeping the wings level. Using a highway two thousand feet below as a marker, he illustrated how to make S-turns, one hundred and eighty degrees at a time. Surprisingly, Dana kept the trainer fairly steady and didn't lose or gain much altitude. Later, Griff knew they had to work on landings and takeoffs, and ordered Dana back to the pattern where the air was going to become increasingly bumpy. At least twenty other trainers were in the pattern circling the field, further chopping the air with their props.

Within a minute of getting into the pattern, Dana was sick again. When she'd recovered, Griff was on her to stay level and maintain the correct altitude. He yelled at her for not seeing a trainer coming in from the starboard side, flying too close to them.

Shaken, Dana forced herself to rise above her own physical misery and concentrate on the sky around her. Every bump made her stomach roll. Every snapping order from Griff drove her closer to tears. The first time she tried to land, she brought the trainer in too high. If not for Griff's lightning response, Dana was sure they would have crashed. As it was, the wheels kissed the runway like a lover. She wondered if she would ever land half that well.

The second time around the pattern, lined up properly, Dana tensed, her hand gripping the stick so hard her fingers were aching. Fifty feet from the runaway, she felt Griff jerk the stick violently.

"Ease up, Coulter! Stop strangling the stick. Use two fingers to land this thing!"

Two fingers? Dana panicked, momentarily losing track of her altitude. The runway rushed up at her. The stall buzzer rang harshly in her ear. The nose was too high!

Griff cursed richly, rescuing Dana from another lousy landing. Again, he'd gotten them down in one piece. Once they'd landed, he ordered Dana to try it again. No sooner had she gotten the trainer airborne than she got sick a third time.

"That's it," he growled at her. "Land this thing! You're no good to yourself or me, and I'll be damned if I'm going to die in this cockpit because you can't concentrate on your flying. Get us down, Coulter."

"No!" Dana gulped back the bitterness in her mouth. "I can do it! Let me have one more chance!"

"No way. Land this thing. Now!"

Dana hadn't meant for emotion to enter her voice, but it did. "Griff, give me one more chance! Just one! I know I can do it. Please..."

Her plea tore at him. Sitting in the rear seat, he glared at her helmeted head through the cockpit plexiglass. "You're weak, Coulter. You don't have what it takes."

"I do, too! Let me prove it to you. I promise I won't get sick again. Just let me try one more landing. If I do it right, will you let me have another hour in the air?"

Griff wanted to say no, but another part of him admired her courage. "You get sick one more time, and I'm grounding you, Coulter," he warned gruffly.

"Okay," Dana agreed. "But let me land and prove I can do it!"

"Do it."

"Yes, sir!"

For the next hour, Dana forced herself to concentrate as never before. Her flight suit was wringing wet with sweat at the end of that time. After the last landing, she sat in the cockpit, so weak she couldn't move. All her emotions, her feelings, had been extruded and used up in forcing her body not to react to her airsickness. She threw up one last time taxiing back to the ramp, but Griff said nothing as long as she continued to steer the plane back to its slot without incident.

Griff climbed out first, moving around to the nose of the trainer, finishing out his report and grade on her. When Dana didn't move, he scowled and came around to the port side of the trainer.

"Coulter?"

"I'm coming." Dana willed herself to move. Feeling incredibly weak, she was afraid she'd collapse. Grasping the windshield and side of the cockpit, she forced herself to stand. Her knees were shaking so badly she wanted to sit back down again, but Griff's glare made her decide otherwise. As she stepped onto the wing, Dana was afraid to see the grade he'd given her. Wiping her hands on the damp thighs of her flight suit, she forced herself to take off the helmet. Her hair was wet, plastered against her skull beneath the cotton helmet liner.

Griff came forward, thrusting the board toward her. She took it with a trembling hand.

"You can't take this, Coulter."

Dana's entire focus moved to the grading box. A 2.0! At least he hadn't failed her. Not yet. The last three landings had been decent, but not great. Those he'd graded as 2.1s. All the others were 1.9s. The average came out to a barely passing grade. Swallowing back the sudden tears of relief, Dana searched numbly for the pen in the pocket of her left sleeve.

"Here," Griff growled impatiently. "Sign the damn thing. I'm in a hurry. I've got things to do."

Stung, Dana took his pen, her name illegible because of her shaking hand.

Taking back the board, Griff pinned her with a dark look. "Admit it. You can't make the grade, Coulter."

Her nostrils flaring, Dana held his gray gaze. "I'll make it." The words were bitten off and flung back at him.

"I'm not putting up with another two hours of airsickness from you."

"I'll make sure I don't get sick."

"You don't get it, do you?" he rasped. She looked frail and pale, standing there, the suit clinging to her tense form. "Students like you never make it. Your body isn't adjusting to flying. It's just a matter of time before I wash you out."

The irony that it might be her body betraying her ability to get her wings frustrated Dana to the point of tears. She swallowed hard, holding Griff's accusing look. "Lieutenant, I'm not giving up. I'm not throwing in the towel." She jabbed a finger at him. "Dammit, I'm not a weakling! You've accused me of it enough that I swear I'll *never* quit."

He flung her a lethal smile. "If you don't, I'll make sure you do."

Dana's eyes widened enormously. As he turned away, she reached out, jerking him to a halt. "Is that a threat, Lieutenant? I've heard that kind of tone before, and I don't like it. If you try and wash me out for any reason other than a fair one, I'll press charges."

Griff froze, glaring down at her. The set of her mouth and those blue eyes narrowed with defiance told him she was serious. Wrenching his arm out of the grasp of her hand, he snarled, "Coulter, you're going to fail yourself. I'm not going to have to do it for you. Airsick students don't last more than two weeks."

Dana stood there, her chest heaving with the need to cry. Damn him! She spun away, heading back to the trainer to pick up her helmet bag and the embarrassing burp bags. AVM Parker was standing there, holding them out to her.

"You okay, ma'am?" he inquired.

"I'm fine."

Parker shrugged his thin shoulders and offered her a slight smile. "Buck up, Miss Coulter. He gave you a passing grade, didn't he?"

"Yes." *Barely.*

"You know he Boarded both his other students on this last session, didn't you?"

Stunned, Dana stared up at the young crew chief. "Uh, no. No, I didn't."

"Mr. Turcotte's a stickler on learning landing procedures. You know, he was Top Gun at Miramar two years ago."

Dana's heart sank. "No, I didn't know that."

"Yes, ma'am. He's a Top Gun. One of our best." Parker offered her a bit more of a hesitant smile as he patted the trainer affectionately. "If you can see his job through his eyes, and what he was to accomplish with you in six short weeks, maybe you can understand his driving need to qualify you. It's a hard, thankless job. I watched your landings. You did pretty good for a first time."

Tension bled out of Dana. She knew she had a friend in Parker, and she was grateful for the information about Griff. "I—thanks, Parker."

"You got a little problem with airsickness?"

With a groan, Dana said, "It's not a little problem."

"It'll go away, Miss Coulter. Don't you worry about it." He watched Griff in the distance. "Be strong for him. If you are, he won't fail you."

Strong. Dana quietly thanked Parker and dragged herself back to the ready-room locker area. How could she maintain this degree of high emotional drama every other day and survive? The last hour had been accomplished on nothing but pure adrenaline. Suddenly, Dana was whipped. After taking a hot shower and changing into her summer uniform, she felt numb. Forcing herself to move, she hurried to make her class on egress procedure.

Griff watched Dana critically as she circled the trainer Friday morning. She looked pale as hell. Her hands shook as she took the discrepancy log from Parker and signed it off. Guilt nagged at him. He'd made up his mind that if she was airsick today, he was going to force her to quit. Still, the stubborn set of her mouth and her blue eyes armed with challenge gave him second thoughts. He'd find out soon enough if the airsickness problem was going to gradually fade away, or remain.

Dana was all business in the cockpit. She'd barely slept the past two nights, having nightmares about getting a 1.9 from Griff for not landing correctly. Worse, she was in a heightened state of panic about her airsickness. Manny had told her that a lot of other students had acute airsickness and had gotten over it. Ignoring the building cumulus hanging around the airport, Dana concentrated on the takeoff. It was perfect! As she had done so many times throughout her restless nights of sleep, she automatically went through the motions of flying. Griff was deadly quiet, but Dana had come to expect that—until she did something wrong. Then he'd leap on her without mercy. Would she get sick? Griff would Board her if she did, and he'd have a right to do it. There was nothing she could do to appeal his decision.

To her delight, the takeoff had been uneventful. Only silence sounded in the headphones. Dana was about to ask what he wanted her to do when he said, "Touch and go's, Coulter."

The battle lines were drawn. The trainer shook and shuddered as it hit a series of air pockets.

"Level it out!"

Immediately Dana corrected, getting the wings level again.

"You're too high!"

Her gaze shot to the altimeter. She was thirty feet above the correct altitude. Down went the nose.

"Make it smoother, Coulter. Don't jerk my plane around like that."

His plane. Dana wanted to cram it down his throat. Her stomach rolled ominously as she entered another series of airpockets. She called the tower for landing permission and got it. Other trainers were about a quarter mile in front of and behind her. The turbulence of being so close to other planes was increasing by the second. Dana pulled back in the throttle and tried to stop closing in on the other aircraft. Why was it slowing down? Stymied, she got into trouble because with loss of power, the trainer began to lose altitude.

"Get this plane up to altitude!" Griff snapped.

Dana pushed the throttle forward. "But we're closing too fast on that other trainer!"

"He'll get out of your way in time," Griff drawled. "Just stay in line and don't screw it up."

The trainer hit another violent air pocket. Dana became just as violently ill. She heard Griff curse and take the controls from her, yanking the trainer around in a tight bank and taking them out of the landing pattern.

"That's it, Coulter!"

Gripping her stomach, Dana gasped, "No it's not!"

"Ensign, you're grounded."

Despair washed over Dana as Turcotte landed the plane and taxied them back to the ramp. Anger overwhelmed her as they descended from the aircraft. Parker gave them a worried look but said nothing, going to service the trainer. Griff stalked off without a word. Dana ran to catch up, gripping his arm.

"Just what the hell do you think you're going to do?"

Griff wheeled around. "Ensign, you are a medical liability. I intend to recommend to the Board that you be relieved of your student status and sent somewhere else. Face it: You're cut out to be a swimmer, not a flyer."

Enraged, Dana leaped forward, jabbing her finger into his broad chest. "Lieutenant, I'm not Carol Turcotte."

Griff blinked, assimilating her tortured cry. He saw the tears in Dana's eyes and winced.

"I'm not weak, and I'm not a quitter. And I wasn't born with a damn silver spoon in my mouth, either. I expect to earn my way through life. Do you understand me? And I'll be damned if a pigheaded instructor who's angry over his divorce is going to nail *me* in order to get even! Do we understand each other, mister?" The tone of voice she took was that of an upperclassman to a plebe back at the academy. Griff looked as if he were in shock.

Dana backed off. "I intend to go to Dr. Collins right now and tell him about my airsickness. If you try and hang me before I get an official response from him, I'll slap you and VT2 with a sexual-harassment suit it will never survive."

Griff studied her in angry silence. Technically, Dana was correct. But dammit, she'd dragged up Carol's name and thrown it into the arena of their combat issues. God, but Dana was a fighter. Admiration warred with his fury. "You do that, Ensign. Have Dr. Collins call me with his assessment."

She eyed him warily. "And if he okays me for flight status?"

"Then we fly."

"What kind of grade am I getting today?"

Griff almost smiled. Dana never let up. If he'd been in her shoes, he'd have asked the very same question. "Incomplete."

"Fair enough."

Dana started to walk away.

"Ensign?"

Halting, she turned slowly in his direction. "Yes, sir?"

"Don't ever bring up my wife's name again."

"Then don't ever compare me to her again." Dana saw her comment hit him like a bomb. Taking advantage of the silence, she added, "Try to see me as Dana Coulter—not every other woman in your life."

Griff pondered their angry exchange as he watched Dana walk away. He was furious with her; and yet, her strength was something he'd never encountered in any woman, except perhaps his mother. Behind him, he heard Parker begin to service the trainer. The crew chief was young, but enthusiastic about his duties.

"Parker?"

The crew chief was at the top of the ladder. "Yes, sir?"

Griff walked back over toward the plane. "You've been here at Whiting how long?"

"Almost three years, Mr. Turcotte."

"And you've seen a lot of flight students come and go?"

With a smile, Parker nodded. "Plenty of them, sir."

Griff mulled over his next question. Ordinarily, he'd never consult an enlisted person about one of his students, but he needed a double check on Dana.

"What's your assessment of Ensign Coulter?"

"She's got what it takes, sir."

"No question in your mind?"

Parker's smile broadened. "Sir, despite her being sick, she's flying well. I was watching the two of you in the flight pattern earlier. If she can hang in there, I think she'll do it. Don't you?"

Griff scowled. "I don't know, Parker. Thanks..." And he turned away, heading back to the ready room. Parker's enthusiasm over Dana dampened him considerably. The crew chief had a lot of time around Whiting, and had worked with more students than Griff had on the walk-around. Griff knew from his own experience that enlisted people with time in grade often knew more than the officer in charge. Disgruntled, he walked past the sentry, flashing his identification. What would the flight surgeon recommend on Dana's case? Would he ground her? Griff sincerely hoped so.

"Ensign, you're suffering from acute airsickness," Dr. Collins said.

Relief made Dana sag against her chair, across the desk from the officer. "When will it go away?"

Collins shrugged. "It's different for everyone. I'd say that in another week or so you'll be over the worst of it."

"What will make it go away faster?"

"More flights."

Dana grinned. "You're serious?"

Collins smiled back and rubbed the bridge of his prominent nose. "Word's gone around about the battle between you and Lieutenant Turcotte."

"It's more like a war, sir."

"He's an excellent instructor with a lot of pressure on him recently."

Dana studied the doctor and realized he wasn't going to say anything more. "Well, sir, I don't think there's a student here who isn't under equal pressure."

"I would agree with you, Ensign."

"So your prescription for me?"

"Fly every day until you get over the airsickness."

"Will you put that in writing?"

Collins's grin widened. "Yes, I will."

On the way to the chow hall at noon, Dana met Molly. Maggie was still out on a flight.

"Hey, did I hear some scuttlebutt about the Turk!" Molly told her conspiratorially after they sat down at the table to eat.

Still upset from the morning flight with Griff, Dana picked at the fried chicken in front of her. The chow hall rang with talk but little laughter. Flying was serious business, and the students were low-key and uptight.

"What did you hear?"

"I was over at the library earlier and read an article in the newspaper. Two and a half weeks ago a Lieutenant Toby Lammerding was killed in an air accident over at Pensacola. He was teaching a woman student to fly." Molly frowned. "It mentioned in the article that Griff Turcotte was a close friend to Toby's family and would deliver the eulogy in Atlanta, Georgia, at his funeral. Get this, Dana: The day you tangled at the airport with that thief was the day Turcotte was coming back from his best friend's funeral."

"My God," Dana whispered. Rapidly the pieces fell into place. "His wife divorced him six months ago. His best friend was killed while teaching a woman student a few weeks ago." Shutting her eyes tightly, Dana added, "No wonder he's having trouble dealing with me. I'm Carol and I'm the woman who killed his best friend all wrapped up into one."

"From the sounds of it, Turcotte's got a lot of anger and grief bottled up inside him. It looks like he's taking it out on you."

Opening her eyes, Dana stared over at her friend. Miraculously, all her anger toward Griff dissolved. In its place was a heart-rending pain for the loads he carried. "I'm glad you told me this, Molly."

"I don't know if it will help," she said doubtfully, digging into her chef's salad.

"Oh, it will," Dana replied softly. Grief and pain were things she understood well. She'd seen her mother carry awful loads alone. And Dana had struggled with her own load because of her father. "Men don't handle crying or letting loose of feelings very well."

"So he's aiming it at you."

"Yes."

With a grimace, Molly stopped eating, the fork poised midway to her mouth. "What are you going to do?"

With a sigh, Dana shrugged. "I just threw his ex-wife's name at him this morning."

"Ouch."

"God, why didn't I figure it out sooner?"

"Give me a break, Dana. No one in their right mind could have guessed all that had happened to Turcotte. For all we knew, he was born that way."

Dana shook her head sadly. "No, I should have taken my cue about him at the airport. He was so kind and—gentle."

"Men can be, occasionally," Molly teased.

"My experience differs from yours, remember?"

"Roger that. Still, I think Turcotte's trying to be fair with you under the circumstances."

Dana gave her a flat look. "Oh?"

"He gave you an incomplete today. If he was really riding roughshod, he'd have Boarded you. And what about Wednesday? He gave you a second chance on landings."

"Only because I fought back, Molly. The man thrives on waging war. You shouldn't have to scream and yell at someone to get through to them."

"Maybe that's the only thing he respects right now—your ability to match him, blow for blow."

Dana sat grimly, her appetite gone. What a lousy situation to be caught in. She was struggling with her own body so that she could get a decent shot at her wings. On top of that, Griff had been wounded in action twice. Mortally, from the looks of it. And like most men, he'd bottled up his emotions and wasn't dealing well with the rest of the world as a result. Except, she was his world and the focus of his anger. There was no easy answer. All she could do was persevere, try to keep her temper and not screw up at the controls. She couldn't give Griff reasons to lash out at her. Dr. Collins had said more flying would help. What was Griff going to do when she handed him the sick chit ordering him to fly with her daily?

Chapter Six

Dana resolved not to allow her own defensiveness and anger to surface around Griff. God knew, the man would test and push her beyond her known limits of patience and endurance. He already had. Taking the sick chit to his office, Dana inhaled deeply before knocking and entering.

Griff was at his desk, as usual, piles of paperwork neatly stacked at both elbows. Dana supposed one was the In file, the other the Out. When he looked up, his face darkened. She came to attention.

"Ensign Coulter reporting as ordered," she said. She put the chit down in front of him, then came to parade rest in front of his desk. Griff's expression changed considerably when he read Collins's medical report.

"You're to fly every day?" he muttered incredulously. Normally, an instructor had three students, each flying three days a week. That left the IPs time on the other two days to corral and process the mountains of paperwork demanded of them. Not only that, but Griff had classes to prepare for and teach, and tests to grade. The two students he'd washed out had already been replaced with two new candidates. What was Collins doing?

"Yes, sir. The doctor felt my airsickness is a passing thing, and that the more flying time I get in now, the sooner I'll get over it." Dana hoped he couldn't hear her heart pounding in her chest. She watched his brows knit with obvious dissatisfaction. A large part of her felt sorry for him.

"This can't be right!" Griff threw a glance up at her. "Wait outside, Coulter."

"Yes, sir." Dana turned and left, guessing that he'd call Collins.

Griff waited impatiently for the doctor to come to the sick-bay phone.

"Collins speaking."

"Doctor, this is Lieutenant Griff Turcotte."

"Ah, yes. You're calling about Ensign Coulter, no doubt."

"I am. Since when have you ordered an airsick student to fly every day? You've never done that before." Collins had questioned Griff earlier about his feelings about Toby's death, and Griff had avoided the topic. Could Collins be concerned that Griff wasn't treating Dana fairly?

"Yes, that's right, Griff."

"Why?"

"I think it's a healthy prescription for both of you."

His hand tightened around the phone. "Look, Doc, I'm fine."

"Pilots are an interesting breed, Griff. When a trauma hits them, they swallow it, pretending it's not there. As a flight surgeon, I'm concerned about the psychological effects that Toby's death has had on you."

"I'm over it," Griff protested.

"It's only been three weeks since he died. No human gets over something like that so quickly."

Rubbing his brow, Griff looked up toward his office door, knowing Dana stood on the other side. "Look, Doc, I appreciate what you're trying to do, but it's not going to work. Coulter is . . . well—" He hesitated, trying to find the right words to walk around his sharpened feelings about women since the divorce. He didn't want Collins putting *him* on flight waivers for some harebrained reason like grief or anger at his ex-wife. It wouldn't look good in his service jacket, and he badly wanted another carrier assignment when he'd finished as an IP at Whiting a year from now. "I just don't feel she can handle the airsickness."

"My professional opinion is that she's the right person to work through some of these problems you're holding on to, Griff."

Needled, Griff controlled his frustration. "Coulter's only pulling 2.0s. I seriously doubt she'll last another week."

"I think that young lady has what it takes to be a fine officer and pilot. She's got grit, and I know that's something you respect."

Saying nothing but "Goodbye," Griff hung up the receiver. He stared at the opposite wall where his certificates and diplomas hung. Not knowing who to bite first, and feeling a deluge of incredible pressure building in his chest, he shoved his chair back and stood.

Dana jumped to her feet when the door was jerked open. Griff was angry—as usual. But she saw something else in his eyes that made her simply want to take him into her arms and hold him—a highly unusual desire on her part. Pain was reflected in his gray eyes, she realized. Raw pain. She stood uncertainly, flexing her fingers into her palms, trying to hide her nervousness.

"Come in here."

She came and shut the door quietly behind her, watching Griff closely. Ordinarily, Griff's shoulders were thrown back with pride, but now they looked slumped, almost broken. The silence built.

"Dr. Collins thinks flying every day will help you."

"Yes, sir."

Griff had spoken hoarsely, his back to her. Now he turned around. There was such compassion in Dana's blue eyes that it nearly broke him. His withheld emotions were so close to the surface, that he could feel tears pricking the backs of his eyes. "You approve?"

"Well . . . does it matter what I think?"

"Yes."

He was struggling to be fair. Dana could see it in every line of his face. That terrible pain and grief he carried inside him was eating him alive. Softly, she answered, "I know I can fly, Lieutenant. I never expected my body to rebel on me. Airsickness didn't exist in my vocabulary." She opened her hands toward him. "I feel Dr. Collins is right: Let me fly often. I'm *sure* I'll adjust."

Griff stood tensely, Dana's husky voice washing over him like warm waves of water after a freezing night. There was such a powerful, invisible attraction between them. For a split second, he almost asked her personal questions. Where did she come from? What kind of life experiences had molded her into the person who stood before him? Griff found himself hungry to explore Dana on a private level. She fed him something he desperately needed: a feeling of peace and serenity. When her lips parted, he drew in a ragged breath and turned away. He walked to his desk and sat down. "This is going to put me on the line, Coulter. I've got my hands full with two new students, plus you. I'll have to squeeze in those extra flights on a catch-as-catch-can basis."

"You tell me when you want to fly, and I'll be there."

"It won't be the same time every day."

"That's all right."

He saw the resolve in Dana's eyes and in the set of that full, ripe mouth—a mouth he wanted to explore intimately; to kiss, to feel the texture of. Jangled at his inability to keep

Dana at arm's length as he did every other student passing through his life, he growled, "Be at the ready room at 0700 tomorrow morning."

Her smile conveyed her hope and thanks. "Yes, sir."

Dana was given orders to leave her aeronautics class fifteen minutes early in order to catch another flight with Griff. It was Friday afternoon, and she eagerly left to reach the lockers in the ready room. The last two days had been a miracle of sorts. On Wednesday she'd pulled a 2.0 and was airsick only twice. Yesterday Griff had awarded her a 2.1, and she'd been ill only once. Everything was improving.

Or was it? Dana slowed her walk as she entered the ready-room building. She had to hurry and change into her one-piece flight uniform, grab her helmet bag and hurry out to where Griff was waiting for her by his trainer. The past two days he'd been moody and snappish, giving her instructions only when necessary. Dana knew she was rapidly improving on her landings. Perhaps that was why he hadn't been "screaming" at her. Still, the pain lingered in his eyes.

On the tarmac, Griff nodded to her as she came up to him. "We're going to do touch and go's over at Pensacola," he told her abruptly.

Eager to prove she could handle the denser traffic situation at Pensacola, Dana nodded. "How long can we fly?"

"Two hours."

"Great!" She flashed him a smile and began the walk-around.

Moodily, Griff watched Dana. Everything about her was confident and sure. Going over to Pensacola wasn't "great" in his opinion. It scared him to death. But it was part of the curriculum to use Pensacola's busy flight pattern to get the Whiting students used to heavy air-traffic situations. Normally, Griff wasn't ever nervous, but today he was. He was hoping that since it was Friday afternoon, fewer students would be in the air, with the instructors taking off a few hours early for the forthcoming weekend.

Griff's plan backfired. As Dana flew the trainer to the Pensacola air station, the pattern was stacked with at least two hundred aircraft circling the huge airport facility. Groaning to himself, he felt sweat pop out on his upper lip. The urge to grab the controls from Dana was very real. Automatically, he began rubbernecking around, checking other aircraft flying in the vicinity. Over the past year, there had been three air collisions and innumerable close calls.

"Stay alert!" he snapped to Dana. "This airspace can kill you."

"Yes, sir."

Her voice was calm and steady—unlike his. Toby's crash kept blipping in front of him. Griff turned off the intercom momentarily, releasing a curse, and then switched it back on.

Tension thrummed through Dana as she entered the busy flight pattern. The headset crackled with constant communications between the airplanes and harried controllers in the tower below. Griff had told her earlier that Pensacola was one of the busiest airports in the U.S. Looking at the hundreds of planes spaced no more than a quarter or half a mile apart, she believed him. Turbulence was constant. Luckily her stomach was responding with only minimal queasiness. Dr. Collins had been right; with more flights, her body was adjusting to flying conditions.

"Look out!"

Griff's cry ripped through her headset. Dana saw another plane loom in front of her cockpit windshield. Gasping, she wrenched the trainer to the left to avoid the collision. The controls were ripped from her gloved hands, and she felt the plane being banked in a tight right turn, out of the pattern. Griff was breathing raggedly. So was she.

"I—I'm sorry. I didn't see it," Dana whispered shakily.

"I've had it! This is the last time, Coulter! You damn well should have seen that aircraft! How in the hell could you miss it? It was coming right at you!"

Shamed, Dana knew he was right. "I—I'm sorry."

"'Sorry' doesn't cut it, Coulter! I'm giving you a 1.9 for this flight. There was no excuse for your failure to see that plane!"

A 1.9. She'd be Boarded. Dana bit down hard on her lower lip to stop from protesting. Griff was still breathing raggedly, his normally unemotional voice lined with feeling. Abruptly, Dana remembered that his best friend had died in a similar accident in the flight pattern.

"Give me another chance, Lieutenant."

"No way! We're going back to Whiting."

"I can do it! You can't tell me you haven't made mistakes flying. This was my first time in a busy pattern. Let me go back and try it again. Please!"

Sweat stung his eyes. Griff blinked them a couple of times, his hand tight around the stick. He wasn't even going to allow her to fly the trainer back to Whiting. For the first time in his life, he'd been scared out of his wits. Although he was unafraid to land an F-14 Tomcat fighter on a heaving carrier deck in the worst kind of weather, this incident had struck real fear into him. He was coming apart at the seams; he could feel it. A terrible shaking, quivering feeling filled his gut. Nausea stalked him. Dana's pleading request only fueled his desperation and anxiety.

"I said no!"

"You think I'm weak, don't you?"

"All women are!" he roared back.

"I'm not! And there are a lot of other women who aren't, either!"

Desperate, unable to steady his breathing, Griff grabbed at straws. "I'll prove it to you, Coulter. Right here and now. Take the controls."

"I've got the controls."

Reaching over, he shoved the throttle back to idle. "All right, you have an in-flight emergency." He leaned down, holding the manual landing-gear release lever. "You lost all hydraulics, and you've got to crank down the landing gear by hand. Do it." He knew without a doubt that with him holding the lever, Dana would never be able to budge it. He knew it was a rotten trick, but he didn't care. She was pushing him too hard. He couldn't go back into that pattern at Pensacola. Not today. Not with a woman. Not even with Dana, who was competent and didn't deserve this. When she couldn't get the lever down, it would prove she was weak, and he could wash her out of the school once and for all.

Torn by his conscience, Griff held the lever tightly, feeling her struggling with it. It moved fractionally, but Griff applied brute force.

"Come on, Coulter!" he shouted. "Get the landing gear down! You're at one thousand feet and falling! Hurry up!"

The bastard! Dana almost said it. She knew without a doubt Griff was holding the lever on purpose. All right, if that's the game he wanted to play, she'd do it his way. Straightening, Dana pulled her left foot away from the rudder, bringing it back against her body as far as she could. Carefully, she aimed the heel of her polished black flight boot at the lever alongside the fuselage. With all her strength, she slammed it down on the mechanism. She heard Griff grunt over the headset. The lever popped free! With a cry of triumph, Dana manually lowered the landing gear. When she reached two hundred feet, she pushed the throttle forward and took the trainer back to one thousand feet, vindicated.

Griff cursed, holding his aching hand. He stared down at the bruised flesh around his left index finger. Dammit, it felt as if she'd broken his finger! Angrily, Griff touched it. The pain was too great. Damn her!

"Get this plane down on the ground," he snarled.

On the ground, Dana waited warily for Griff to grade her. He held the board awkwardly in his left hand, fumbling with the pen. She saw a bruise forming on a couple of his fingers and took satisfaction in the knowledge that he'd paid dearly for trying to trick her.

"You're getting a 1.9, Ensign." Griff shoved the board toward her so she could see the grade and sign it off. Her eyes rounded with shock and then fury.

"I don't deserve a 1.9! I refuse to sign it!" Dana thrust it back at him.

"You screwed up! We nearly got hit by another plane."

"Well, did it ever occur to you that the other plane might have been at the wrong altitude?"

"It doesn't matter," Griff roared back at her. "You should have seen it!"

Breath coming in ragged gulps, Dana marched up to him. "Damn you, Turcotte! Damn you to hell! You're trying to wash me out when it's not me you're really angry with! I know all about your best friend dying at Pensacola with a female student! Don't you think I can put two and two together? You're full of grief and loss and anger—and I just happen to be the closest thing in your gunsights to shoot at!" Dana struck her chest with her thumb. "I'm not stupid, Lieutenant. You're projecting anger over your divorce and the death of your friend on me. It's not fair! I don't have it coming!" Her nostrils flared. "And I'll be damned if I'm going to take this 1.9 lying down. I'll fight you at the Board of Inquiry. I'll spill everything. Even Dr. Collins knows what you're doing! I'll drag him in on this."

It hurt to feel. Griff stood, Dana's hoarse cry, her pain, consuming him. When he saw the tears in her eyes, he backed away. His hand was throbbing and on fire. His heart felt as if it would burst inside him. Spinning on his heel, Griff stalked away, afraid to say anything because he wasn't sure he could get the words out. A sob lodged in his throat, tightening it, and he tried to gulp it away. It was no use. He owed Dana an apology. He owed her a hell of a lot more than that. She was right, his conscience railed; and he was wrong.

Dana stood alone by the trainer, watching Griff walk quickly back toward the ready room. Tears stung her eyes, then trickled down her cheeks.

"Damn him," she whispered painfully, turning and retrieving her helmet bag. What would happen now? Would he push through with the 1.9 grade and demand a Board?

"Broken index finger," Dr. Jamison said, pointing to the X ray. He eyed Griff critically. "How'd you say you broke it?"

Griff muttered, "I got my hand jammed around the manual landing-gear release by mistake." Jamison looked doubtful and scratched his head. Griff was ashamed to tell him the rest of the story.

"Well, it's going to take a cast."

With a groan, Griff protested, "A removable one?"

"You want a crooked finger?"

"No, dammit."

"It'll be on for six weeks. Maybe five, with good behavior." Jamison grinned slightly. "Come to the casting room with me, and we'll take care of it."

Humiliated, Griff shuffled along behind the small, wiry doctor. It was Friday evening, and sick bay was nearly deserted. Students generally got sick during the week, before critical flights, not before a weekend. He remained silent while Jamison created a cast that went up to his elbow. It was going to be in the way on flights. Angry with himself, not Dana, Griff wanted to escape the base and get out to the beach to think. And feel.

"Don't get this baby in water, Griff. No showers, just baths."

"Are you serious?"

"Want to go through this all over again?" Jamison asked, his hands and arms splattered with damp plaster. He quickly wrapped Griff's fingers and wrist with yards and yards of gauze before applying the wet plaster.

"No, I don't."

"Then be a good fighter pilot and take a bath for the next six weeks."

"I prefer a shower."

"Of course." Jamison chuckled. "Pilots like things quick and fast. A bath takes too much time and trouble. You can whip in and out of a shower in about five minutes—just like every other situation in life."

Griff wasn't in the mood to appreciate Jamison's philosophical humor. Right now, all he wanted was to escape to his beach and think. Think about Dana's accusations—and search his soul for the raw truth and some answers.

Needing the security of the ocean, Dana had chosen Strawberry Beach, one place she was sure Griff wouldn't show up. The Friday-evening tourists lined the white sand, offering little privacy. It didn't matter. Although many children played in the knee-deep warm water and a few body surfers dove beyond that, no one swam past the breakers where she planned to go. She would have all the privacy in the world. At least she didn't have to worry about running into Griff here. Dropping her flowery print towel on the sand, Dana shrugged out of her white cotton shorts and gauzy lavender blouse. Her tennis shoes came off with a nudge, and she was ready to swim.

Children's laughter caught Dana's attention as she waded into the water. Part of her anxiety dissolved beneath their spontaneous joy as they played tag with one another. Dana halted, unable to remember a happy time like that in her own childhood. Pushing down those memories that could never be changed, Dana sank into the water, beginning a lazy freestyle stroke. The past was gone. She could only change the present.

Griff morosely studied Strawberry Beach and the many groups of Friday-evening families. He knew Dana wouldn't be here. She would avoid the crowds. Not wanting to risk running into her by accident, yet needing the soothing quality of the water to aid his thinking, Griff spread out his small blanket. The cast made it awkward, but he had no one to blame but himself.

Looking toward the beach, Griff sat down. The laughter of children rang around him. They were so innocent and happy, Griff reflected. Dana's face wavered in front of him, and he sighed heavily, allowing his head to drop forward. Staring down at the red cotton blanket, Griff recalled their last blistering conversation. Dana was right: He was using her as a scapegoat for his inability to cope with his own emotions about his divorce and Toby's death. He'd caused her to cry. Guilt jabbed sharply at him, and Griff compressed his mouth.

Somehow, he had to stop hurting Dana. She had nothing to do with his problems. He was projecting them on her. Looking down at the cast on his arm, Griff knew he deserved the broken finger. He'd never pulled that kind of stunt on a student. His anger had overridden his sense of fairness. Never had he hurt someone with that kind of intent. Normally Griff prided himself on his sensitivity to others, but Toby's death had set him into a tailspin, and he'd lost all sense of direction, allowing his dark feelings to rule him.

Rubbing his temple, Griff stared toward the choppy water. The sun would set in another hour. The clouds along the horizon blocked some of the light. Dana's eyes had turned cobalt with anguish when the tears had formed, he remembered. He'd made her cry. What a rotten bastard he'd turned out to be. Dana was a strong, good person with clear values. She played fair. He hadn't.

As his gaze perused the filled beach, Griff wanted to find a way to apologize, to get things back on track between them. He laughed abruptly. Whatever gave him the idea Dana would have any interest in him after the way he'd behaved toward her? And yet Griff dwelled on that very thought, that fragile emotion that had stubbornly refused to be destroyed in his heart since meeting her. He wanted to know Dana on a personal basis.

Dana was right: She was nothing like Carol. Repeatedly, Griff had seen her strength and resilience. My God, she was strong, he admitted finally. Lifting his chin, he realized now part of why he was drawn to Dana. She possessed that internal strength he'd always searched for and never found in a woman.

"Great, Turcotte, just great. And you've damned near destroyed her because you were so blind," he whispered, his voice raw with self-disgust. There was nothing to dislike about Dana, Griff finally admitted. She had courage—and she was a damn good flight student. Her ability to learn quickly and not get rattled under tremendous pressure was the mark of a successful Navy-pilot candidate.

Griff's eyes narrowed against the sun shining brightly across the ocean in front of him. He saw a lone figure just outside the breakers, striking toward shore. Was he seeing things? Griff's heart picked up in beat at the realization that it was Dana. He'd recognize her long, graceful swimming style anywhere. Unconsciously Griff rose to his feet, flexing his hands against his denim clad thighs. Fate sure knew how to play a hell of a trick. Dana had come to the same beach—probably to avoid him.

Shading his eyes against the sun, he watched as Dana bodysurfed on a small wave, then rose to her feet in the waist-deep water. A smile shadowed Griff's mouth as he saw Dana lean over and talk to a little blond girl in a bright orange life jacket, who was paddling happily back toward the shoreline.

Griff waited tensely. Fate was offering him a second chance. As soon as Dana came out of the water, he would go over and talk with her. Whether she wanted to or not, she would hear his abject apology. He didn't hold out hope that she would either believe or accept it. Words were weak compared to actions, and Griff knew he still would have to prove himself to Dana on a daily basis while they flew.

"Riptide!" the lifeguard in the tower blared through his bullhorn. "Everyone out of the water! A riptide is coming in! Parents, get your children out of the water!"

Griff started, his gaze pinned on Dana, still in the waist-deep water. A riptide! Anxiously he looked beyond her. With the sun glaring off the ocean, the reddish-colored riptide could barely be discerned. The lifeguard hadn't seen it in time, and now the murky, crimson-colored water was snaking silently toward unsuspecting swimmers. Knowing that a riptide could jerk people right off their feet even in ankle-deep water, Griff sprinted toward the beach to help get the children out of its way. The cold currents of a riptide came out of the depths of the ocean, swept ashore at the speed of a freight train, then moved just as rapidly back out to sea. Victims caught in their grasp could be drowned by the terrific undertow. Those who survived the initial undertow had been known to be taken out to sea for ten or fifteen miles before the current dived back down where it had originated from.

As Griff sprinted through the sucking, heavy sand toward the people scrambling to heed the warning, he glanced to his left and saw Dana turn, looking out to sea. She stood poised like a statue.

Dana saw the ugly, reddish-colored riptide moving toward her with deadly speed. In water this deep, she could be killed. Instantly Dana lunged toward shore, striking out in sharp, quick strokes. Already she could feel the pull of the water at her legs and feet, trying to suck her back out to sea. Grimly, she fought the ocean's ruthless strength. Finally, in knee-deep water, she stood, shaking her hair free of the brine and rubbing her eyes. Looking up, Dana's mouth fell open.

"Griff!" There, no more than a hundred feet from her, he was running into the surface, rescuing a six-year-old child playing on an inflated dragon. It had to be her imagination! What was he doing here? His arm was in a cast up to his elbow. So many thoughts collided in Dana's head. Screams and shouts sounded all around her. People were running to rescue their children from the spreading red tide.

Dana's eyes widened. The blond girl she'd talked with earlier was swimming unconcernedly a hundred feet offshore. The reddish fingers of the riptide spread toward her, and Dana watched in horror as the child was yanked quickly back toward the waves and the open sea. The girl had a life jacket on, but that wouldn't necessarily save her from the savage undertow.

"Vickie! My God! Vickie!"

A young blond woman raced by Dana, jumping awkwardly through the water. It had to be the girl's mother. Dana sized up the situation immediately. The mother was overweight and in bulky clothes, while Vickie was already caught in the undertow, her small head bobbing between a series of breakers. Without thought for her own safety, Dana wheeled and leaped after the mother.

"I'll get her! You stay here," Dana gasped, pulling the woman to a halt in the ankle-deep water.

Sobbing, the woman pointed to her daughter. "But—Vickie! My God, she'll be killed!"

Dana released the woman's arm. "I'll get her for you," she said calmly. "Stay here and tell the lifeguard to get us help."

Griff had just lifted a ten-year-old boy out of the riptide's grasp when he saw Dana dive into the surf and begin swimming out to sea. He put the boy down on the beach.

"Dana!" he roared. His voice carried, but she either didn't hear him or ignored his cry. What the hell was she doing? Panic riffled through Griff as he took two steps into the water. Then he saw why she'd returned to the ocean: A child had been captured by the riptide, and was already a quarter mile out to sea.

Griff's throat closed with fear for Dana's life. He knew she was a strong swimmer with a lifetime of knowledge about the ocean, but riptides didn't respect experience. Standing helplessly, he watched as the red water pulled Dana beneath the surface.

"No!" he shrieked, tears jamming into his eyes. He ran into the water, now up to his knees. "Dana! Dammit, Dana!" His screams reverberated across the breakers that spilled their foamy lives out on the sand. His heart aching in his throat, Griff nearly lost his balance in the swift-moving current.

"Vickie!" the mother shrieked. She turned, running toward Griff who stood no more than fifty feet away. "Get help!" she cried. "My daughter, Vickie, is out there. The woman said to get help!"

Chapter Seven

The last thing Dana heard was Griff's thundering voice riddled with panic, calling her by name. She had her own fear to contend with as the riptide violently twisted around her, jerking her downward. Luckily, Dana had taken a deep breath of air into her lungs seconds before the action occurred. She was being dragged against the sand at startling speed, going deeper and deeper. Her lungs began to hurt, a sign that the riptide had drawn her at least fifty feet beneath the surface. The need to strike back up toward the surface was imperative. Within a minute or so, Dana no longer would have the strength to break the tide's hold.

Her eyes tightly shut, her mouth thinned to retain what oxygen was left, Dana rolled onto her belly as she scraped the bottom of the ocean. Tucking her legs tightly against her chest, she used the sand as a springboard to lunge upward. It worked! She felt the current lessen slightly as she used powerful strokes to break the initial bond.

There was no such thing as being free of a riptide. The cold water refused to completely release Dana, and every stroke was a superhuman effort. In her heart, she remembered Griff, and rallied. Another part of her remembered the girl, Vickie. Would the life vest prevent her from being sucked down as Dana had been? Dana prayed it would.

Dana shot out of the water like a projectile, a huge gasp tearing from her. She flattened out to make herself less of a target for the current and dog-paddled in a circle, catching her breath.

"Vickie!" she screamed. The waves were three-to-four feet high all around her. The sun was directly parallel to the horizon, sending a sheet of blazing, blinding light into her eyes.

"Vickie, where are you?" Dana's voice cracked. She had to divide her attention between avoiding the tricky current, still trying to pull her down, and keeping her head out of the water to suck in precious, life-giving air.

"Here..."

Dana craned her neck. There, a hundred yards away, Vickie bobbed on the surface, her thin blond hair plastered against her frightened face.

"Hold on, I'm coming!" Dana called, swimming toward her. The child's green eyes were huge with fear, and she clung tightly to Dana's neck when Dana reached her.

"It's all right," Dana whispered soothingly, treading water. "You're safe now, Vickie, safe—" But they weren't. Dana twisted her head toward the shore. It was rapidly disappearing from sight. The current held them tightly in its grip. The water around them remained murky red.

With a sob, Vickie cried, "Mommy—I want Mommy!"

"Hold on and I'll take you back to her, honey."

"P-promise?"

Dana forced a smile for the child's benefit, gently prying Vickie's fingers loose from around her neck. "Piece of cake, Vickie. Now, come on, relax. You aren't going to drown.

My name's Dana, and I'll get you back to the beach."
Reaching down with her free hand, Dana loosened the belt
around her suit. Vickie cried out when Dana released her
momentarily to slip the belt through the top of the child's
life jacket.

"I'm going to tie you to me, honey," Dana explained.
Her legs were beginning to feel a bit tired. Shifting, she
floated easily on her back, giving them a rest while she
fashioned a sling around the left shoulder strap of her suit,
buckling it back up.

"I—I'm scared." Vickie sobbed quietly, grasping for
Dana's shoulder and clinging tightly to her.

"So am I. Now, listen to me, Vickie. We both have to be
big girls about this. We're going to make it to shore, but I
need your help. Okay?"

Sniffing, Vickie wiped her watering eyes. "O-okay,
Dana."

Leaning over, Dana pulled her into her arms and kissed
her salty temple. "That's my girl. We have to be brave. No
more tears, because it wastes the water you have in your
body. Understand?"

With a nod, Vickie released her death grip on Dana's
shoulder. The belt became an umbilical cord and lifeline
between them.

"See, you can float right along beside me," Dana pointed
out, watching the fear slowly dissolve from Vickie's eyes.

"H-how soon can I go home? Mommy'll be worried."

"Lots of people are worried about us, honey." Dana
knew there was no use fighting the riptide carrying them
miles out to sea. The sun had set, making the horizon a layer
cake of lavenders, blues and pale violets. Looking around,
Dana realized Santa Rosa Island was one long, thin stretch
of land lying horizontal to the coast of Florida. The riptide
was carrying them out from it at a ninety-degree angle.
From her own experience, she knew riptides could shoot ten
or twenty miles out to open sea before dipping back down.

Until then, she and Vickie were its unwilling passengers and prisoners. There was no way she could humanly fight to break free from the violent current. They'd simply have to ride along until the tide surrendered them.

Blinking, Dana continued to float on her back, trying to conserve every ounce of her energy. The current was icy cold, chilling her, and she worried about losing precious body heat. Hypothermia could sap her energy to stay afloat, much less make it to shore. The more she analyzed their precarious situation, the more worried Dana became. Night was coming on, and Coast Guard rescue would be difficult in the dark.

The one thing Dana clung to was the fact that Griff had seen her swept out to sea with Vickie. If his tone had been any indication of his concern for their lives, he'd do everything in his power to get them rescued. The trauma stripped away her anger toward Griff. As she floated beside Vickie, an overwhelming need to cry struck Dana. Choking back the reaction for the little girl's sake, Dana closed her eyes, feeling the hot prick of tears behind her lids.

Please, Griff, help us! I know you can....

Griff stood in the air-conditioned office of Coast Guard Search and Rescue. Barely holding on to his disintegrating temper, he kept his voice low. "What do you mean, you can't get out an SAR chopper to hunt for Ensign Coulter and the girl?"

The chief behind the desk gave him an apologetic look. "I'm sorry, Lieutenant Turcotte, but there's been an emergency fifty miles south of us. Our two choppers are on that rescue mission. Two yachts collided, with fifteen people on board."

Half an hour had passed since Dana had been swept out to sea. Griff had driven to the nearest CG station, thinking it would be easy to get an SAR under way immediately. Vickie Tandy's mother, Veronica, stood beside him.

"But can't you do *something* to help me? My daughter's only seven years old! My God, she could drown out there!" she cried.

Griff placed his arm around the distraught mother. He glared at the chief. "How about calling in a chopper from another station, then?" he suggested tersely. Fear was knotting his stomach. Dana was at risk. What if she got cramps from the icy-cold current or what if sharks loitered around them? Portuguese men-of-war, the highly deadly jellyfish, plied these waters with great regularity. One sting, and Dana could die.

"I've already tried, sir. Look this is a day for emergencies. You know how it is on Fridays: Everyone's heading out to the beach for the weekend. Our SAR demands are more than we can handle. We're operating on a shoestring."

Flashing him an irate look, Griff acknowledged that the chief was correct. It wasn't that he didn't want to send a helo out to look for Dana; recent budget cuts meant none were available. "All right, then help me figure out where they might drift on that current."

"We can't do anything until a helo drops a data buoy in the water and gives us that information, Lieutenant."

Griff bridled. He led Veronica to a wooden chair and sat her down. "Look, Mrs. Tandy, I'm going to make a few calls. Stay here."

Sniffling, Veronica released his hand. "My baby's out there. My God, how could this be happening? Why isn't there a helicopter available?"

Patting her shoulder awkwardly, Griff whispered, "I'll find one somewhere." He had to. He couldn't lose Dana. Not now. Not ever. Moving back to the desk, Griff asked to use the phone. The chief nodded, pushing it over to him. Making a quick phone call to Pensacola, Griff got in touch with Commander Evans, an old squadron friend who had flown F-14s with him off the USS *Enterprise* several years ago. Griff knew Evans was in a key position at Pensacola, and told him the problem. The Navy kept several rescue helos, in case students crashed their trainers into the gulf. Keeping his fingers crossed, he asked Evans to authorize the release of an SAR team to begin looking for Dana and Vickie.

Night came quickly. Dana could still feel the undertow tugging relentlessly at her legs, but it wasn't as strong. Above her, the stars hung close and twinkled like precious, faceted diamonds. Her teeth chattered uncontrollably. The temperature of the riptide was stealing the heat from her body. Dana said nothing, maintaining a floating or treading position to conserve as much of her physical strength as possible. Vickie's teeth chattered, too. Dana brought the girl to her side, putting her arm around her and trying to warm her by keeping her close.

Dana's heart dwelled on Griff. Why had they fought so much? Something good and wonderful existed between them, but they'd never had a chance to explore it. She stared up at the night sky. Would her life end this way—never knowing what real love was like? She felt cheated, and it hurt. Closing her eyes, trying to remain relaxed, Dana allowed the entire airport scene to well up in her memory. She clung to the image of Griff's concerned face, and remembered his gentle touch. Would making love with him be like that? Somehow Dana knew instinctively that Griff was capable of giving, not just taking.

Disgusted with her rambling thoughts and feelings, Dana forced her eyes open. *Remember,* she told her heart sternly, *he's the one who called you weak, incapable of being successful.* And just as quickly, her heart recalled those rare moments when Griff had proved hauntingly human, drawing her to him, man to woman. Dana sighed in frustration. She was too streetwise to hang on to those rare occurrences. Griff had been a bastard ninety percent of the time, and she knew her roommates would agree that those were bad odds.

Right now, Dana realized, she *had* to rely solely on Griff for help. She'd expected an SAR helo to be up and looking for them. Lifting her hand out of the water, she checked the luminous dials on her Rolex watch: eight o'clock. Three hours had passed since they had been captured by the riptide. Rescue was looking dimmer by the moment. A frisson of panic struck Dana. She didn't want to die! Not this way, and certainly not now! And Vickie was only seven. She had a whole lifetime in front of her.

Abruptly, Dana felt the water temperature change, and the current eased, releasing them. The ocean rose and fell constantly around them. The wind had ceased at sunset, the sea calming to mere one- and two-foot wave patterns.

"I think we're free," Dana told Vickie.

"Free?" she queried in a tiny voice.

Sitting up and treading water, Dana pulled Vickie into her arms, giving her a tight squeeze. "The riptide's gone deep. We're through being pulled out. Now I can start swimming us back toward land."

Vickie clung to her. "Land? Where?"

Only dark ocean surrounded them. Dana looked up, finding Polaris, the North Star. She grinned, then realized Vickie couldn't see her smile through the moonlight night. "Honey, I know which way to go. The stars will show us. You ready?"

"I guess so...."

Dana admired Vickie's courage. Would Dana have been so trusting if it had happened to her at that age? With slow, measured strokes, she started heading toward a shore she couldn't see. She had no idea how far away from land they were. She didn't want to know. With Vickie attached to her suit's shoulder strap, her ability to swim properly was hampered. Not only did Dana have to stay afloat, but she had to drag Vickie with her. What if Santa Rosa Island was too far away? What if the tide worked against them? The current could drain her physical stamina and sooner or later, Dana knew she would sink and drown.

"Mommy said sharks live out here," Vickie said in a small, quavering voice.

"They do," Dana replied, her own voice ragged as she gulped in air. And on a smooth, quiet ocean like tonight's, they would definitely be drawn to the splashing sounds made by her swimming motion.

"Do they eat at night?"

"No," Dana lied. "Just during the day. They sleep at night like we do." They were night feeders, primarily, never really sleeping, always on the prowl for food. Dana changed the angle of how her hand hit the water, trying to minimize the slapping sound. The belt tugged at her, creating drag, taking a little bit more of her strength with each stroke. It couldn't be helped.

Vickie grew quiet, completely trusting the belt that strung them together. She lay on her back at Dana's urging, her small arms crossed over her tummy, her long, slender legs floating out in a relaxed fashion. The darkness was consummate. Dana couldn't even see her hand in front of her face. Her senses switched to the warm ocean surrounding them. She'd always had acute sensitivity to all things, but tonight Dana shifted her entire focus to her senses of touch and hearing. Occasionally she felt a small jellyfish brush one of her legs. Inevitably, minutes later, Dana would feel the hot sting of the gelatinous sea animal. Jellyfish usually hung about three feet beneath the surface. If touched, they reacted instantly with many of their long tentacles. Luckily, she wasn't allergic to jellyfish stings.

Each time her hand sliced through the dark water, Dana felt for anything that might be floating in their way. She was sure Portuguese men-of-war were in the Florida area. The water was too warm for them not to be around. If she or Vickie blindly bumped into one, it could mean death. It would take a while, but gradually, if the sting was bad enough, Dana knew it would cripple her enough to stop her from swimming. And then, they'd drown.

Quickly pushing those terrorizing thoughts out of her head, Dana tried to figure out how far out to sea the riptide had carried them. For three hours, they'd been pulled along by the current. How many knots had it been? Fifteen or twenty miles per hour? It was impossible to know the speed of the current. Rapidly doing some mental calculations, Dana felt her heart sink. Could it be they were twenty miles offshore? Dana had swum ten miles, and a couple of times, fifteen, but never twenty. And certainly not with a seven-year-old girl in tow.

Panic edged her resolve. Dana switched her thoughts back to Griff. He had such an incredibly strong, confident face. His eagle-gray eyes were beautiful, in Dana's opinion. She clung to her good memories of him. Still, the nagging thought persisted that if they were twenty miles out to sea, she couldn't possibly make it back to shore with Vickie. Maybe by herself, but not with the girl.

Yet, there was no question in Dana's mind that she wouldn't try to make it. Even if her magnificently trained body gave out, she might get Vickie close enough to the beach that the current might sweep them ashore, and save Vickie's life. Dana had to try. There was no alternative. If only Griff could have helped. If only...

"Okay, the SAR helo's up and searching," Coast Guard Chief Adams informed Griff.

Pacing back and forth in the small office, Griff gave a curt nod. Hours ago he'd told Veronica Tandy to go home and wait for word from the CG. Contacting the personnel office at Whiting, Griff had gotten the names of Dana's two roommates and dialed their number.

"Hello?"

Griff cleared his throat, his hand a little tighter on the phone. "This is Lieutenant Turcotte calling. Who am I speaking with?"

"Ensign Maggie Donovan, sir."

Griff heard the surprise and question in her voice. "I'm calling about your friend and roommate, Dana Coulter," he explained.

"Dana? Where is she? We've been worried sick, Lieutenant."

As quickly as possible, Griff explained the situation.

"We're coming down there," Maggie said.

"No. There's no use—"

"Lieutenant, she's our friend. It doesn't sound like the Coast Guard is doing much about rescuing Dana. Maybe we can estimate where Dana will come to shore."

Griff nodded. He'd been thinking the same thing. The passion in Maggie's voice was clear, and he knew there was no use trying to convince them to wait patiently at their apartment for word on Dana.

"All right, come on down. With three of us combing the beaches tonight, we might find her."

"We'll be right there."

Griff hung up the receiver, staring at it. Dana had some good friends, and he was glad for her sake. Dana was too important to him to leave in the Coast Guard's hands. He was going to stay the night, if necessary. Earlier, a Navy SAR helo from Pensacola had made a search and found nothing. The CG pilots had just returned from another rescue and come back to plot where Dana might be located.

Lieutenant Commander Storm Gallagher was at the controls, assuring Griff that she and her helo crew would do everything possible to find Dana and the girl. Griff had searched the woman pilot's features, reading between the lines: Time wasn't on their side. One thing Gallagher did give him hope on was dropping the data buoy. Armed with current speed and direction, which would be called in via radio, the chief might be able to plot a course to search for Dana. Griff looked at his watch. It was eight o'clock, and darkness had fallen.

He turned and stared out the windows that overlooked the ocean. It looked so calm, while he felt as if a hurricane was ripping him apart inwardly. Changing the focus of his eyes, Griff stared at his reflection in the glass. He looked tired and exhausted. What about Dana? Was she still fighting to stay afloat? Griff's last memory of Dana had been her surfacing from the undertow near Vickie. Then both of them had disappeared. Tears leaked into his eyes, and Griff wiped them away with the back of his hand. Why had he treated Dana so badly?

Griff grew very still, feeling something he'd never experienced before. He savored the frail tendril in his heart. What name could he give to this new feeling? After five years of marriage to Carol, Griff thought he'd gone through every possible human emotion. But this incredible sensation that made his heart burst open like a blossoming flower was entirely new. And beautiful.

"Dana..." He said her name softly: "Danielle..." Why hadn't anyone ever called her by her full name? It was beautiful and exotic, like her. Griff raised his eyes, seeing the fear in his reflection—fear that she could be dead or dying out there alone on that black, merciless ocean. The azure beauty of her eyes promised him so much—so much. Clenching his fists, he stared at himself several seconds and digested the new feelings Dana had miraculously brought into his life.

Whirling around when the radio crackled to life with Storm Gallagher's voice, Griff headed back to the counter. The chief was quickly writing down data buoy information. Griff took out his small pocket calculator. He and the chief went to the wall-size map of the ocean together.

"Ms. Gallagher is going to search this area, sir," Evans said.

Griff frowned. "Didn't she just say the riptide's gone?"

"Yes, sir."

"Then this latest data buoy info is useless."

"Not quite. All we can do is hypothesize the speed of the current. We know the direction," the chief said, tracing the area with his finger. "It's just a question of speed."

Dissatisfied, Griff figured the information on his calculator. He moved around the chief. "If the riptide moved faster than you think, she could be over there—twenty miles offshore."

The chief shook his head. "Sir, that's a long shot. Normally, riptides go for a couple of miles. The climatology and oceanographic people said this was a big one, so we've allowed up to twelve knots of speed. That still would put her only fifteen miles offshore. And that's the area Ms. Gallagher is searching."

Frustrated, Griff stuck to his intuitive feeling. "And if they find nothing?"

"She'll either shorten or lengthen the next search pattern."

"Dana could be dead by that time!" Griff hadn't meant to bark at him. He studied the map critically for several minutes in silence. Finally he said, "I think Dana will be in this area, which puts her twenty miles offshore. Which way is the present current and tide running if she was there?"

The chief scratched his dark brown hair and said, "If she's able to make it to shore, it ought to be in the area of Parham beach on Santa Rosa Island." He stared up at Griff. "That's a big if, Lieutenant."

"If Commander Gallagher doesn't turn anything up on this first search, will you ask her to check that area next?"

The chief shrugged. "Sir, it's up to her, not me."

Griff wanted to scream. He wanted to cry. "Look, call it a hunch, but I think the riptide took Dana out a lot farther than anyone realizes." At that moment, two women dressed in jeans, blouses and lightweight jackets entered the office.

"Lieutenant?" Maggie came forward. "We're Dana's friends. This is Ensign Molly Rutledge. Have you heard anything yet?"

Griff nodded toward the blond woman, whose eyes were huge with worry. He moved over to the map and gave them the information he'd just received, adding his own hunch.

"So if we spread out in this area," Maggie said, tracing it with her index finger, "we might be able to spot her when she comes ashore?"

"That's right."

"Let's agree on a search pattern," Molly suggested quickly. "Lieutenant, why don't you take the beaches east of Parham, and we'll patrol the ones west of it?"

It was a sound plan. Griff liked the way the women reacted to the crisis. But then, he had to remind himself they were Annapolis graduates. A bit of hope trickled into his chest. "Good idea." He turned to the chief. "Have you got a couple of extra two-way radios we can carry in our cars in case we find Dana?"

The chief nodded. "Yes, sir." He went into another room and came back a few moments later with handsets for Maggie and Griff.

Griff thanked him, then turned back to the women. "The chief will notify the local hospital about Dana and Vickie. I'm sure they'll have a medical team standing by. Whoever finds them, call the hospital and tell them you're coming in. Once you're under way, call the other car."

"And be sure to call us, too," the chief added.

"Of course," Maggie said. She gripped the handset. "Let's set our radios for the same frequency, Lieutenant, so we can communicate with each other when we do find Dana."

Smiling to himself, Griff felt buoyed by the woman's clearheaded thinking. It gave him stability. Dana couldn't have a better team out looking for her.

Griff drilled Evans with a lethal look. "Tell Commander Gallagher where we're focusing our search, will you?"

"Yes, sir."

Griff left the office, followed by the two women. They hurried in silence to the well-lit parking lot. Raising his hand to them, he got into his car. Parham Beach was forty miles north of here. What could he do if he did find Dana and Vickie? He had a flashlight, a beach towel and a blanket. With his arm in a cast, he couldn't swim; but that didn't matter. He'd comb the beaches above Parham one at a time with a flashlight, yelling for Dana, hoping she would hear him. If he did find her, he'd swim out and rescue her, cast or no cast.

It wasn't much of an alternative, Griff admitted, driving well over the speed limit along the interstate. He had to believe that Dana would make it to shore. She wouldn't give up. She wasn't a quitter like Carol.

"I'm cold, Dana," Vickie cried softly.

"I know, honey. Just hang in there." Wearily, Dana rolled over onto her back. An hour ago she'd spotted a low-flying helicopter five miles away. She was positive it was a Coast Guard helo. Her spirits, ebbing after four hours of swimming, rallied. But they plummeted when the helo continued the search pattern away from where she trod water.

Her arms felt like lead weights, and Dana allowed them to rest across her body as she floated on her back to take a needed breather. Vickie's small hand reached out, searching frantically for contact with her. Gently, Dana grasped her small, wrinkled hand, squeezing it.

"I want Mommy," Vickie said, beginning to cry.

"Shh," Dana whispered, bringing the girl against her. With a shaking hand, Dana tried to smooth Vickie's salty, stiff hair off her face. "We're going home now, honey."

"But I don't see Mommy."

Glancing at her watch, Dana saw that it was now midnight. They'd been in the water for seven hours. Her flesh was badly wrinkled and puckered. Thirst was clawing at her throat, her mouth torturously dry. Dana tried to think coherently. She knew she was losing electrolytes, which would impair her mental faculties. Repeatedly Dana checked the stars for direction. Her eyes were playing funny tricks on her; the stars were sometimes growing hazy and out of focus.

"I'm sure your mommy is praying for both of us," Dana soothed the girl. Her left leg cramped suddenly, and she bit back a groan, automatically flexing into a treading position to rub the protesting calf. Her muscles were shaking, telling her she had very little reserve strength left. As she rubbed the knotted muscle, the pain brought clarity back to Dana.

Looking up, her heart skittered briefly. She could see lights. A cry clawed up Dana's throat.

"Look, Vickie! Look! You see those lights?"

"Y-yes."

"That's home." Dana's voice quavered as hope pounded through her exhausted body.

"It looks so far away."

Managing a croak that was supposed to be a laugh, Dana said, "Maybe six miles, Vickie." *Six miles.* How far had they come already? Dana had no idea. Her arms and legs were stinging with welts from jellyfish. Dana had swum through at least ten groups of the floating creatures. At least the stinging sensation helped keep her mind focused.

"Is Mommy there?"

"I'll bet she is," Dana gasped, turning over and kicking her feet to propel them both forward. The lights glimmered and twinkled in the darkness. Hope, along with the need to survive the ordeal, soared within Dana. The stars hadn't led her wrong.

Now, each time she lifted her arm over her head, Dana's shoulder protested with sharp, unremitting pain. She was sure the sockets were inflamed by the constant strain of towing Vickie. Six miles was too much to think about. It seemed too far to Dana, so she concentrated on each stroke. Griff's challenging words—that she was weak and couldn't do what a man could—infiltrated her state. Dana played his angry voice and challenge over and over again in her mind until she was muttering it out loud. She allowed his hatred of her, his fury because she was a woman, to infuse her with fresh resolve. She'd show him that she and Vickie *could* survive! Gasping with each stroke, laboring heavily in the water, Dana kept her watering eyes focused on the black shore that twinkled with lights here and there. Somehow, they'd survive this. It was going to feel good to throw this entire event in Griff's arrogant face. He would never be able to call her weak and incapable again!

Chapter Eight

Frantic with worry, Griff swung his sports car back toward Parham Beach. The narrow strip of road that covered the length of Santa Rosa Island looked black beneath the headlights of his car. Griff already had stopped at eight other beaches, calling for Dana. Sweeping his powerful flashlight across the sand, Griff had looked, waited and listened, but had heard no cries for help and seen no one in the surf, although he'd waded waist-deep into the water. His throat hurt from yelling hour after hour as he ceaselessly combed the beaches. To be honest with himself, his throat also ached with unshed tears.

Gripping the steering wheel, Griff felt a surge of grief such as he'd never felt before. Dana could be dead. No! Dammit, if anyone could fight that riptide, it was Dana. She wouldn't let Vickie die, either. Glancing at his watch, he saw it was 0400. In another hour the horizon would lighten to a dull gray—a warning that the sun was on its way to give light to this endless night.

The hours had stripped away any pretense of how Griff felt toward Dana. Praying wasn't one of his strong points. He'd stopped going to church on a regular basis when his mother died. Before then, he'd only gone because she'd asked him to. Often he'd wondered why a God who was supposed to love humanity so much would allow his mother to suffer as she did. It never made sense to him. But tonight Griff felt the need to reach out to something beyond himself. He was doing all he could. Praying was an extension, filling a need in him, for Dana's sake. For his own sake.

Gravel crunched beneath the wheels of the car as Griff stopped, and he left the headlights on and the engine running. The twin beams stabbed down across Parham Beach, illuminating the dark. As he got out the warm, humid gulf air surrounded him. Griff took the flashlight and walked down across the sand to the shoreline itself. Inside, he was crying—crying for a chance to find Dana alive and start all over with her.

"Dana!" His voice carried strongly across the quiet beach. "Dana, where are you?"

Dana's legs were cramping with terrifying regularity. Each time they knotted, she had to expend her precious remaining physical strength and roll over on her back to float. Her teeth chattering constantly, her body jerking and convulsing as if it had a mind of its own, Dana floundered weakly, trying to force herself to keep her head above the waterline. Vickie was sleeping. Somewhere in Dana's shorted-out mind, she knew the little girl was dehydrated and had probably lost consciousness. The only good thing about their situation was that it was night. Sunlight would have sapped her strength twice as fast, and Dana knew she'd never have made it even this far.

The blinking shore-lights were much closer now. Her eyes were playing tricks on her, and so were her ears. The beach was so close, so close. It hurt to lift her arms; her shoulder sockets were fiery with constant pain. Her flesh was badly wrinkled, her lower lip split in several places from the salt water. Every now and then, she tasted the blood on it, wondering frantically if it would draw sharks.

Her legs were numb from so many jellyfish stings, and Dana dully worried if her gasping for air was actually an allergic reaction to all the venom she'd absorbed. Every part of her was breaking down. Each sloppy splash of her arm hitting the water could bring a shark. As much as she tried not to make a sound, Dana no longer cared. Either they would reach the beach soon, or she would sink like a rock, unable to control the eroding reflexes of her exhausted body. Shark or drowning. Which did she prefer?

Kicking feebly, Dana forced her dissolving concentration onto lifting one arm at a time over her head, bringing it down into the water, pulling herself and Vickie a few more feet toward the shore. Griff's face wavered in front of her, and hope trickled through her. Somehow Dana knew he wouldn't give up on her. He might be a stubborn cuss who was in so much internal pain that he lashed out unconsciously at others, but he would never deliberately allow her or anyone else to die.

Thinking about Griff gave her hope, and Dana doggedly pushed on, Vickie in silent tow next to her shoulder. The beach was so much closer. If only...if only she could make it. Less than a mile of dark water remained. Her Rolex read 0430. A cramp started in her upper arm, and Dana groaned. The entire extremity reflexed on her. Unexpectedly, Dana sank into the water. The salt rushed into her nostrils and down into her throat, burning and choking. Fear jerked her head out of the water, and she flailed around, coughing violently, retching up the salt she'd swallowed.

Every movement sucked precious, last minutes of energy from her. Dana wanted to cry, but she had no tears; her body had used the water as a resource to feed itself. She sank below the surface again. Feebly, fear forcing her to respond, Dana fought back. If she sank, Vickie would drown. Gasping for air, Dana sobbed. Should she release Vickie? The cramp in her arm stopped. Immediately, Dana struck out toward shore. Could they make it? Or was she going to die a half mile from making it home?

The gray ribbon along the horizon told Griff it was 0500. Dejectedly, he stopped at an unmarked beach above Parham and climbed out of his car. His eyes burned from lack of sleep. Taking the binoculars, he rested his elbows wearily against the top of his car to steady his hands. He swept the length of the deserted beach, looking, always looking. With light came the awful realization that Dana probably had drowned. He had kept in contact with the Coast Guard and Dana's friends on a hourly basis via the handset. The CG hadn't spotted Dana, although they'd widened the search as far as twenty miles off the island. Storm Gallagher had refueled and was now making a low pass close to the beach for a thirty-mile stretch of the island, saying that if Dana had survived, she would be closer to shore. The words from the seasoned Coast Guard pilot gave Griff renewed hope.

His mouth coated with bitterness, Griff felt a heaviness in his heart that threatened to crush him. Tears squeezed into his eyes, and he pulled the binoculars aside, letting the moisture run freely down the stubble of his cheeks. Griff hadn't been able to cry over the divorce. He hadn't cried at Toby's funeral. Now the stinging, burning sensation gathered momentum, and a sob, like a fist pushing up through his chest, tore out of his mouth. Griff laid his head in his arms, and allowed the punishing sobs to continue. His shoulders shook. Like an injured animal, he surrendered to the glut of emotions he'd tried so long and hard to suppress.

The harsh sounds were absorbed into the peace of the beach parking lot. How long he stood there crying, Griff didn't know. Nor did he care. Finally, the storm within him abated, and he lifted his head, blinking away the remnants of the tears. Inside, he felt cleaner, less pressured. His mother had always told him it was good to be able to cry, but the military saw it as a weakness, so he'd stopped doing it long ago.

The sharp pain left in his heart was for Dana. Miserably, Griff looked out toward the beach. He blinked once. His heart thudded heavily in his chest. Was he seeing things? The gray light must be playing tricks on his watery eyes.

Lifting the binoculars, Griff saw a dark lump of something in the shallows. It could be a huge pile of kelp washed ashore. Or an old log that had come to rest after a long journey across the ocean. The light was still too weak to make out any details. Quickly, he jumped into his car and jammed his foot down on the accelerator. Hope warred with dread. Griff had predicted Dana would come ashore somewhere in the area of Parham Beach. Whatever had washed ashore was a mile from that point. Could it be? *Oh, God, please, let it be Dana! Let it be her.... Let her be alive....*

The screech of brakes biting into the asphalt of the parking lot filled the early-morning air. His hands shaking, Griff scrambled out, leaving the door open and sprinting toward the dark shape in the water. It hadn't moved. If it were kelp, or a log, it should move back and forth with the tide. Taking huge strides, his heels sinking deeply into the sand, Griff quickly covered the distance. In his hand he carried the beach towel—just in case.

Squinting, Griff saw the darkened shape begin to take form. His heart soared. It was Dana! She lay on her back in the shallows, Vickie sitting beside her, huddled close for warmth. Griff wished for more light. As he slowed, splashing into the ankle-deep water toward them, he saw the stark exhaustion on Dana's unconscious features. Her eyes were closed, one arm around the girl.

"Dana..." he whispered, crouching in the water. Her hair was stiff and plastered around her skull. As he placed his fingers against her neck, his breath suspended. He waited, trying to feel a pulse at the carotid artery point. There! A faint, weak pulse. Griff hauled Dana upright and cradled her against his body. Her head lolled against his jaw, and Griff became alarmed. Her flesh was cold. Cold as ice. She was shaking so badly that he automatically placed his other arm around Vickie.

"It's going to be all right," he said quaveringly, holding them, pressing both of them against his chest. Neither answered. Pulling away, Griff quickly assessed Vickie, who rested against him with her eyes closed. She was in good shape by comparison. He had to get them out of the water and up on the beach.

"Can you stand, Vickie?"

"I—I think so...."

Gently Griff lifted Dana into his arms. She was completely unconscious, little more than a feather in his arms. "Follow me," he told Vickie hoarsely, waiting for her to grip his pant leg to help herself stand.

Once on the beach, he laid Dana back down on her side and covered her upper body with the towel. Vickie fell beside her, starting to sob, her small arms around Dana.

"I'm going to get the blanket from the car, Vickie. I'll be right back for both of you. Understand?" Griff crouched down, his hand on the girl's shaking shoulder. Anxiously he stared at Dana. Her teeth were chattering, her limbs jerking spasmodically. She was in deep shock.

"Y-yes...."

Griff left, running as fast as he could through the thick, dry sand. Grabbing the blanket, he hurried back to them. Tucking the blanket around Dana, he devoted the rest of his attention to Vickie. Gently crooning to the little girl, Griff extricated her from Dana's side. Lifting her into his arms, he wrapped the thick beach towel around her and carried her toward the car, trying to assure the child that she was safe. Vickie only sighed and rested her head wearily against his chest.

Once at the car, Griff placed Vickie in the driver's seat and ran back out to where Dana lay unmoving. Fear made his hands shake as he reached down and gently eased her into the shelter of his arms. She was like boneless putty.

"Easy, easy," Griff coaxed, pressing her tightly against him. Searching her face, he realized her eyes barely opened. Did she know it was him? How could she? How many hours had she been swimming? Griff wrapped Dana in the warm, thick blanket.

"I'm going to take you to the nearest hospital, Dana. Do you understand me?" He was frightened at how cold her flesh had become. Hypothermia was a real possibility. "God, I thought I'd lost you, Dana...." And he choked up, unable to say anything further as he lifted her. Time was of the essence. His left arm ached like hell beneath her weight, but he didn't care if he broke the finger all over again.

As Griff hurriedly started his trek back to the Corvette with her, his alarm turned to panic. The blanket had slipped away from her thigh. The light was improving, and he could see huge, long red welts crisscrossing her leg. Jellyfish? Griff had never seen so many stings on a person before. His fear paralleled his admiration for Dana's raw courage and indefatigable strength. His arms tightening around her, he pressed her closely against him, wanting to share his body heat with her.

"Dammit, Dana, you've got to hang on," he told her in low gasps as he jogged toward the car. "You're safe now. Vickie's going to make it. Fight back, sweetheart. Fight back for both of us...."

It had to be one of her hallucinations. Dana emerged momentarily from the numbness and cold surrounding her to hear Griff's low, urgent voice. She felt weightless, as if someone were carrying her. Impossible. Had she drowned?

Or was she still fighting to keep her head above water? It was simply too much to lift her weighted lids. *Griff.* How badly she wanted to make it to shore to see him again. All her anger toward him had been used up. All her hope had gradually been stolen away by the chilly ocean. Where was Vickie? Dana stirred, moving her fingers, feeling her flesh stretch in protest. Pain reared up her arm as she tried to find Vickie.

"Don't fight me, Dana."

Who? Dana felt her cheek pressed against something warm and solid. It wasn't water. Where was she? Was she really dying and imagining that Griff was holding her? Dana didn't even have the strength to cry out his name any longer. The ocean had swallowed her cries of anguish, her cries for help.

"Relax. Relax, sweetheart."

Unable to find the necessary spark of strength, Dana stopped trying to locate Vickie.

Griff gently placed Dana in the passenger side of the car. Vickie was sitting up, looking at him with huge eyes. He came around the car and gave her what he hoped was a smile.

"Where's Mommy?" she whispered.

Taking the girl into his arms, he shut the door. "I'm going to call her right now, honey. My name is Griff, and I know yours is Vickie." He wrapped the towel around the child, and kept her tucked beneath his arm.

Dana heard a man's voice again. It had an emotional tone. How could it be Griff? She was still at sea, trying to reach the shore that was so close and yet so far away.

The calls to the hospital, to Maggie and the Coast Guard station had been made. Griff drove his car down the Santa Rosa Island highway as fast as possible. Vickie was content to sit in his lap, snuggled deeply in his arms, seeking his warmth. Worriedly, he glanced over at Dana, who was unconscious, her head tipped back against the seat, her lips parted. Griff tried to quell his mounting panic. As he neared the hospital emergency entrance, the light had improved enough to show some of the torture Dana had endured. Long red welts covered her slender, lovely throat. Her flesh was a blue gray, a telltale sign of hypothermia. Everywhere were jellyfish stings, her flesh swollen around the marks. Was Dana allergic to them? If she was, she could die from the venom alone, much less the physical hell she'd endured in endless hours at sea.

Griff brought the Corvette to a screeching halt at the emergency entrance. To his relief, two gurneys and several nurses and doctors were waiting for them. He saw Veronica Tandy, her hands pressed to her mouth as he handed Vickie out of the car to one of the waiting medical teams.

"Get to Dana," he ordered the other team hoarsely. "She's in shock and unconscious."

Griff stood helplessly by, watching the quick actions of the medical people. His heart leaped when the doctor with sandy-colored hair barked at his team to take Dana to ICU.

As he hurriedly followed them in, one nurse turned and held her hand out.

"I'm sorry, Lieutenant Turcotte, you can't come with us."

"But—"

"We'll take good care of her."

Frustration thrummed through Griff. "But she needs me!"

With a sad smile, the tall nurse said, "Of course, she does. But give Dr. Falk the time he needs. She appears anaphylactic and hypothermic. It will take at least an hour before we'll know anything. In the meantime, why don't you go to the third-floor ICU waiting room? We'll be in touch with you as soon as is humanly possible."

Angry and concerned, Griff paced the waiting room endlessly. Maggie and Molly arrived fifteen minutes later and he explained the situation. An hour went by. And then another. He badgered the nurse on the floor, trying to eke out some information on Dana's condition. Finally, toward the end of the second hour, an ICU nurse by the name of Bannister intercepted his pacing.

"Lieutenant Turcotte?"

Griff's head snapped up from its position against his chest. "Yes?"

"You brought Dana Coulter in. Is that correct?"

He studied the older woman. She had a pinched face, looking painfully prim and proper. "Yes, I did."

"Dr. Falk has her stabilized."

Griff saw Maggie and Molly come up beside him. "When may we see her?"

"Are any of you related to the patient?"

Frowning, Griff said, "No." He looked at the women. Both shook their heads.

"But we're Dana's closest friends," Molly pleaded.

"I'm sorry, Dr. Falk can only release information about Ms. Coulter's condition to her family."

Griff's anger got the better of him. "That's a bunch of bull! Dana's condition *is* my business, Ms. Bannister!"

Her brows dipped. "Her mother has been notified, I understand. Unless you're a member of the family, I can't allow you to see her."

Glancing quickly at the two women standing tensely beside him, Griff made a decision. In a low voice he snarled, "I'm her fiancé." Dana would need someone when she woke up. He wanted to be there for her. Would her friends dispute his lie?

Maggie's eyes narrowed on him, speculative and assessing. Molly's widened with shock and her mouth dropped open. Griff gave a bare shake of his head.

"Well...uh, I'll have to tell Dr. Falk that. He'll have to decide."

"Do that." Griff stood, his hands tense on his hips as he watched the nurse walk back toward the ICU doors.

Maggie stepped up to him as soon as the nurse disappeared. "You aren't her fiancé."

Griff felt heat crawling up his neck and into his face. He held her challenging green gaze. "No. But how else was one of us going to get in there to see how she is?"

Molly gripped Maggie's arm. "It's a good idea. Let him do it. I'm sure Dana will forgive him."

Griff sincerely hoped so. He saw Maggie's face soften. Molly's eyes were filled with understanding. What loyal friends Dana had. "Thanks," he whispered.

Minutes later, Falk came out. His face lined with worry, he managed a slight nod.

"I understand you're Ms. Coulter's fiancé?"

"That's correct, Doctor. Tell me what the hell's going on. It's been two hours! How is she?"

Falk motioned him to sit down, but Griff refused. So did the women.

"She's hypothermic, Lieutenant. That means her temperature dropped below a survival level. When that happens, the body's organs hoard what heat is left. That's what has taken so long. We've had to slowly bring her back to a normal body-temperature level. Luckily, she's young and strong."

"Dana was in the water for twelve hours," Griff said, afraid of what else Falk might say. "When I got her out of the surf, she was unconscious. Is she awake now?"

"Not yet. That's part of hypothermia. The brain shuts down all but the most vital of systems in order to sustain organ life. I'm more concerned about the jellyfish venom in her bloodstream at this point."

"Is she allergic to it?" Maggie barged in, her hands on her hips, upset.

"If she wasn't, she is now. I've got her on anaphylactic drugs, combating her body's reaction to the venom. Her breathing is depressed, and we're monitoring her closely."

Griff's throat constricted. "You mean she could suffocate?"

Falk barely nodded his head. "It's possible."

Terror ate at Griff. "Well . . . how long before we know anything?"

"The next six hours will be the most critical."

"Oh, dear," Molly whispered, pressing her fingertips against her throat.

"Then I want to be with her," Griff said. "I don't want her going through this alone."

"She's unconscious."

"Dana will know I'm there." Griff dared the doctor to dispute his growling rejoinder. He took a huge risk. "I want a chair brought into her room. I'll stay there with her."

With a shrug, Falk slowly got to his feet. "She won't know you're there, Lieutenant. You'd be wiser to go home and get some sleep and call me in six hours."

Griff nearly cursed the doctor's lack of sensitivity. Instead, in a low voice, he stated, "I'll stay, Doctor. Just get me a chair, and I'll sit next to Dana's bed and hold her hand. She'll know I'm there."

"Whatever you want, Lieutenant."

"Wait. . . . Couldn't Maggie or Molly stay with her, too? They're her best friends," Griff argued.

Falk shook his head. "Sorry, it's against hospital rules."

"Bastard," Maggie murmured softly under her breath when the doctor was out of earshot. She gave Griff a black look. "And you'd better treat her right or you'll answer to us."

Griff managed a strained smile. "Dana's in good hands."

Grudgingly, Maggie stepped aside so he could pass. "We're going to stick around, Lieutenant."

"Fine. Let me get situated in there with Dana, and then I'll come out and give you a report."

"Thank you," Molly whispered, tears in her eyes. "Dana's gone through so much.... We just don't want her to think she's alone."

He gave a jerky nod. "Yeah, I know." He was the bastard who'd made her life miserable.

The beeps and sighs of the equipment kept Griff on edge. Rubbing his burning, bloodshot eyes, he looked at his watch. It was eight o'clock, Saturday morning. His hand tightened protectively over Dana's limp fingers. Slowly, her skin was beginning to fill out again, losing its saltwater wrinkles. His gaze moved up her long, sculptured throat to her face. At least she'd lost that blue-gray pallor. For that, he was grateful. But in the past three hours, she hadn't regained consciousness, and that worried him. Was she simply sleeping? Or was she in a coma? No one could tell him for sure.

Stroking her thin fingers, he stared down at her. Dana was so small. Everything about her appeared fragile—from her heart-shaped face to her small, aristocratic nose and delicate lips. They had bathed her earlier, and her salt-stiffened black hair now lay slightly curled and clean around her skull. Griff thought she had the most beautifully shaped head. He didn't stop himself from gently running his hand across her thick, silky hair.

"Dana, it's Griff. Do you hear me? I know you can." His hand tightened around hers. "Listen to me. You're going to pull through this. I'm not going to let you go. You're safe now. And so is Vickie. She's gone home with her mother—" A lump formed in Griff's throat, and he halted, swallowing hard as he absorbed her serene features. "Sweetheart, you're something special. I don't know how you did it, being out there in that ocean for twelve hellish hours. I knew you wouldn't give up. I knew you wouldn't...."

The door to Dana's room quietly opened and closed. Griff looked over. It was Nurse Bannister.

"Lieutenant, Mrs. Coulter is on the phone at the desk, long-distance. She just got done talking to Dr. Falk. She'd like to speak to you."

Heat fled up into Griff's face. Dana's mother. Hesitantly he rose. "Okay...." Reluctantly, he released Dana's hand and halted a few steps from her bed.

"I'll stay with her," the nurse assured him in a low voice.

Maybe Bannister wasn't so bad, after all, Griff thought, giving her a weary smile meant to thank her. "I won't be long," he promised, and left.

Griff had been without sleep for over twenty-four hours. He was staggering when he walked. Stopping at the visitors' lounge, he didn't find Maggie or Molly. When he reached the nurses' station, the nurse on duty told him they'd gone down for coffee in the cafeteria. Griff picked up the receiver and stared at it. He didn't know what to say.

Finally he held it to his ear. "Mrs. Coulter? This is Lieutenant Griff Turcotte."

"Thank God, you came. This is Ann Coulter. I'm Dana's mother. They said you're her fiancé. Dana never told me about you."

Stumbling, Griff said in a very low voice, hoping the nurse wasn't listening, "Well...it's been kind of recent, Mrs. Coulter...."

"Please call me Ann. How is she, Griff? Dr. Falk seemed so uncertain...."

Gripping the phone, he heard the terror in Ann's voice. He tried to tell her everything—and to reassure her. "Right now their biggest worry are the red welts from the jellyfish stings, Ann."

"Oh, God. Red welts?"

Griff nodded. "Yes." He heard Dana's mother begin to cry. "Mrs. Coulter? Ann, it's going to be okay. I know Dana will make it. She's tough. And she's got so much heart. Her best friends, Maggie and Molly, are here with her, too. They're down getting coffee right now, or I'd let you talk to them."

Sniffing, Ann whispered, "I'm so glad they're with Dana. Griff, has she told you about her father, Frank? About the welts he used to inflict on her?"

Griff froze. "Welts? What are you talking about?"

"Dana took so many beatings from my husband. I—I was afraid to leave Frank, and Dana was always protecting me from him. Even as a little seven-year-old, she'd stand between me and my husband, trying to help me, Griff...." Ann wept inconsolably.

A terrible, sinking feeling gripped his stomach. Griff shut his eyes tightly. He heard the guilt in Ann's voice; the anguish that again, her daughter was suffering.

"Look, it's different this time," he promised her hoarsely. "Dana saved a little girl from sure death. Something good came out of these welts. Come on, Ann, it's going to be okay. Dana's going to make it." *She has to!* Griff's mind whirled with old conversations he'd had with Dana, and he remembered her reactions to him, as a man. How awful he must have appeared to her. A brute bullying her around— just as her father had. With a groan, he buried his face in his hand, only now beginning to realize the full impact of his actions on Dana—on any possible future he wanted to pursue with her.

"Should I fly back to be with her, Griff?"

"I don't think so. The doctor has said she's in good condition, not critical." Then he tried to joke: "She has me."

"And for that, I'm so grateful. You sound so wonderful, Griff. Not at all like her father. Frank was a sick man. I—I finally got the courage to leave after he put her in the hospital when she was seventeen. If it hadn't been for Dana believing that we could make it on our own, I'd never have been free of him. Oh, God! I feel so horrible about all this."

Tears burned in Griff's eyes. He didn't try to hide them. He didn't care who saw them. "Look," he rasped, "Dana's in the best of hands down here. I'll take good care of her. I promise."

"She's so leery of men, Griff. You must be special. Frank instilled her with a fear of them. I'm sure she's told you about Jason Lombard and the way he used her. I felt so helpless then, listening to her cry over the phone after it happened. I—I just wished I could have prepared her better for the world—for men. But you sound so sensitive and wonderful. Knowing my daughter as I do, I think she probably was going to wait awhile longer before telling me about you. This time, she wanted to make sure."

Griff shut his eyes. "I can promise you one thing, Ann. I'll never make your daughter call you, crying."

"Bless you. Dana deserves some breaks. She worked so hard to get good grades at Annapolis, but so many of the men resented her. Once she wrote me a letter and said they all reminded her of her father. I'm so relieved that you were able to get through her defenses and prove there are good men, too."

Tears dribbled down Griff's face, catching in the bristly growth of his beard. "Let me get your number," he said hoarsely. "The minute Dana wakes up, I'll get back to you."

Chapter Nine

Dana felt as if she were coming out of a long, dark tunnel. She had little energy, and she shifted her limited focus to tactile sensations. Someone was holding her hand. It was a large, rough hand that continued to softly stroke the underside of her wrist. Tiny prickles moved up her arm, reminding her she was alive. Stretching her state of awareness, Dana was surprised she could feel her legs once again.

When the hand caressed the top of her head, Dana groggily realized she really was alive, and not dead, after all. The gesture sharply reminded her of the way her mother used to do that when Dana was sick, or had been hurt by her father. Relaxing beneath the gentle ministration, Dana absorbed the hesitant, trembling touch across her hair, relishing the sense of protection.

Gradually the tunnel lightened, and Dana forced her eyes open, looking up through her thick lashes. Her lips parted. It was Griff Turcotte sitting at her bedside, holding her hand and stroking her hair! Shock made her gasp.

Griff froze. "Dana?" His voice was hoarse. It was nearly ten in the morning. An hour ago, Falk had expressed his worry that Dana might have gone into a coma from the venom absorbed into her bloodstream.

It hurt to think, much less talk. Dana felt the warmth of Griff's hand, and a tremor passed through her.

"You're going to be okay," Griff told her, hearing the raw, undisguised emotion in his voice. He saw a spark of life in her barely opened blue eyes. "God, I was worried about you." Managing a sliver of a smile, he rasped, "You're one hell of a lady, do you know that? Vickie's fine. She's back home with her mother. It's you we're worried about. You took so many jellyfish stings. Maggie and Molly are waiting for you outside."

Too much information was coming too fast. Dana clung to his dove-gray gaze, feeling the incredible care surrounding her from Griff. How could this be? He was the way he'd been before—at the airport. Confused and groggy, Dana turned her head to one side.

"Go away..." she whispered.

Griff froze, his hand loosening around Dana's. *Go away.* The plea in her voice was real. Griff pushed back the chair and stood uncertainly, digesting her words. The past thirty-six hours of his life had been a living nightmare. He had so much he wanted to say to Dana, to share with her about his feelings for her. The apologies would have to come first.

Reaching over, he barely touched her gowned shoulder. "The war's over between us, Dana," he rasped. Unwilling to leave and knowing he must, Griff walked dejectedly to the door. As he opened it, he turned. Dana was staring at him, her azure eyes filled with tears. Bowing his head, Griff knew he'd made her cry. God, all he'd offered her had been brutal male punishment on a mental and emotional level. He was no better than Frank, who had levied physical punishment upon her instead. There were many kinds of cruelty.

Opening his mouth, Griff swallowed against his constricted throat.

"I'm going to tell Molly and Maggie you're awake. I promised them I'd let them know when you became conscious." Griff blinked back tears. "Just get well, Dana. I'll handle everything for you at the station. I don't want you to worry about flying. When you're well, we'll start all over again. I promise you, it'll be different."

The door closed. A small, ragged sound escaped Dana. Turmoil raged within her, and she closed her eyes, tears coursing down the sides of her face. Right now, all she wanted was to see her two closest friends and tell her mother that she was okay. Her brain was only slightly functioning. Why was Griff here with her? What time was it? What day? He'd said Vickie was fine, and for that she was more than grateful.

Lifting her right arm, which had an IV in it, Dana frowned. Her arm was covered with red welts. The nightmarish swim came back to haunt her. As Dana floated back to sleep to heal, the only thing that gave her solace was the memory of Griff's anxious features as he watched her. Had she really seen tears in his eyes as he'd stood at the door?

Molly brought a huge bouquet of flowers, and Maggie brought Dana her favorite chocolates—Turtles. The women were in civilian attire, standing around Dana's bed when she awoke the second time. Their smiling faces, wreathed in welcome, helped her rally.

"We're so glad you're going to make it!" Molly whispered, leaning over and hugging her tightly. "We were worried sick!"

Dana managed a slight smile through her chapped and cracked lips. Maggie was next, giving her a hug and then ruffling her hair.

"Talk about a sleepless night," she teased.

"Sorry," Dana croaked.

Molly sat on the side of the bed and held Dana's hand. "Lieutenant Turcotte saw you swept out to sea by the riptide."

"Yes." She cleared her throat and thanked Maggie for the glass of orange juice. Dana was too weak to hold it, so Molly steadied the glass, allowing her to suck the cold, sweet juice through the straw. Dana was still exceptionally thirsty. Earlier Dr. Falk had come in, checked her over and told her to drink as much liquid as possible. She was on her way to recovery.

Maggie took the glass, then expertly fluffed the three pillows behind Dana's back, arranging them so that she could sit up in bed. "Yeah, the Turk called us. Can you believe that? We didn't miss you at first, because you normally swim down at the beach at that time. When he called, we both hightailed it down to the Coast Guard station."

"Was he ever panicked!" Molly agreed.

With a soft snort, Maggie sat down on the opposite side of the bed, facing Dana. "He was so upset, he was almost in tears."

"That doesn't make sense," Dana protested. "He hates my guts."

Molly pointed to a small desk opposite Dana's bed. "Odd for somebody who hates you to send thirteen yellow roses." She raised one eyebrow at Dana.

Staring at the huge yellow rosebuds, Dana was speechless. A small white card, unopened, was propped against the vase.

"Maggie, could you—"

"Sure." She smiled, got off the bed and retrieved the envelope.

Dana was none too steady yet, so Maggie opened it and handed her the folded card. With trembling hands, Dana read it. It was Griff's scrawl, all right. She knew her friends were waiting to hear the contents, so she read it out loud to them. "Dana, there's a poem I want to share with you sometime when you get better. Get well. Griff."

"A poem?" Molly sighed. "How romantic."

Maggie grimaced. "Give me a break, Molly. The Turk isn't what I'd call the romantic sort."

Running her fingers across the handwritten card, Dana felt a tug within her heart. "Earlier," she whispered hoarsely, "when I woke up, he was here. He looked happy to see me."

"That's a miracle in itself." Maggie laughed.

"Wait a minute," Molly said. "Remember, Griff was the one who got the Coast Guard involved in trying to find you. And then, when they couldn't come right away, he threw his weight around and got the commander over at Pensacola to release one of the Navy SAR helos to search for you."

Dana's eyes widened enormously. "He did?"

"Come on," Maggie protested. "The guy isn't a complete ogre! He might dislike you as his student, but he wasn't going to let you or that little girl drown out at sea! Dana, you're acting as if Griff wants you dead and buried, and his actions prove just the opposite. Something isn't making sense here."

Molly rubbed her chin, thinking. "She's right, Dana. Griff was the one who figured out where you might wash up onshore. He pinpointed Parham Beach. We searched below it for you, and he searched above it."

Disbelieving, Dana sat there, digesting the revelations. "He did that for me?"

"Hell of a guy," Maggie stated. "He came through for you when the chips were down. If he hates you, it sure doesn't show." She gave Dana a probing look. "Are you sure he wants to wash you out?"

It hurt to shrug her shoulders, but Dana did anyway. "This morning—early, I think, when I first awakened—he told me something," she admitted in a raspy voice.

"What?" Molly asked eagerly.

"Griff told me that the war's over between us."

"Well, there you go!" Maggie grinned. "It looks like you proved yourself in his eyes, Dana. Maybe he'll ease up on trying to Board you."

"You know you're in the headlines, don't you?" Molly dug into her huge canvas purse. "Front page, too. Look!" She placed the paper on Dana's lap.

Dana's mind still wasn't functioning properly. Falk told her it was due to the severe electrolyte imbalance, and that in a day or two, she'd have all her mental faculties back. Picking up the small regional paper, she gawked at the headline: Woman Survives Twelve-Hour Ocean Ordeal. There was a photo of Griff talking with a Coast Guard official. Dana studied his photo. He was unshaven, and his clothes were wrinkled as if they'd been worn for a long time. His left hand was in a cast; she wondered why. Had he broken his arm?

Reading the article, Dana began to realize the enormity of her and Vickie's rescue. As Molly had said, Griff was responsible for raising hell to get an SAR helo out to hunt for them. Then he'd plotted a possible trajectory curve along Santa Rosa Island, based on wind direction, current speed and tide, to estimate where she might finally come ashore.

"Did you read the part where the mayor of Pensacola is going to award you a medal for saving Vickie's life?" Molly said excitedly, pointing to the last paragraph of the large article.

Dana read the rest of it, setting the newspaper back in her lap. "Griff deserves the medal, too," Dana protested, feeling her anger stir. "I could have died, maybe, if he hadn't found us when he did."

"Take it up with Griff and the mayor," Maggie suggested, getting up. "Dr. Falk isn't allowing any reporters to come and talk with you, yet. There's a slew of them out in the hall waiting for a chance to do just that, you know."

Dana closed her eyes wearily. Griff's note was still in her hand. "I don't want to talk to anyone except my mother."

"I'll dial the number for you, and then we'll leave, Dana," Molly offered.

Maggie gave her a warm smile. "You're looking tired. I think you need more sleep."

Dana told Molly the number, glad of her friends' sensitivity to her condition. They left just as the phone call went through to her mother. As she talked to her, Dana gazed across the room at the lovely yellow roses. Griff had given them to her. Why?

Griff awoke late Sunday morning, his roomy apartment quiet as usual. He rolled over in bed and turned on the radio. Instrumental music flowed through the room. He lay there, hands behind his head, and stared up at the white stucco ceiling. After coming home from the florist's shop in Pensacola yesterday afternoon, he'd taken a hot shower and staggered into bed. Looking at his watch now, he realized he'd slept nearly fifteen hours.

Glancing at the phone on the table next to his bed, Griff had a driving urge to call Dana, but it was only 0600. Let her sleep and heal. Unable to stand not knowing how she was, he rolled over, punching the buttons of the hospital's phone number. Maybe the nursing station could give him some info. They should be forthcoming with news on Dana's condition for her "fiancé."

After making the call, Griff sat on the edge of the bed, his feet on the polished wooden floor, assimilating the information the nurse had provided. Yes, Dana had gotten the roses he'd sent over. Yes, she was improving rapidly, and no, she wasn't awake yet. No, the reporters wouldn't be allowed to see her today. Perhaps tomorrow. And yes, her two women friends had visited her.

Sunlight lanced through the white sheers on the windows, highlighting the simplicity of his bedroom. Tall, graceful palms and ficus trees added life and color. Griff rested his elbows on his thighs, his hands hanging loosely between his legs. All he'd done last night was dream of Dana's response to him. She'd turned her head away and told him to leave. Staring down at his feet, Griff didn't blame her. Somehow he was going to have to get through the day without calling or visiting Dana. If she wanted to see him, she'd have to call him. It was the only way. If he chased her, he'd only end up losing her.

Making a harsh sound, Griff stood, the reddish highlights of the wooden floor glaring in the morning sunshine. He hated weekends now. After five years of marriage, he'd gotten used to a certain fixed order to his life. Now, he felt as aimless as an unraveling ball of yarn. As he padded through the apartment to the bathroom, Griff thought Carol might be right about one thing: He was the marrying kind—a man who was happier and better off in a marriage than without one. Carol had told him he'd be damned lonely after she left. She'd been right on that call, too.

Curbing his desire to call Dana at 0800, Griff decided to go over to Whiting Field to prepare for the next week's classes. If he didn't busy himself, he knew he'd call Dana, and that couldn't be done.

At his office, Griff found Yeoman Johnson at his desk.

"What are you doing here, Ray?"

Johnson looked up and grinned. "Working. What are you doing here, Mr. Turcotte?"

"Working."

"That's some story about Miss Coulter and how you rescued her," Johnson pointed out, handing him the Sunday edition of the newspaper.

Scowling, Griff saw his photo on the front page. With a grimace he handed it back to the yeoman. "Dana...I mean, Miss Coulter, rescued herself. All I did was find her washed up near Parham Beach."

Leaning back in his chair, Johnson nodded thoughtfully. "How is she doing in the hospital?"

Griff hesitated at his door. "Okay."

"When do you think she'll be back to try and get her wings?"

"Dr. Falk said it would probably be two weeks."

"Whew! That's putting her three weeks behind in this class."

"I'll fly extra hours with her to make it up."

"You still want her as a student?"

Griff nodded, his hand tightening momentarily on the doorjamb. "Yes." *More than ever.* The admission had come out low, laced with barely closeted feelings. He saw the yeoman's thick black brows rise fractionally.

"Then you've changed your mind about her?"

"She changed it for me," Griff answered abruptly, not wanting to discuss the tender topic any further.

At noon, Johnson brought in part of his sack lunch and shared it with Griff. Griff thanked him, but really didn't have much of an appetite. The phone on his desk was so close, and he wanted so badly to call Dana. The need to hear her voice, to see if she was still angry with him, was eating at him. But why wouldn't she be angry?

"If Ensign Coulter is going to be back on the flight schedule two weeks from now, do you want me to slot her in daily?"

"Yes."

"Two hours?"

"No, three."

"But...that's going to impact your schedule an awful lot, sir. You're teaching two classes this time."

With a shrug, Griff muttered, "I don't care."

"Okay, sir...it's your decision," Johnson said, and left the office.

Griff stared at the phone, wondering what Dana thought about the roses he'd sent her. And what if her mother told her of his lie about being her fiancé? Griff groaned. He couldn't wait two weeks before admitting the lie he'd told Ann Coulter. Dana might not agree with why he'd done it, but he owed her an explanation—in person.

His heart pounding in dread, Griff decided that confessing his fib at least was a good excuse to go and see Dana. Damn, but he needed to see her.

Vaguely Dana heard the door to her room quietly open and close. The nurse had awakened her fifteen minutes earlier to draw blood. In fact, her sleep had been interrupted repeatedly until she wondered how any patient ever managed to recover. Lying on her side, she slowly rolled over onto her back, the chill of the air-conditioning making her wish she had more than just a light blanket and sheet across her. Dana heard someone walking toward her bed.

She opened her eyes. Griff Turcotte stood before her, his eyes bloodshot, but his face scraped free of the beard she'd seen him with earlier. Dressed in a white cotton shirt with the sleeves rolled up, a pair of dark brown slacks and loafers, he looked casual and devastatingly handsome. The uncertainty in his eyes made Dana swallow her anger.

"What do you want?" she croaked, her voice still hoarse and sore.

"Well...I just wanted to come over and see how you were doing." Griff motioned nervously toward the roses he'd sent. "I see you still have them."

"Why wouldn't I?" Dana struggled to sit up in bed, the physical weakness making her feel helpless, a feeling she detested. The white gown she wore was coarse cotton and chafed her sensitive skin. Pulling the sheet and blanket up to her waist, Dana clasped her hands in her lap.

Griff motioned to the white steel chair. "Uh, mind if I sit down for a minute?"

"I guess not...." Dana felt like a heel. Griff was unsure of himself in a way she'd never seen in a man before. He sat tensely on the edge of the chair, facing her. Trying to be civil, Dana muttered, "The roses are pretty. Thank you." She saw him rub his hands together in what appeared to be a nervous gesture. Dana wouldn't have believed Griff had a nervous bone in his body—or any emotions other than those made of cold, angry steel.

"It was the least I could do." Wiping his sweaty brow, Griff managed a poor semblance of a smile. "You look better. Got a little color in your cheeks. And your arms don't look so bad." Indeed, the puffy red welts had gone down, leaving a series of red lines instead. Dana's black hair shone with blue highlights. Although she was still pale, her cheeks were two spots of color. Hungrily, Griff absorbed her vulnerable state. He still had a tough time reconciling Dana's delicate features with that iron resolve that had kept her alive during her twelve hours in the gulf.

"Falk's got me on enough antibiotics to kill a horse," Dana muttered defensively. She looked at Griff. What did he want from her?

With a shake of his head, Griff whispered, "It was too close, Dana. Too damn close. I almost lost you ... I mean, *we* almost did."

Shaken, Dana lay against the pillow, unable to absorb, much less think coherently, why Griff was behaving in a caring fashion. "I thought I was going to die," she admitted.

"I never prayed so hard in my life." And then Griff managed a lopsided grin—the first genuine one since the incident. "Praying isn't one of my strong points."

"Mine either. But I did a lot of it last night."

"My mother was sick all her life. And as a kid, I used to wonder why a so-called loving God would let her suffer the way she did after having me. After she died, I quit going to church. I felt it was hypocritical."

The look in his eyes told Dana he wasn't lying. When Griff mentioned his mother, his face lost its usual harshness and turned tender with memories. "I was never one for church, either," she muttered, avoiding his sharpened gray gaze. "Things got rough for my mom, and I was like you: I couldn't understand a God who'd let her live in that kind of hell."

Griff grew quiet. Dana always tiptoed around her abusive homelife. Even now, she saw her mother's trials in the marriage but not her own. Was it an instinctive reaction? If Dana didn't remember it, the pain was less, perhaps. Griff could understand that. He'd never forgotten the pain of his mother's long, tortured illness. Clearing his throat, he glanced up at her.

"Look, the reason I came over was to see how you were."

"I'm better," Dana admitted quietly, holding his searching gray eyes. "And I read the newspaper this morning. I owe you a lot for helping save my hide."

"You don't owe me a thing," Griff protested.

"Sure, I do."

"Why?"

"There isn't a man alive who doesn't want something in return for what he gives a woman."

Startled, Griff sat a long minute, considering the probable feelings behind her words. Finally he said, "You don't owe me a thing. I'd have done it for you and Vickie whether I knew you or not."

Then, why are you here? The words were almost torn from Dana, but she couldn't bring herself to ask the question. "Well, whatever your reason, I want to thank you. I could've lain unconscious in the water and drowned before someone discovered us. I didn't have any strength left." Dana managed a twisted smile. "Frankly, I don't even remember you rescuing us. I heard snatches of your voice, your touch..."

Wringing his hands together, Griff took a deep breath. "You were pretty much in shock," he agreed quietly. "Listen, there's a second reason why I came."

Automatically, Dana tensed. "It's about my flight status, isn't it?"

Surprised, Griff sat up, hearing the tightness in her voice. "Why . . . no."

"You're still going to Board me, aren't you?" It hurt to breathe as she waited for Griff to confirm her worst fear.

He looked at Dana in amazement. "My God, you've just been through an incredible hell where you almost drowned, and you're worried about me Boarding you?" His voice had risen with hurt laced with anger.

Glaring at him, Dana rasped, "Just because you helped save my neck doesn't change a thing between us, Mr. Turcotte. I know you hate my guts. Believe me, I had twelve hours at sea to think about a lot of things. I had no interruptions, no distractions. All I could do was swim and think. Just give me the bottom line, will you? Am I going to be on the Board list when I return to the station?"

Disbelief shattered Griff. He stood up, dragging in a ragged breath. "Hell, no! You won't be on that list!"

Wincing at his explosive reaction, Dana stiffened.

Immediately, Griff was sorry he'd blown up at her. Had her father cursed at her? Yelled at her? Obviously, or she wouldn't have reacted so violently to him. "I'm sorry," he whispered, holding out his hand toward her in a gesture of peace. "I didn't mean to yell. It's just . . . well, the last two days have been hell on me, too."

"What's my status at Whiting, then?" Dana demanded bitterly, watching him begin to pace the length of the room. There was such a powerful, coiled tension in Griff. He walked like an explosion ready to detonate at the slightest provocation. Her father had been the same.

"You're officially listed as hospitalized."

"Dr. Falk says it will be two weeks before he'll authorize me to continue my schooling. You could Board me for that."

"I won't."

"Why? It's a perfect opportunity to get rid of me."

Swinging around, Griff carefully controlled his body language and voice. He saw the shadow of fear lurking in her dark blue eyes. More than anything else, he didn't want Dana to be afraid of him. "Do you remember what I told you after you regained consciousness?"

Frowning, Dana said, "Yes."

"What did I say?"

He was treating her like a child, and she resented it. "You said the war's over between us."

"I meant it, Dana."

Her heart beat hard once, underscoring his use of her name. What the hell was he up to? Surely he was playing some head game with her to keep her confused and off balance so that when she did get back to flying, she'd Board herself.

"Look, we're getting off the reason I came here," Griff continued. He halted at the end of her bed and wrapped his hands around the cool metal footboard.

Sullenly, Dana looked up at him. "Right now, Mr. Turcotte, I don't know what to think about you. One minute you're screaming at me in the cockpit, trying to Board me. The next minute you're playing Mr. Nice Guy. I can't trust you."

He hung his head. "I've been a royal bastard," he admitted, "for the wrong reasons. This last two days cleared a lot of things up for me, Dana. The morning when I brought you to Emergency, I called over to the station and got the chief on duty to get me your file. I had them notify your mother about you."

"I know, she told me."

His heart started a slow, dreaded pound. "Did she say anything else about me?"

With a grimace, Dana looked away, staring at the venetian blinds on the window. "She thought you were a very nice man." The words came out flat.

"That's all?"

"Isn't that enough? Do you think I'm going to tell my mother how rough it is here on me and my friends at Whiting? How rough you are? She's gone through enough hell in this lifetime, Turcotte. I don't intend to give her my sob story and make her start worrying about me. She worried enough about me growing up." Feeling exhausted by the emotional contact with Griff, Dana waved her hand wearily. "I'm just glad you called her. Thank you."

"She's a nice lady," Griff began awkwardly, "and she has your voice."

"My mother and I are very much alike."

"You're made out of some pretty special material, in my opinion." When Dana's eyes rounded in confusion, Griff knew he had to own up to his lie. "The morning after they took you into Emergency, Maggie and Molly arrived about fifteen minutes later. We couldn't get anything out of them about your condition. I asked the nurses, and they wouldn't say anything. Falk said only your family could visit you and be told of your true condition."

"That's standard policy," Dana stated, refusing to look at him. Why didn't Griff leave? It was painful being around him, because such a huge part of her needed him. What would it be like simply to fall into his strong, welcoming arms and be held? Just be held? No one had ever held Dana. She had held her mother when she sobbed in the bathroom or some other out-of-the-way place where her father wouldn't hear her crying.

"Yeah, I guess it is normal policy." Griff absently ran his hand along the white metal railing of the footboard. "They wanted us to go home, but we said no. I didn't want to leave you, Dana. You had no one, and I wanted to be there for you. So—" Griff sighed heavily, holding her gaze "—I did a really stupid thing."

"What?"

"I lied."

"Lied?"

"Yeah, I lied to the nurses and doctor. You'd gone through so much by yourself, I wanted you to know someone was there for you after all that. I told them I was your fiancé so I could find out about your condition and hang around until you regained consciousness."

Dana's mouth fell open. Then she snapped it shut. "You what?"

"It gets worse," Griff assured her in a low tone. "I had the nurses' station notify your mother. She called here and the nurse at the desk answered. She told her your 'fiancé'—me—was with you." He kept his eyes lowered, unwilling to see Dana's reaction. "As soon as I got to the phone, your mother started crying. All I could do—wanted to do—was try to make her feel better. She thought I was your fiancé, and I didn't have the heart to tell her differently. I—I guess I didn't want her to think some stranger was with you, who didn't care what was happening to you. I assured her you were in good hands, that I'd be with you until you woke up, and then I'd call her back." Risking everything, Griff forced himself to look up, trying to prepare himself for Dana's righteous anger. He knew that telling her the truth probably would destroy the last goodness left between them. What would she say?

Chapter Ten

Speechless, Dana stared at Griff. He looked embarrassed and awkward, and she felt compassion instead of anger over his lie to the hospital and to her mother. There was a dull red color to his cheeks, and his mouth quirked, as if he were waiting for her to chastise him thoroughly. Her mind whirled with options. He'd said he lied because he cared for her and didn't want her to be alone; but he'd proved just the opposite—until now. Maybe he'd done it out of guilt. Confusion clouded her feelings.

"Maggie and Molly didn't say a thing about your lie."

Moving uneasily, Griff mumbled, "I asked them to go along with it. I told them I'd tell you the truth as soon as you felt better."

Dana remembered her friends' responses to Griff's helping her. Neither of them would have let Griff lie if they thought it was going to hurt her. She glanced up at him.

"Did Maggie challenge you on your lie?"

"Yes."

If the situation hadn't been so shocking, Dana would have smiled. Maggie was a real guard dog if she felt Dana or Molly was threatened. It was in her nature to protect those she felt were defenseless. If Maggie let Griff get away with the lie, she must have felt there was a good reason behind it.

"Molly wasn't too keen on it, either," Griff said quietly. "I convinced them it was in your best interests. Someone had to get in to be with you. I was the only likely candidate, under the circumstances. I think they weighed me being with you against no one being there, and that's why they went along with my lie."

Silently, Dana agreed with his assessment. "I'm sure Maggie raised hell with the nursing staff to see how I was."

He managed a slight nod, deciding not to tell Dana he'd raised even more hell to get to see her. "She was pretty dogged about it."

Mulling over the situation, Dana was silent for a long time. Finally she whispered, "I don't know what to think about you."

"You aren't mad?"

"I don't know what I am."

Hope pounded through Griff. Dana looked nonplussed. "I intend to tell your mother the truth, too. Today, as a matter of fact. I've got her number, and I'll call her when I get home. I know what I did was wrong, but I didn't see any other choice under the circumstances."

"Why don't you wait?" It was her turn to blush and not meet his gaze. "When I talked to my mother later that day, she was pretty happy I had a fiancé."

"Then . . . you knew!"

Dana nodded. "I was just wondering if you'd own up to it or not. . . ." A decent person would. Maybe a decent person wouldn't have lied in the first place, but the circumstances were extenuating. A large part of Dana heaved a sigh of relief Griff had admitted his lie at the first opportunity.

Risking a glance at him, Dana said, "She was probably pretty happy when you told her, huh?"

"Yes, she was. She stopped crying then." Griff cocked his head, studying her intently. "I don't understand. Why don't you want me to tell her the truth?"

With a shake of her head, Dana whispered, "If you don't mind, just let it remain this way—for a while. It won't hurt anything." Chewing on her lower lip, Dana added, "Mom wants to see me happy. She knows the four years of hell I've gone through to graduate from Annapolis. It's just a small dream. Let her hold on to it—just for a little while."

Relief, mixed with an incredible tenderness, flooded Griff, as he watched Dana wrestle with her feelings. "Everyone should have dreams," he said. The silence grew stilted. Softly, Griff added, "It doesn't sound as if you had a very happy childhood."

With a grimace, Dana lay back, closing her eyes. "Who did, Turcotte? I've never met anyone who had an apple-pie-in-the-sky time growing up."

"I can't disagree with you." Dana appeared positively worn-out. "I've overstayed my welcome," he murmured. "You need to rest."

Dana barely opened her eyes. "Griff?" He hesitated at the door, turning his head toward her. "Did you mean it? The war's over between us?"

"Be at the ready room at 0700 two weeks from now and find out," he challenged her softly. Griff saw her blue eyes lighten and her lips part, as if she were going to cry. "It's the least I can do for you," he whispered unsteadily. "I'll teach you how to fly, Dana."

"I've got some bad news, Dana." Maggie entered the hospital room several days later and gave her friend a slight smile of welcome. She had just come from Whiting Field and still wore her light blue uniform skirt and blouse.

Dana was in bed, several aeronautical books spread across her lap. "Hi. What's wrong?"

Bringing over a chair, Maggie sat down. She folded her garrison cap and placed it on the bed table. "It's about Molly." Her lips compressed. "She got Boarded today."

"No!" Dana cried. Sitting up in bed, she clenched her fists. "What happened?"

Maggie gave her a glance. "It's been coming for a while, Dana. I was hoping I was wrong, but—"

"You're talking in circles. What's wrong with Molly's flying? She seemed really happy—I thought she was taking the flights real well."

Maggie sighed. "She just doesn't have what it takes, Dana. You and I skirted this issue before we ever came to Whiting. Molly's different. She's...softer. Hell, I don't know. She doesn't have that steel backbone you and I have."

Quirking her lips, Dana lay back against her pillows. "Poor Molly. You know how much her father and brother have been pushing her."

"Dammit, I know!" Maggie got up, unable to sit still. "I wish to hell they'd leave her alone! So what if her father's an ex-Navy pilot? So what if her wheelchair-bound brother had the appointment to Annapolis in the first place? Molly took his place for *them*."

"She's living her life for them," Dana concluded.

"Well, Molly's hit a brick wall," Maggie muttered angrily. "She's falling apart behind the stick."

Dana rubbed her face, her heart breaking for Molly. "I hate when bad things happen to good people. Molly's the best. She's got the most generous heart, the most giving—"

Maggie halted, staring at Dana. "Look, all we can do is support her the best we know how. I think this Board will break her. Once her family gets wind of it, the phone calls and letters will start. You know how that dramatic little scenario goes."

"Damn her family!" Dana laughed bitterly. "Of course, I'm one to talk."

"You came out of a different situation. Whatever happened made you tough and resilient, Dana. Molly's rich family coddled and protected her."

"Annapolis sure took off that veneer," Dana pointed out. She held Maggie's worried green gaze. "But no matter how much strength she's got, it can't help her win her wings."

"Well," Maggie muttered, "her grades are too high for the Navy to throw her to the wolves."

"When's her Board?"

"Friday."

Tomorrow. "I wish I could get home. I hate staying here. I could be of more help to Molly if I were around."

"Just sit here and get well, Coulter, and quit your bitching. I'll take care of Molly until you get home. It's only four more days."

"If Molly feels up to it, bring her over later, will you?"

Maggie leaned over, giving Dana a hug. "Okay. I'll bring a box of Kleenex with me, too. We'll have a good, therapeutic, group cry."

The room grew quiet after Maggie left. Dana stared blackly at the aeronautical books she was studying in order to keep up with the schooling phase of her training while she recuperated. Loneliness stabbed at her. Although her friends visited her on a daily basis, something was missing.

Dana didn't look at why. When she closed her eyes, Griff's face appeared. When she wasn't studying, he inevitably filtered into her unguarded mind and heart. Since owning up to his lie, he hadn't visited her. Well, what had she expected? The need to talk to him about Molly overrode her cautious nature. She would call him Saturday, on his day off.

When the knock came at her hospital door, Dana's heart thumped hard in her chest.

"Come in," she called. She stood by the window, dressed in her pale pink velour robe, her feet bare.

Griff stepped into Dana's room. He gave her a warm, hesitant smile, unsure how she would receive him. Her phone call had been brisk and businesslike; she hadn't told him what she wanted to talk about. She nodded a greeting, and he noticed that she appeared to be equally nervous. It made him feel slightly better.

"Hi. How are you feeling?"

Griff wore charcoal-gray slacks with a white short-sleeved shirt. Dana stared at the huge bouquet of springtime flowers in his hand. His hair was recently washed; his face was free of the dark five-o'clock shadow he usually had at this time of day. Her mouth went dry, and she made a weak gesture with her hands.

"Better," she murmured. She reached hesitantly for the bouquet he offered her. He seemed so shy—it made her want to forget their past and start over. "They're beautiful. Thank you."

Griff glanced meaningfully around the room, finding his yellow roses still in the cut-crystal vase, the note he'd written, beside it. "I was hoping you'd keep the roses."

Dana moved around him, placing the bouquet on the tray next to her desk. "Why wouldn't I?" She sat down on the edge of the bed. Griff turned and stuffed his hands into the pockets of his pants. Despite his size and bulk, he seemed somehow vulnerable.

With a shrug, he muttered, "Oh, I don't know. I've been a real bastard to you, for starters. That's reason enough to throw them out."

"I hoped they were a peace offering," Dana said in a low tone, watching his shadowed face. When he lifted his chin, his gray eyes a smoky color, her heart expanded in a wild, giddy feeling.

"They were. Yellow roses are reserved to say, 'I'm sorry and can we start all over again?' "

Uncomfortable, Dana looked away. Griff's change was too much too soon for her. He'd offered the olive branch in more ways than one, but could she trust his gesture? "I needed to talk to you about something, Mr. Turcotte."

Griff's heart sank. It was back to military formality. He tried not to show his hurt. "Sure. What is it?" Didn't Dana believe that he wasn't going to Board her? He saw that she had a cardboard mock-up of the trainer cockpit in the corner of her room. Even while recovering, she was drilling herself on flight procedures. It showed her spunk and resolve, and he admired her fiercely for it.

Dana stared down at her tightly clasped hands. "I don't even know if it's proper to talk about this, or if you can...."

Griff walked nearer. He was careful to keep a comfortable distance between them, although it was the last thing *he* wanted. Dana was looking much better, with color in her cheeks and some of the old defiance in her blue eyes. He saw little evidence of the red jellyfish welts because the velour robe effectively covered the rest of her small form.

"You can talk to me about anything," he said, meaning it.

Lifting her chin, Dana held his warm gaze. How she wanted to believe him. Just being in his presence threatened to expose her carefully closeted emotions. The overwhelming need to throw herself into his arms and be held surprised her. Stumbling over her escaping emotions, Dana blurted, "It's about Molly. She was Boarded yesterday. One more, and she's out of flight school."

"Oh...that." Griff frowned, avoiding Dana's searching look. "I'm sorry, Dana, I can't discuss another student with you. It's against regulations. I know you understand."

Yes, she did. Frustration thrummed through her, and she stepped toward Griff. "Then tell me how we can help her."

Struggling, Griff turned and walked toward the window. Outside, the May afternoon was hot and humid. Pink and white oleanders framed the window. He'd heard about

Molly's Board. She just didn't have the ability to fly well, according to her IP.

Dana read Griff's silence as serious. She walked up to him and placed her hand momentarily on his arm. "I know how you feel about wanting to wash students out, but Molly's my friend. She's like family. If you could tell me what Maggie and I could do at home to help her—"

"It's not that simple, Dana." Griff turned his head, staring down at her. He saw the pain his words caused in every feature of her face, and he hated himself once again for inflicting hurt upon her. "Listen to me." He turned, facing her. "We get a lot of people through here who would make great private pilots, even commercial pilots. But we're charged with finding those few who can take off and land on the deck of a damn carrier no matter what the weather. You don't have an understanding of what that means yet. Maybe Molly has good flight skills for private or commercial aviation, but not necessarily for combat flying."

Dana absorbed his emotion-laden words. Griff could have blown her off, as he'd done previously in her own case. Instead, he was being as gentle as possible with her while still being honest about Molly's chances. "I see," she whispered.

"Being a Navy pilot requires a combination of guts, steel backbone, lack of fear and an unknown quantity you can't teach or drill into a person, Dana. Molly may not have that unknown ingredient. It's the only thing we can't teach a fledgling pilot."

Her heart hurt for Molly. "I know what you're talking about," she said, and turned away.

Helpless, Griff stared at Dana's back. She always looked so small to him, pitted against him and the world he knew. Despite that, her back always remained ramrod straight, her small shoulders thrown back. There was nothing weak or apologetic about Dana. "Sometimes," he added, "a Board scares students into reaching down to see if they possess that unknown quantity inside themselves. Maybe this will do it for Molly. I hope it does.''

Griff's sincerity shattered another wall around Dana's heart. She managed a small smile. ''Thanks for coming over here and being honest.''

''You're welcome. I don't like being the bearer of bad news. You've had enough lately.'' He didn't want to leave. The past few days had been hell on him. He'd wanted to call and visit Dana daily, but he knew better. She didn't trust him, and he wouldn't push himself on her.

''I was raised on bad news, Lieutenant. I've learned to roll with it, and still land on my feet.''

''Maybe your luck's changed.''

Dana smiled wryly. ''I'm a realist. I don't think so.''

Griff headed slowly toward the door, grasping for a reason to stay, or to see her again before she came back to the station. His hand on the doorknob, he suddenly had an idea.

''The doctor's releasing you two days from now, right?''

''Yes.'' Dana gave him a quizzical look.

''Great. How about if I pick you up and take you to your apartment?'' He held up his hand, seeing shock register in her eyes. ''I've already talked to the doc. They're releasing you at 1000. Your friends will be at the station, but I'm free at that time. I can pop over and get you, drop you off at home and be back at the station in time for my next class. How about it?''

Dana's first reaction was to say no. The look, the expectancy on Griff's face made her mutter, ''I guess it's all right.''

''I'll be here at 1000 on Monday morning.'' His pulse bounded unevenly, celebrating the bit of trust Dana had just placed in his hands.

''Wait!'' Dana faced him. ''Why are you doing this?''

Griff held the door open with the toe of his shoe. ''Because I want to.''

"Out of guilt?"

He refused to be drawn into an argument. Griff saw the confusion and fear in her eyes. "Never out of guilt," he said quietly.

Taking a shaky breath, Dana stared at his strong, dark features. His eyes were a soft dove gray, as they had been at the airport. The same kind of care exuded from them, making her feel as if she were being embraced in a warm, protective blanket. "I can't stand anyone doing anything for me out of guilt or pity," she warned.

His mouth curved into a slight smile. "I'll never do anything for you because of either of those feelings. Okay?"

"Okay."

Dana stood, watching the door close, the silence once again settling around her. The room seemed empty without Griff's larger-than-life presence. What was he up to? And why? Chaos reigned in her. Two days from now they'd meet again, square off again. Dana couldn't shake the feeling that Griff wanted something from her. But *what?*

Griff tried to contain his surprise at seeing Dana waiting at the curbside outside the hospital doors for him at 1000 Monday morning. She wore a pair of light gray slacks and a blouse covered with pink, red and yellow hibiscus, which complemented the high color in her cheeks. Her hair was tousled, obviously freshly washed and dried. She held her cardboard mock-up of the trainer cockpit under her right arm. Her left hand grasped her purse. Beside her sat one piece of luggage.

Getting out of the Corvette, Griff smiled. "Looks like you're raring to get home," he teased, coming around and opening the trunk of his sports car.

Dana nodded and managed a brief smile. "I'm more than ready, believe me." Griff looked handsome in his tan slacks and short-sleeved shirt. His garrison cap, set at a jaunty angle on his head, shouted that he was, above all, a fighter pilot. Dana's gaze settled on the set of gold wings above his left breast pocket. In or out of uniform, Griff was definitely a head turner—and dangerous to her traitorous heart, which was picking up in sporadic beat every time he looked at her with his warm gray eyes.

"You look beautiful this morning." He took her cardboard cockpit and carefully stowed it in the rear of the Corvette with her luggage.

Dana didn't know how to respond to his husky compliment. She quirked her mouth and turned away so he couldn't see her response. Surprised that he came around to open the door for her, she looked up at him. His smile was devastating.

"A gentleman always opens a door for a lady," he told her, "even in this day and age."

With a groan, Dana got in and strapped on the seat belt. The leather interior of the Corvette and the cockpitlike instrument panel made her realize why Griff had chosen this car. It was probably as close as he could come to a plane on the ground.

Settling into his seat, Griff buckled up and eased the car away from the curb. "Now, what was that groan for?" He wanted to keep things light and easy between them. If the heightened flush across her cheeks was any indication, Griff was delighted with her reaction. At least she wasn't glaring at him.

"I thought the caveman era was dead." Dana tried to concentrate on the lovely avenues of trees and palms. Brightly colored oleander bushes surrounded most of the homes.

"My parents drilled it into me that a gentleman always does certain things for a lady."

"I'm sorry, but after four years at Annapolis where we were treated as if we weren't female, it's lost on me."

"I don't believe that. You're out of Annapolis now. It'll get easier."

She gave him a questioning look. "Really?"

It was Griff's turn to flush. "It will," he promised her softly. Glancing at her profile, he saw that her lips were pressed together, as if waiting for a blow. Frustrated he wondered how long it would be until she started lowering her guard toward him. Scrambling, he asked, "What will you do with your week of enforced rest at the apartment?"

"Try to keep up with Maggie's and Molly's workloads."

"Good idea." He pulled a piece of paper from his pocket and handed it to her. "I've given admin orders to release all curriculum material to you on the subjects you need to stay up on."

Dana stared at the crisp, neatly typed orders with Griff's scrawl at the bottom. "Thanks—"

"My yeoman, Johnson, will bring over some text material to your apartment this afternoon and get you up to speed so that when you step back into the arena next Monday, you'll be caught up."

Stunned, Dana stared over at him. "Tell me something. Would you do this for any other student?"

"Yes."

She studied the orders, still feeling there were reasons behind his more-than-generous actions. Griff could have let her get this information on her own. He could have made it tough for her.

At the apartment, Griff insisted upon carrying her luggage and mock-up into the apartment. After putting them in her bedroom, he was able to look around. Dana's room held posters of flowers and pastoral landscapes. Her desk was neatly stacked with books and papers. The shelves were lined with books needed for flight training. Next to her double bed, covered by a crocheted afghan in lavenders, violets and pale pinks, were several music boxes. Here was a side to her he'd not been introduced to, but wanted desperately to know.

Out in the living room, Dana waited for Griff to saunter back to where she stood. His eagle gaze missing nothing, and it left her feeling naked beneath his inspection. She saw his interest in her room, and she didn't know how to feel about it. He could use any and everything against her in the cockpit. Having him in her apartment was like inviting the enemy to view her Achilles' heel. But was he her enemy?

"I like your place," Griff said, meaning it. He placed his hands on his hips. "Mine looks like a morgue in comparison. You've got lots of green plants and flowers in here. That's good."

Her heart went out to him. "Plants seem to make things come alive."

Griff shrugged and headed for the screen door. "It's been my experience that it's the person you share your life with that makes it come alive." Afraid he'd said too much, he gave her a mock salute. "Stay home and continue to get well. I'll see you Monday. And wipe that worry out of your eyes, all right?"

Dana managed a grimace. "I don't think it will ever go away."

"Sure, it will. See you around, Dana."

"Goodbye... and thanks."

"Any time."

Dana's heart finally settled down after Griff left. Her spirit was buoyed by the fact that he was making sure she got the classroom assignments. Was the war really over? How badly she wanted it to be. Monday would tell her everything.

Chapter Eleven

Dana had thought she was nervous before, but Monday, as she sat in the ready room, tension had her sweating. All around her, students waited, talking in low voices or studying their flight manuals before the instructors came for them. It had been a week since she'd last seen Griff. Dana felt as if his absence had created a huge hole in her.

A week at her apartment had helped Dana regain her old strength and mental toughness, but the ocean had taken something from her. She couldn't define it exactly, but she felt softer, more vulnerable after almost dying. Molly, despite her own problems with flight training, had mentioned the change in Dana a number of times, and Maggie had seconded it. Had it come from herself, or was it something Griff had given her? The new Griff, she corrected herself. Dana wiped her sweaty palms against the thighs of her flight suit. She wanted peace between them. For the past two weeks she'd wondered about the poem Griff wanted to share with her. Perhaps it would give her the insight into him she so desperately sought.

"Miss Coulter?"

Dana jerked her head up. Griff stood a few feet away. Dressed in his olive-green flight suit, he looked unbearably handsome. When his mobile mouth drew into a slight curve of welcome, heat swept up Dana's throat and into her face. Unsure, she rose, forcing a smile in return.

"Hi."

Griff wanted to reach out, touch her shoulder and tell her it was all right; but under the circumstances, that was impossible. The wariness in Dana's eyes tore at him. "Hi, yourself. Are you ready to fly?"

Nodding jerkily, Dana gripped her flight log. "Yes, sir." His eyes were a nonthreatening dove gray, and she managed a strained laugh. "Yes, I'm ready, Mr. Turcotte."

As they walked out to the ramp where the trainers were parked, Griff shortened his stride for Dana's sake. "You look healed and as good as new," he told her. "How are you feeling?" He tried not to stare at her like a gawky teenage boy, but it had been a week since he'd seen her—an eon, to him.

"The truth?" Griff's easy demeanor gave her the courage to respond.

"I never wanted anything but honesty between us."

Dana wanted to believe him. Measuring her words carefully, she said, "I'm fine."

"Any nightmares?"

"Yes." His insight, when he chose to use it, never failed to amaze Dana.

"Common after a near brush with death."

The morning was bathed in a peachy glow along the horizon. Unaccountably, Dana felt her hopes soar. "As a pilot, have you come close?"

Griff nodded. "I was one of the pilots who challenged those Libyan planes and shot one down a few years ago. Yeah, I had nightmares afterward."

"Oh."

Halting at the trainer, Griff motioned her toward it. "Go ahead with the walk-around."

It was a dream, Dana thought. It had to be. Griff was acting like a normal human being with her. Was it all an elaborate trick to catch her off guard so he could give her a 1.9 after the flight? She also wondered if her airsickness would resurface. She would find out soon enough.

AVM Parker was there to welcome her back, handing her the discrepancy log to look over and sign. His smile was full, and she responded effortlessly to his welcome. The walk-around was completed, and she waited tensely for Griff to gig her on some small thing she'd overlooked. He remained silent, hands clasped in front of him, a neutral look on his face.

Climbing into the trainer, Parker helped Dana get the harness buckled. It was the first time the crew chief had done it, and she waited to hear Griff yell at him to get down and let her do it herself. The order never came. Parker gave her a smart salute and stepped down the ladder.

"Have a good flight, Ms. Coulter."

She gave him a thumbs-up. "Thanks, Parker." Her mind raced with the next thing she had to do. Her headphones were silent. Was Griff just waiting? Pushing the start button on the instrument panel, she heard the trainer's engine cough, and the propeller started turning.

The morning air was choppy because at least twenty other planes were in the flight pattern. The trainer felt good in her hands, but Dana knew she was gripping the stick too hard. As if reading her mind, Griff said, "Two fingers on the stick."

Dana obeyed, relieved not to hear the grate of anger that usually accompanied the order. Her stomach churned as they bumped along. Was he going to keep her in the flight pattern, making airsickness a more likely problem?

"Take us out over the gulf, Dana."

Dana. Normally, it was Coulter—and even then, ground out like glass being smashed beneath the heel of his boot. He'd called her Dana, his voice civilized, unruffled—no sign of emotion in his tone. For the next two hours, he drilled her on basics, a ninety-degree turn, a one-eighty and three-sixty. She worked hard to keep her altitude even and the wings level. The temperature was climbing, and with it came more turbulence.

Toward the end of the two hours, Dana couldn't hold her stomach down. Pressing the button on the stick that linked her to Griff, she croaked, "I'm going to be sick."

"I've got the stick," came his calm reply.

Humiliated, Dana could do nothing but let him fly until she stopped retching and had stowed the burp bag. Wrapping her hand around the stick, she said, "I've got the stick."

"Roger."

Dana waited for him to start haranguing her about being weak. Silence. She gulped a couple of times.

"Parker stowed some water on the starboard side down by your seat. Take a drink of it, Dana. I've got the stick."

Stunned, Dana sat frozen for a moment, not believing her ears. Finally, she forced herself to move. Unsnapping her oxygen mask, she located the plastic bottle, drinking deeply from it, washing her mouth out in the process. Capping the bottle and stowing it, she took back the stick.

"Thanks, Mr. Turcotte."

"You're welcome. Okay, let's head back. You've had enough for one day."

Dana swung the trainer around, in shock. The difference in Griff was like night and day. Was this a ruse to gain her trust before going back to his old tactics, or was he really changing? Dana knew the grade he gave her would reflect a great deal of where Griff was really at.

"You're giving me a 2.2?" Dana gasped.

Griff smiled as they stood next to the trainer after the flight. "You put in two tough hours, Miss Coulter. Your landings were above average for being rusty, and your ninety, one-eighties and three-sixties were excellent." Griff balanced the board against his cast, and signed off his name. Dana's eyes were huge and beautiful—and God, how he wanted to drown in them.

Stunned, Dana signed off the grade and turned to speak to Parker, who was already servicing the plane for Griff's next flight. She excused herself and walked over to the AVM.

"I just wanted to thank you for putting that bottle of water in there for me, Parker."

"Ma'am?"

"The water in case I had to use the burp bag."

"Oh...the water." Parker flashed her a big smile. "That was Mr. Turcotte's idea, ma'am. I just played gofer and hunted it up for you. He's the one you should thank."

"I see...." Dana turned, nonplussed. She walked up to Griff, who was busy filling out the rest of the report for Ops. "Parker said it was your idea to put the water in there for me. Thank you."

He glanced up. "You're welcome. Come on, let's get back to the ready room and discuss the particulars of your flight."

Dana shook her head and said nothing. On the way, she glanced up at Griff, and noticed his walk seemed lighter. He almost seemed happy.

"Lieutenant?"

"Yes?"

"I keep thinking about you—I mean, us. This grade isn't a joke, is it?"

Griff held Dana's serious azure eyes. "You earned the grade."

"You didn't scream at me today in the cockpit."

"No." Griff slowed to a stop as Dana confronted him, frustration mirrored in her eyes. He longed to reach out, stroke her cheek and tell her how sorry he was for the way he'd behaved the past month.

"What's going on, then?" Dana demanded tightly.

Griff looked around. The humid gulf breeze stirred, and several F-15 Eagle fighters flashed overhead, making the air vibrate in their path. The breeze gently mussed Dana's ebony hair. Griff sharply recalled how soft its strands were.

"I'm trying to make amends to you."

"Amends? What's changed?" she demanded hoarsely. "Ever since I got swept out on that riptide, you've been acting funny."

Griff understood her reaction. If he told Dana the truth—that he liked her, wanted to know her on a personal and intimate level—she'd run from him. "Yes, that incident forced me to look at a lot of things," he agreed.

"If you gave me that grade because you felt sorry for me, I won't accept it!"

He held her mutinous gaze. "I feel anything but pity for you, Miss Coulter."

Dana made a strangled sound and moved away from him. "This is crazy!"

"We're starting over."

Dana stepped into his path. "All right. What do you want from me?" she rattled.

Griff saw the shadow of fear in her eyes. "Nothing."

"You want something, dammit! I can feel it."

Her cry serrated his heart. Griff wasn't in a position to pull her into his arms and calm her down. "What I want from you is a smile."

"What?"

"I've never seen you really smile."

Shaken, Dana looked up at Griff. "This whole situation isn't making sense to me!"

Laughing, Griff said, "Maybe. Oh, there's one more thing."

"What?"

"I want to hear the sound of your laughter. If it's half as pretty as your mother's, then I'll be happy." With that, Griff eased around Dana and left her standing on the tarmac to digest their conversation.

"Oh, Miss Coulter?" He saw Dana turn, her eyes narrowed with confusion. "Be at the ready room at 0700 tomorrow morning."

Dana was afraid to look at Griff's assessment of her flying skills as he handed the paper to her after the morning flight. Her suit was damp, and she'd sweated heavily, expecting him to catch her off guard and start screaming at her again. It hadn't happened. In the cockpit he was all business, his voice low and, at times, even supportive. When she needed correction, he gave it to her. When she didn't, silence reigned on the headset in her helmet.

"A 2.2? Another one?"

"What's the matter? Don't you like it? If you're going for anything but helo-pilot status, you have to strive to make 2.3s or 2.4s, Miss Coulter."

Griff was deliberately teasing her, wanting to ease some of the tension he saw in every line of her body.

Dana glanced up from the board, catching the smile in his fathomless gray eyes. She had gotten airsick once on this flight, but it hadn't affected her grade. And just as before, the water bottle had been stowed for her use.

"I had my heart set on fighters, Mr. Turcotte. How did you know that?"

"Griff," he corrected, and looked around the mostly-deserted ramp. "When we're alone, I want you to call me

Griff. And as to you wanting jet status, I think you've got the ability to go for it.''

Wanting to believe that he wasn't setting her up to Board her, Dana signed off the paper, frowning. He wanted to be on friendlier terms with her. Why? ''And you'll call me Dana?''

Griff didn't miss the edge of sarcasm in her voice, the wariness. He remembered Ann's words about Dana, how she'd been pursued and tricked by Lombard. ''I'll call you anything you want me to call you,'' he answered softly.

Handing him the board with her grade on it, Dana turned away, confused. ''Tigers don't change their stripes, Mr. Turcotte. I'm not going to believe you're changing yours.''

Time, Griff cautioned himself as Dana walked away from him. *Give her plenty of rein and time. She'll come around.*

Dana suddenly halted, glancing at him across her shoulder. ''When can we fly again?''

He grinned. ''When do you want to?''

''Tomorrow?''

''How about tonight? Your first night flight?''

Dana frowned. ''Is this some kind of trick?''

''Meet me at 2100 and find out.''

The ready room was quiet when Dana arrived at 2050. She had changed flight suits earlier after grabbing dinner at the apartment. At exactly 2100, Griff appeared at the door. Was it the thrill of making a possible breakthrough with Griff that made her heart pound so hard? Or the fact that he looked so stalwart in his flight suit?

''I see you're a lady who likes to live dangerously. You decided to meet me and see if we're taking a night flight.'' As Griff approached, he saw less wariness in her eloquent eyes.

''I've lived dangerously all my life, Mr. Turcotte. Why should it change now?''

Griff nodded sagely. "No argument out of me. Let's get out there and do it together, shall we?"

Excitement dissolved her distrust. Dana saw the challenge in Griff's eyes and heard it in his voice. He was supporting her! "I'm ready," she whispered with feeling.

The night flight was a completely different experience from day flying. Griff had her switch from visual observation outside the cockpit, to beginning to rely totally on the instruments. He showed her how the horizon gauge would move if they nosed up or down. For the next two hours she lived in the cocoon of the darkness, relying on waving arms, dials and the soft red light illuminating the cockpit so she could see them.

The flight lasted two hours. Dana couldn't suppress her wonderment at the stars that sparkled outside the cockpit. And for once, she didn't get airsick. She noticed, however, that her bottle of water was faithfully stowed in the starboard side next to the seat. Taxiing the trainer back to the ramp after the flight, she couldn't suppress her joy.

"Griff, it was so lovely up there. I can see why you like night flying so much. Did you see the stars? They were so close I felt like I could reach out and pluck them right out of the sky."

Unsnapping the oxygen mask so that it hung to one side of his helmet, Griff smiled at Dana's spontaneous use of his first name. He'd made the flight a positive experience for her. His plan to get Dana's trust was working. Gratitude that she still had the ability to trust any man at all made him feel humbled as never before. "Night flights are fun—except for refueling with a tanker at thirty thousand, or making a carrier landing."

As Dana brought the trainer back to its parking slot, she hesitantly asked, "Griff, you never said how you broke your arm."

"You never asked."

"I want to know."

"I'll tell you on the ground. Let's unstrap and get out of here."

The field was darkened and quiet, except for lights around the control tower and the security gate. Dana felt so much heaviness lift from her shoulders as they slowly walked back to the ready room. She waited patiently for him to tell her about the cast. After they showed their badges to the guard, Griff said, "When I held the manual-release landing lever that day during the emergency landing order I gave you, and you hit it with your boot, it broke my finger."

Dana gasped and halted. "Oh, no!"

Griff grinned and held up his cast. "I had it coming, Miss Coulter."

Stunned, Dana said nothing else and followed him into the ready room. Under the fluorescent lights, Griff looked tired, strain evident around his eyes. She sat down opposite him at one of the many report tables to discuss the flight and wondered what kind of grade he'd give her.

"I didn't mean to hurt you, Griff. I knew you were playing a rotten trick on me, and I got mad."

With a laugh, Griff pushed the grade board in her direction. "Don't worry about it. It taught me a lesson I'll never forget."

Dana's gaze flew to the grading box: 2.1. Not bad for a first night flight! Not bad at all, in Dana's opinion. Maggie had gotten a 2.0, and so had Molly. Her lips curved upward as she signed the board and handed it back to him.

"That's what I've been waiting for." Griff sighed and leaned back in the chair.

Stymied, Dana asked, "What?"

"That beautiful smile of yours. What a gift."

The tenor of his voice told her he was being honest. His returning smile was devastating. Suddenly, Dana felt more beautiful than she could ever recall. She avoided Griff's brazen appraisal of her. "You just gave me the greatest gift *I* could ever have," she whispered.

Relaxing, Griff simply enjoyed the time he was able to spend with Dana. "What's that?"

"I know you've got a lot of pressure on you, Griff. Taking extra time to help me log the hours I need to catch up is something...well...special." She held his dancing gray gaze. "The gift of treating me fairly after our rotten start over a month ago. I really believe that the new Griff is here to stay."

"None of it was your fault," he told her quietly. "I had too many problems I was refusing to deal with, Miss Coulter. I blamed you for them, and I shouldn't have."

"You can call me Dana..." And then she added shyly, "If you want to."

Griff ached to reach across the table and kiss her. There was such vulnerability in Dana beneath the tough facade she wore to protect herself. With a careless grin, he said, "I'd like that." The need to love her was excruciating. Right now, Dana was unsure of herself as a woman. Her lack of experience was touching.

"Does your arm hurt you very much?"

"No. My pride got hurt a hell of a lot worse than my finger."

With a laugh, Dana stood. "That I can believe!"

Her breathy laughter sang through Griff, and he absorbed it like a starving man. It was late, and both of them had to be at the station early tomorrow.

"So, when's our next flight?"

He liked the new easiness flowing between them. Some invisible hurdle had been spanned. "I've got a break at 1500 tomorrow. The air will be rough, but I think your stomach's ready to handle it."

Dana nodded, placing her garrison cap on her head. She picked up her helmet flight bag. "I'll see you then. Good night, Griff. And thanks."

Griff sat alone in the ready room for a long time after Dana had left. Rocking back in the aluminum chair, he savored the tendrils taking root in his heart. Dana was finally beginning to trust him. She'd started calling him by his first name. Good. Despite his exhaustion, Griff felt happier than he could ever recall. Tomorrow afternoon couldn't come too soon.

Dana tried to quell her desire to look at the grade Griff had given her after the afternoon flight. They had flown for three hours. Her logbook was starting to rack up flying hours, and she was beginning to catch up with the rest of her class. The ready room was empty at 1800, everyone having gone home for the day. She sat down at a table and took off her garrison cap. Her flight suit wasn't quite as damp as usual, and Dana was grateful that she hadn't gotten airsick. Dr. Collins had been right: The more regularly she flew, the more her body adjusted to the new and different sensations.

Griff handed her the board, then walked to the coffee dispenser. "You did well," he congratulated her, pouring himself a cup. "Want some?"

Dana looked up. "No...thanks. A 2.3?"

Sauntering back to the table, he gave her a reckless grin. "Your landings at Pensacola were excellent."

With a grimace, Dana read his individual comments on her flying ability. "I was scared to death when you told me I had to fly us over there."

Sitting down, Griff sipped the hot, black coffee. "Why?"

"After the last incident over there, I sweated it."

He lifted the arm of his flight suit and pointed to the dark stain beneath the armpit. "We both did," Griff said with a wry smile.

Dana studied him. "You believe in confronting your fears, don't you? I know your best friend was killed in a midair collision over that field. And I just about got us killed by not seeing that other trainer the first time we flew over there."

Spreading out his long legs beneath the table, Griff nodded. "Just to set the record straight, when we got back that day, I lodged a flight protest on your behalf."

Dana gawked at him. "You did?"

"Yes. You were cleared of any wrongdoing. The other student pilot was at fault. And so was his instructor." Frowning, Griff added, "I don't want you thinking you caused a possible midair collision, Dana."

"When did you find out about this?" Had he hidden the information from her? Dana hoped not, for it would indicate he was still playing games with her.

Griff reached into his pocket and dug out a neatly folded piece of paper. "I got their judgment this afternoon," he said, handing it to her. "I thought you'd like to see their determination. It will go in your jacket."

Gratefully, Dana read the official report and handed it back to him. Even more important, Griff wasn't holding out on her. "You don't know how terrible I felt. I didn't want you to think I was like the student who killed your friend. I had a lot of fear. . . ."

"Fear can get you killed," Griff agreed. "Going over there at the busiest time of day today, we were both able to work through some of our hangups—together."

"I admire your courage," she admitted.

"What else do you admire—in a man, that is?" Griff baited.

Dana leaned back in the chair and rolled her eyes. "You're asking the wrong person that, Griff."

"I don't think so."

Shaking her head, Dana muttered, "All my experiences with men have been bad ones."

"Even with me."

Dana heard the regret in Griff's voice. "I finally figured out that you probably weren't angry with me personally. I just happened to be a convenient whipping post."

"And for that, I'm sorry."

"You're paying me back by being fair now."

"I'm trying to be. So, what qualities do you admire in a man?"

Dana's mouth twitched and she spoke hesitantly. "Honesty. I don't believe *any* relationship can survive without it. Maggie and Molly have said they've met men who have a streak of sensitivity in them. I've never seen it personally, but I'd like to see that in a man, too."

"Sensitivity?"

Dana struggled to qualify what she meant. She rested her elbows on the table. "Why can't a man see the beauty of a sunset and the different colors in it? And why can't he feel as deeply as I do, and be able to tell me about it? I don't believe there's that much difference between us. We all have a heart that feels...."

"Men had been taught to ignore a large part of themselves," Griff offered quietly. "We feel just as deep and hard as any woman. We just don't share it—sometimes even with ourselves."

"Well," Dana grumped, "it's stupid to hide how you feel. When things were going bad at home, Mom always was able to cry. She taught me it was okay to express myself, even if it was just to her." Then, avoiding Griff's sharpened gaze, Dana added softly, "Crying helps me release the pressure cooker inside myself."

Griff held his breath for a moment. The fact that Dana would discuss her homelife with him at all told him how much she was beginning to trust him. "When I was out searching the beaches for you and Vickie, I got in touch with a hell of a lot of feelings I'd stored up. Just before I discovered the two of you, I stood by my car and cried for a long time." Giving a bashful shrug, Griff said, "In a way, Dana, you helped me release the grief I'd been carrying around for the past six months."

Openmouthed, Dana stared at him. Griff was toying with a pen in his hands, avoiding looking at her. "You cried?"

she asked, then chastised herself for asking such an inane question.

"It's been known to happen," he answered wryly. Looking up, he held Dana's compassionate gaze. "It felt good. It had been a long time coming. In a way, Dana, you helped heal me." Griff shoved the pen into the upper-sleeve pocket on his left arm. "Hopefully, you'll let me help heal some of the damage I did to you."

Touched, Dana sat in the soothing silence. Griff was exquisitely human—and she realized her heart had never given up on believing there was innate goodness in him. "Maybe," she offered hesitantly, "we'll be able to heal each other."

The urge to sweep Dana into his arms and teach her the good things that could be shared between a man and woman sent a keening ache through Griff. Reaching into another pocket of his flight suit, he pulled out a crisp white sheet of paper that had been neatly folded.

"I think now's the time to give you this."

Dana took the paper, slowly unfolding it. "What is this?"

"That poem I wanted to share with you," Griff admitted in a low voice. "It was a favorite of my mother's. I remember learning to read it to her as a kid. She reflected the courage in it, and that night you got swept out to sea, all I could think about was "Invictus." You embody the poem in every way, just as she did. My mother had a hard life with no hope of recovery. You came out of a rough childhood and could have turned out a hell of a lot different than you did, Dana. Instead, you took a negative and turned it into a positive. I admire that in a person. Go on, read it out loud. I always like hearing it."

Tears watered in Dana's eyes as she sat there with the paper stretched between her hands. The fact that Griff would share such a touching, deeply personal part of his life with her had moved her as nothing else could. How he had loved his mother! She must have been a very strong woman to have earned Griff's complete admiration.

"'Invictus,' by William Ernest Henley," she began in a hushed tone.

"Out of the night that covers me,
Black as the Pit from pole to pole,
I thank whatever gods may be
For my unconquerable soul.

In the fell clutch of circumstance,
I have not winced nor cried aloud;
Under the bludgeonings of chance
My head is bloody, but unbowed.

Beyond this place of wrath and tears
Looms but the horror of the Shade;
And yet the menace of the years
Finds, and shall find me, unafraid.

It matters not how strait the gate,
How charged with punishments the scroll.
I am the master of my fate;
I am the captain of my soul.

Tears blurred Dana's vision as she stared at the carefully hand-printed words on the paper. "Y-you wanted to share this with me that day you came for a visit?"

"Yeah, but it didn't seem like the right time."

Closing her eyes, Dana took in a ragged breath. "The poem... It's beautiful."

"It mirrors you." Swallowing hard, Griff felt tears leak into his eyes. He didn't care if Dana saw them or not. "Your mother told me about Frank, and how he used to beat you up." Anger made his voice shake. "You've been under fire since the day you were born, Dana, and it's a wonder you've survived as well as you have. You had to weather Annapolis, and then, when you got to Whiting Field, I did nothing but confirm what you knew about men all over again: We're brutal bastards at best, trying to strip your soul from you.''

It seemed natural to reach out and place her hand on Griff's arm. Such suffering and guilt showed in his eyes and the set of his mouth that Dana couldn't bear his pain. If she'd had any remaining doubts about Griff's sincere desire to treat her fairly, they dissolved. ''There's a difference,'' she whispered unsteadily. ''Once you realized what you'd done to me, Griff, you stopped doing it. My father knew what he was doing and didn't want to help himself.''

Covering her small hand with his own, Griff gently stroked her skin. ''Look, I know I have no right to ask this, but I'm going to anyway. Dana, there's something good between us. Something so damned right that I felt it from the moment we met at the airport.'' He saw her eyes go dark with fear and his mouth went dry. Heedless of his own dread that she would turn and run from his admission, he dived on. ''You've been injured by men all your life. I think it's about time you started trying to get over that fear. Not all men are like your father. I know I'm not a prime candidate because of my behavior for the past month, but I think we can be good for each other.''

Panic seized Dana. Griff's hand on hers felt so right and good. Slowly, she retrieved her hand from his. Unable to look at him, she whispered, ''Griff...I'm scared.... Scared to death.''

''So am I.''

Dana's eyes widened and her head snapped up.

Griff gave her a careless smile that he hoped would relax her. ''I know I'm an arrogant son of a bitch, and I've got one hell of a nasty reputation as a demanding instructor here at Whiting. I've got more than my share of bad points, but I want you to try to see that I have a decent side, also.''

Uneasy, Dana asked, ''Then what do you want from me?''

"Nothing you don't want to give freely and from your heart."

She melted at the timbre of his deep, low voice, but insisted, "Men take, women give."

"Not in a positive relationship. It's never one-sided."

"Then why did your marriage fail?" Though Dana knew she had no business asking, she couldn't help herself. She watched as Griff got up for a second cup of coffee.

"I came from a family where I saw the positives of giving *and* taking, Dana. When I met Carol while I was in training here at Whiting five years ago, she appeared to be a strong, capable woman."

"Like your mother?"

Griff nodded. "My mother was a heroic person. I'm not going to sit here and deny I prefer a woman made from the same mold."

"And Carol was strong?"

"Not really." And Griff explained.

When next he looked at his watch, an hour had gone by. It was past dinnertime, and even though he was physically hungry, he was more starved in an emotional sense for Dana's continued company. "What do you say to going and grabbing a bite to eat over at the Coffee Pot Restaurant off the station? It's 1900."

"Well...I'll have to change back into civilian clothes before I leave here." No one was allowed to leave Whiting in a flight suit. They had to wear either a dress uniform or civilian clothes. No one wore their uniform off base unless absolutely necessary.

Griff looked at his watch. "How about meeting me at my Corvette in fifteen minutes? I'll take you to dinner."

"Yes...I'd like that." Dana felt her heart skipping in her chest. As she rose and went to the women's locker room to shower and change, she experienced a wild, out-of-control giddiness. Griff was taking her out to dinner. They both wanted—needed—this time with each other. Dana didn't know how to respond to him because there were no strings attached. And yet, the hunger that burned like molten silver in the depths of his eyes sent her aching with expectancy.

Mulling it over, Dana changed into her pale pink cotton slacks, sandals and a simple white blouse. Maggie had given her a flowery scarf, and she tied it around her neck, deciding it made her look wonderfully feminine, mirroring how she felt at the moment. As Dana made her way out of the locker room and through the door to the ready room, she ruthlessly considered her attraction to Griff.

She'd been intrigued with him since the day they'd met at the airport. How many times had she wondered what it would be like to be kissed by that flexible, mobile mouth of his, which promised strength and yet, somehow, tenderness? Dana had never wondered about such things before, and she walked to the parking lot deep in thought. Up ahead, she saw Griff waiting patiently beside his sports car. Her pulse quickened as she approached him. His dark brown hair, recently washed, was shining and smoothed against his head from the shower. The five o'clock shadow of his beard gave his rugged face a dangerous look that sent a delicious tremor through her.

Nonplussed by her reactions to Griff, Dana managed a shy smile as he opened the car door for her. His returning smile was one of reassurance, not wolfishness. And the hunger she'd seen in his eyes before was banked. There was genuine happiness reflected in them now, and a ribbon of joy flooded her heart.

"I changed my mind," Griff told her, shutting the door, his hands resting on the frame of the open window.

"Oh?"

"You look so pretty, I think a better restaurant is in order. The White Horse Inn suits you tonight. How about it? I've got a sport coat, so they'll let me in."

Dana unconsciously touched her lower lip. "The White Horse Inn has great food." Griff looked more than acceptable in the lavender long-sleeved shirt and charcoal-gray slacks. He looked wonderful in her eyes. "Why not? It's been a day for new things."

Griff got in and buckled his seat belt. "New starts," he corrected. "We're finally getting off on the right foot—together."

Unsure what he meant by that statement, Dana leaned back against the leather seat as he drove off the station. Nervous and excited, she couldn't seem to think; only to feel. What she felt frightened her more than anything had in a long time. Suddenly Dana paralleled herself with a plane spinning out of control. She glanced over at Griff's profile. The cocky grin pulling at his mouth partly dissolved her fear of him as a man. There was so much to explore about Griff that was good. And now he was giving her an opportunity to do just that.

Chapter Twelve

The candle-lit atmosphere of the posh restaurant was romantic, fitting Griff's mood. Dana sat across from him in the dark maroon leather booth, her features soft and glowing beneath the light. She ate daintily, her every movement graceful and flowing. He wondered hotly what it would be like to love her—then tried to forget that train of thought. As long as Griff stayed on aeronautical topics, Dana was an eager and enthusiastic conversationalist. The minute he strayed to more personal or private subjects, she became quiet, almost withdrawn. So, Griff began to talk about himself in order to draw Dana out.

"When I was ten years old, my sole book-reading centered around World War II airplanes. What did you read at that age?"

Pleasantly full, Dana laid her fork aside and blotted her mouth with the pink linen napkin. "At ten I had a newspaper route and wasn't really reading military topics at all. Matter of fact, I didn't have time for pleasure reading."

"A newspaper route. That's pretty impressive for a young girl."

"Is that chauvinism talking?"

He grinned. "Partly. Still that's a lot of responsibility at such a young age, don't you think?"

With a shrug, Dana waited until the waitress took away the plates. The coffee was poured and then they were alone. "Mom thought it was a good idea for me to take up a paper route."

"Why?"

"It got me out of the house when my father was home. He worked the swing shift at a foundry in Youngstown, Ohio. When I got home from school at three, I tried to be quiet, but somehow I always ended up waking him." Dana's mouth compressed and she finally said, "I'll spare you the morbid details. Mom wanted me away from the house until he left at six. The newspaper route was a good answer."

"Under the circumstances," Griff agreed hollowly. "Glad my father didn't look at me the same way." Right now Dana appeared fragile, her skin translucent and taut beneath the low lighting. Talking about her past was a painful ordeal, he realized. The driving need to hold Dana, to show her that a man could provide something other than fear or pain, was foremost in his mind.

"What's your dad like?" Dana ventured.

With a sigh, Griff replied, "A hell of a lot different from yours. Dad was a blue-collar worker, and he loved my mother deeply. He worked in a copper mine in Jerome, Arizona, while I was growing up. We didn't have much money because of my mother's endless medical bills. Dad worked long, hard hours to make ends meet. I remember every night, for at least an hour, he'd come to Mom's room and we'd all sit and talk or read." Griff smiled fondly. "That's where I picked up my love of reading. Dad read to my mom. When I was older, I read to her, too."

"It sounds so different from my childhood, but you didn't have it easy, either."

Griff wanted to reach out and grip her hand to take away the ravages of pain still shadowing her eyes. "At least my dad never beat me."

Dana lowered her lashes. "That's over now."

"No," Griff countered in a whisper. "You still carry the memory."

"Battle scars," Dana said, trying to make a joke of it, wanting to lighten their somber mood.

"We all carry them, don't we?" Griff muttered. He saw she was uncomfortable with the direction of the conversation.

Dana rallied. "Did your parents support you going to the academy?"

"Yes. Actually, I had it planned years in advance."

"You were one of those kids who knew what you wanted."

"Didn't you?"

Dana sat her cup on its saucer. She folded her hands and rested her chin against them. "No. Not until I got into high school."

"And who aimed you toward a military career?"

"My school counselor. I had excellent grades despite my family life, and the kind of assertiveness he said they were looking for."

"So, you see the Navy as a career, not necessarily because you're military at heart?"

She liked Griff's ability to see between the layers of her. So many people—men in particular—didn't. "Yes, it's a career. I believe in having a military system that is able to defend our country. I don't believe in starting wars, just trying to prevent them."

"My philosophy's the same." He saw her eyes widen in surprise, and then she smiled.

"I'm not a hard-liner."

"Could've fooled me," Dana teased with a laugh. She sobered. "You're easy to talk with, Griff. I've never talked to anyone about my homelife like this."

Fighting the desire to reach out and cup Dana's small hand, he said, "A certain young lady has taught me an awful lot about myself in the past month and a half."

"And so you're here with me because you're grateful?"

Griff's mouth stretched slightly. "I like the way you confront people."

"I believe in honesty, Griff. Are you here tonight for that reason?"

"What if I said no?"

"Then I'd ask why." Dana felt her pulse leap as his eyes smoldered with some undefined emotion in their charcoal depths.

"That's not playing the game, you know."

"What game?"

"One of the many that men and women usually play with one another."

Scowling, Dana sipped her coffee, barely tasting the delicate Colombian flavor. "It only took me one time to see how those games work, Griff. I swore I'd never knowingly play them again."

Leaning forward, placing his elbows on the table, he said, "I agree with you. Carol played a game with me, and I fell for it."

Nervously, Dana fingered the damask tablecloth. "So, if you're not here with me out of gratefulness, what is it?" She forced herself to hold his warm gaze.

"I'm here because I enjoy your company. I like your laughter and I like it when you smile. You're a bright, intelligent woman who has one hell of a backbone. And, if the truth be known, I'm fascinated by you."

Dana sat very still as she digested Griff's admission. "Because I proved myself out in that riptide?"

With a sigh, he sat back. "It took that incident to get me to see a lot of things about myself, and it forced me to look at plenty of other issues, Dana. You were a catalyst for me."

"You've sure been one for me, too," she muttered.

He grinned. "Yeah? In what way?"

Uneasily Dana squirmed in her chair. "I—I'm not prepared to say much about it right now, Griff. At least, not yet."

Satisfied that he meant more to her than just an instructor, Griff was content not to push her. "Fair enough." He glanced at his watch. "Come on. I'd better get you back to the station to pick up your car. We've got a busy day ahead of us tomorrow, and it's getting late."

Reluctant to leave, Dana nodded. "It's been a wonderful dinner, Griff. Thank you."

Rising, he smiled. "A dream come true for me."

As Dana walked at his shoulder through the darkened interior, she gave him a wary look. "'A dream come true'?"

"Now, there you go, giving me that look like I'm feeding you a line—again."

Embarrassed, Dana walked out the door to the parking lot. "I guess I had that coming."

Risking the trust he'd established with her, Griff placed his hand on Dana's elbow, walking close to her. "I guess you did. Not every line is a lie, Dana. Can I help it if I think you're beautiful? Or that you walk with an incredible grace I've never seen in another woman?" He looked down to see the effect his admissions had on her. Her eyes were wide and lustrous with wonder—and trust. Her mouth was unbearably attractive, and he ached to stop her, to take her into his arms and kiss her until she ran like hot honey through his fingers.

Dana slowed as they neared the sports car in the partially filled parking lot. "Sometimes I have a tough time telling a line from the truth," she admitted. Griff's hand tightened momentarily on her elbow, and he drew her to a halt. She turned, mere inches separating them. Looking up into his darkened face, she felt herself go shaky inside.

"There's one way to tell," Griff whispered, placing his hands lightly on her upper arms.

"How?" Dana saw his eyes narrow with intent. Griff urged her forward. It seemed so right to her, the gentleness of his action giving her time to decide whether or not she wanted to partake in what he was offering. Griff was going to kiss her. She saw the look in his eyes; his intention was unmistakable.

Caressing her shoulder, Griff whispered, "Your heart will never lead you wrong." His hand tightened on her arms. Hoarsely he said, "Dana, I want to kiss you...and I promised you I'd never take unless you wanted to give. I meant that." The throbbing heat within him was almost painful. Dana was so close, her lips parted, begging to be kissed. Griff held himself in steely control.

Pressed against his hard, warm body, Dana's mind centered on the shocking, wonderful sensation created by their contact. Drowning in the stormy gray of his eyes, she couldn't find her voice. She felt the powerful beat of his heart against her breasts. This was so different from the way Lombard had treated her. She felt the potent vibration of need telegraphing through every muscle in Griff's body, but she also knew he would respect her wishes. The thought was galvanizing, heated.

Leaning upward, Dana pressed her hands against his chest and whispered unsteadily, "Yes, I want to kiss you...."

A groan vibrated through Griff as her hands grazed his chest. Everything about Dana's reaction was exquisite. Leaning down, he cherished her lips, feeling the soft, giving texture of them. A little rush of air escaped her, and he savored her response. Dana was trembling! Ever so gently, Griff coaxed her lips apart, allowing her time to adjust and get in touch with her own womanly response to him.

Dana's world melted as Griff's strong mouth eased her lips apart. She could taste the coffee they'd drunk. Her breathing ragged, she responded, hearing a groan begin deep within Griff. His tongue caressed the corners of her mouth, and a little cry echoed in her throat—sensations startling and new. Nipping at her lower lip, he cajoled her to come to him, to lean completely against his frame. Wanting more, Dana slid her arms around his neck, kissing him with hungry intent. She wasn't disappointed as he claimed her hotly, his lips devouring her, telling her of his urgent need for her. Surrendering to his arms, Dana followed her feminine instincts.

Her fingers laced through his dark hair. The muscles in Griff's neck were tense, and she felt a fine quiver race through him. As his hands framed her face, his mouth teaching her how to kiss him deeply, her world dissolved and joined his. A world of heat, of lightning striking through her, created a throbbing sensation between her legs that grew to an ache until she felt a languid weakness flowing through her like a molten river of fiery lava. Ever so gently, Griff kissed both corners of her mouth, brushed her lower lip with his tongue and then withdrew, his face inches from hers.

"You're so hot, so beautiful," he rasped. Unsteadily, Griff caressed her short, silky hair. "Dreams are made of someone like you," he admitted near her ear. Running his hand across her small shoulders and down her spine in a gesture meant to help stabilize Dana, he pressed a kiss to her temple. She smelled of a faint, flowery perfume, intoxicating his starved, alert senses.

Gradually Dana pulled away, though Griff's hand stayed on her arm. The smoldering promise remained in his hooded eyes as she tried to reorient herself. Leaning against the car, she gave him a wry look.

"I thought I was going to melt away," Dana admitted in a wispy voice.

"That made two of us, sweetheart." Griff eased next to her. Above, the stars were points of sparkling light on the dark quilt of the sky. The gulf wind ruffled briefly, moist and warm, like the kiss they'd just shared. Griff smiled down at Dana and noticed, even in the poor light, that her cheeks were suffused with a rosy blush.

As Dana stood there, she remembered Maggie telling her once that when the right man kissed her, she'd feel light and wonderful afterward. Well, she did now. Holding his intense gaze, Dana wondered where their budding relationship was going. It scared her. Yet, Griff had done nothing to frighten her; had only made her aware of her own special femininity as never before. Wrapping her arms around herself, Dana said softly, "This has never happened before, Griff. Not this way."

"I like what we shared, Dana. There's no hurry, no pressure. Good things take time."

She slanted an amused glance in his direction. "For a jet jock, your philosophy is the opposite of most guys'."

Griff placed his arm around her. "And 'most guys' haven't found you. You're different, Dana. And I know you're afraid of men in general. If I was in your shoes, I would be, too." He frowned and looked up at the star-laden sky. "I want the chance to explore what we have—on your terms, your time. That's the only way it's going to work, and I know it. If I push you, or start demanding things, you're going to run, and I don't want that."

"Still," Dana whispered, "it's new to me, Griff. You're different, and I don't have any experience with a man who's sensitive and gentle. I'm not used to it."

Wanting to kiss her again, but afraid of pressuring Dana too much, Griff stepped away and opened the car door for her. "Look, for the next couple of months we'll be around each other. That should give you time to see if you want to risk your neck with me."

He was teasing her, but Dana read between the lines as she slipped into the car. Tonight, Griff had allowed her the choice and control of the situation between them. Would it continue, or was it all an elaborate game? Her heart told her to trust Griff. Her wary head suggested caution. In three weeks, if she kept up her flight grades, she would leave Griff's instruction and other instructors from the flight pool would teach her for the duration of the course. As he got into the car, she stared at him.

"You said there was no hurry."

Griff turned, studying her shadowed face. Dana's eyes were luminous from their shared kiss. "That's right. Experience has taught me that time is on my side—not the opposite."

The weight on her shoulders disappeared. Dana leaned back, absorbing Griff's words. Most of all, she remembered the beauty, the gift of the kiss they'd shared. It was a dream, a wonderful dream. Would it continue? She was afraid to know the answer to that question. Besides, her flight training came first. And equally important was her worry about Molly. If Molly got Boarded one more time, she'd be washed out of the program. Dana didn't want that to happen. Molly was like the sister she'd never had, and Dana relied heavily on her in an emotional sense. Shutting her eyes, Dana leaned her head back, content to be swallowed up by darkness as the Corvette growled through the night.

Dana stepped into the apartment a week later and heard crying. Frowning, she placed her books on the couch and followed the sound. It led to Molly's bedroom. The door was open, and she stepped inside. Maggie was sitting on the edge of the bed, holding Molly, who was sobbing her heart out.

"What happened? What's wrong?" Dana asked, moving to Molly's side and sitting down opposite Maggie.

Grimly, Maggie explained, "Molly was Boarded a second time."

It felt as if an ice pick had been plunged through Dana's heart. "Oh, no!" She placed her arm around Molly's heaving shoulders.

"I just got home a few minutes ago," Maggie said, "and I found her in here crying alone."

Alone. Dana knew that situation well herself. Gently stroking Molly's blond hair, she whispered, "I'm sorry, Molly. So sorry...."

Maggie handed Molly another tissue, absently moving her hand up and down her friend's back in an effort to calm her. "She goes before the Board tomorrow morning."

Dana took the damp Kleenex from Molly as she finished mopping her reddened eyes. "I'm sorry, Molly."

"I...it's okay. The IP's right: I'm just not cut out for this." She sniffed, taking another tissue from Maggie. "B-but I worry about my family. What will my father think? And Scott? Oh, God! I've got to call and tell them." And she began to cry in earnest.

Dana took Molly into her arms when Maggie rose and went to get a cold washcloth from the bathroom. The look of anger in Maggie's eyes spoke volumes. Tucking Molly's head against her small neck and shoulder, Dana whispered soothingly to her. Maggie returned and sat down. Dana took the cloth and pressed it gently to Molly's brow and eyes.

Maggie shook her head. Dana knew they had talked about Molly's family pressuring her; and yet, when they tried to broach the topic with Molly, she refused to see what Maggie and Dana saw so clearly: that Molly's life was being orchestrated by her father and brother. She had no life of her own. She was tied to weekly letters and phone calls, held accountable to them, and they always overreacted to her efforts.

Dana sighed heavily, holding Molly as her sobs began to lessen, until finally she quieted. Breaking the silence, Dana asked her in a low voice, "If they Board you, what does it mean?"

Molly slowly sat up and pressed the washcloth to her eyes. "I'll get assigned somewhere else," she croaked, her voice wobbling. She gave them a tearful look. "I'll have to move. I'll be alone. . . ."

The pain in Dana's heart widened. She'd been alone all her life and couldn't wish the experience on anyone. "But you'll have us, Mol. We're write and call you—even if they send you to Timbuktu."

Rallying, Molly tried to smile. Maggie's laugh was forced.

Dana watched Maggie get up and pace, the fury coupled with anxiety in her eyes was evident. Molly was the softest, the gentlest of the three of them. Dana had no doubts about herself or Maggie being able to survive life's punches on the chin. But Molly? The three of them were as close as sisters. Would this Board destroy her? The possibility was real, and it made Dana nauseous. No one deserved this kind of sentence. Especially Molly. There wasn't a mean bone in her body. Her heart was always open and generous to those in need. Dana had been helped by her too many times to count. Now Dana felt helpless. There really was nothing she could do for Molly except be there in the form of moral support.

"You know what I dread more than anything?" Molly whispered, staring down at the cloth in her hands.

"What?" Dana asked hoarsely.

"Telling my father and Scott."

Maggie stopped pacing, her hands placed on her hips in defiance. "Well, those two are just going to have to roll with the punches for once, Molly! I hope they're more concerned for you—for your next duty station or school—than that dream they want you to pursue for them!"

Molly took a deep, unsteady breath, her lower lip trembling. "Tomorrow, I'll find out what the Navy will do with me."

* * *

Dana and Maggie waited tensely on the hardwood bench outside the Boarding room. It didn't take long. Thirty minutes later, Molly emerged, waxen and solemn. They got up, sheltering her as they walked down the empty hallway toward the doors that led to the parking lot.

Dana didn't care whether it was militarily correct or not— she placed her arm around Molly's waist. Maggie put her arm around Molly's sagging shoulders.

"Well?" Dana probed.

"I'm washed out. Th-they were kind about it. Captain Ramsey said I had a fine academic record and that the Navy wasn't going to waste my skills."

"So?" Maggie said impatiently. "What does that mean?"

Molly managed a slight smile. "They're sending me to Patuxent River, Maryland, to try to become a flight-test engineer."

Dana jerked to a halt, her mouth dropping open. "What? Test school?" It was a plum of naval aviation to be a test pilot or a flight-test engineer.

"I'll be damned," Maggie whispered, a grin working its way across her freckled features. "I'll be damned.... That's *great,* Molly! What an opportunity!" She threw her arms around Molly. "Congratulations!"

"Wow!" Dana exclaimed, shaking her head. "That's fantastic, Molly."

With a slight laugh, Molly nodded. "I really thought they'd send me off to some dark corner of the world and forget about me for the next six years."

"Not with your grades," Maggie told her, grinning proudly over at her. "What a hell of an assignment!"

"Wow!" repeated Dana.

Molly laughed uncertainly at Dana. "You always say that when you're at a loss for words."

"I know. Just think of the opportunity you have, Molly."

"For all women," Maggie added seriously. "Do they have any women flight engineers in the Navy yet?"

Molly shook her head, gripping their hands. "No...not yet. I'm really kind of excited about it."

"Excited?" Maggie hooted. "I'd be floating ten feet off this deck! You'll do great there, Molly. I just know it!"

Dana saw the shadow of fear in Molly's eyes. "First you have to get past your family's reaction, right?"

"Right. I think what I'm going to do is drive up to New York City and see them. A phone call isn't going to do it. The Navy has given me thirty days' leave. I'll go home, then drive to Lexington Park, right outside the gates of Patuxent River, and find an apartment to move into."

"I admire your courage," Dana said, "meeting your family head-on." She ruffled Molly's fine blond hair. "Four years at Annapolis gave you a lot more backbone than you ever thought you'd own. You're standing on your own two feet now."

"One step at a time," Molly told them, beginning to walk with them once again. She gripped Dana's hand. "And you're doing great. I'm so proud of you. Lieutenant Turcotte has really turned around and helped you."

Griff. His name haunted her sweetly, stirring her heart as no other man ever had. One kiss—they'd shared only one heated, longing kiss. If Dana was honest with herself, she had to admit that she wanted to kiss him again; but she needed time to learn to trust him. Very shortly, their six weeks together would come to an end. Then she would learn further flight techniques from a pool of instructors. Thinking of that time, Dana missed Griff already, wanting these last few weeks to drag by so she could savor his company.

Dana walked back to the ready room with Griff. They'd shared their last flight together. Her initial six weeks were over. The evening sky was pale gold, lined with building white cottony cumulus clouds. The sun's last rays shot through the ragged line, flinging spokes of light into the pale blue sky above. Dana's heart felt heavy. Since his kiss three weeks ago, Griff had made no attempt to kiss her again, or even to suggest taking her out. The days had been instructive, showing her that *some* men could be taken at their word.

"I don't want this day to end," Dana admitted. She gave Griff a shy look. "The last three weeks have flown by."

He grinned. "Is that a pun? Never mind, I know what you mean," Griff reassured her, thinking how Dana's confidence had soared in the past three weeks. She had caught up in flight hours with the rest of her class, and was keeping a 2.3 average—good enough for her still to be considered for jet training.

Risking a great deal, Dana slowed her stride and halted outside the building. It was Friday evening, and very few people were still around. Chewing on her lower lip, she looked up into his expectant features. "Is it appropriate to celebrate surviving six weeks of flight school with your instructor?"

Grinning, Griff shrugged and placed his hands on his hips. "Normally, no. But this instructor doesn't mind celebrating it with you. What did you have in mind?"

She liked the way Griff's eyes crinkled, and she smiled, some of her nervousness dissolving. "How about an evening picnic at our favorite beach?"

"Is this a formal date?" he teased.

"Well . . . sort of. . . ."

"Sounds great. How about if I bring the wine and you provide the food? The limit of my cooking ability is beans and wieners." Griff quelled his keen hunger for Dana. Keeping his hands to himself had made for the toughest three weeks of his life, but it had allowed her the room she needed to develop confidence in him. His patience was paying off. In a perverse sort of way, he'd enjoyed the waiting, and was learning to appreciate Dana on so many other levels.

Buoyed by his light manner regarding her invitation, Dana rallied, eager to spend personal time with Griff again. "You've got a deal. How about I meet you down there in an hour?"

"You've got it, sweetheart. See you then." Griff threw her a mock salute and turned away, heading toward the admin building.

Taking a shaky breath, Dana hurried toward the ready room, anxious to change into civilian clothes and get home. What would Maggie think of her brazen invitation to Griff?

Maggie sat at the kitchen table making a salad. It was her turn to cook tonight.

"You can't have it both ways, Dana," she said. "You tell the guy this relationship has to come about on your time and terms. And then you get nervous because you've asked him out on a date. He couldn't ask you out, because you set the rules. So why are you nervous?"

Dana shrugged, hurrying to put the final touches on the impromptu picnic. "You're right, and he's been wonderful about not stalking or chasing me."

"Griff has treated you fairly on your flights, too," Maggie reminded her. She got up and moved to the stove to dish baked chicken onto a plate. "I think he's been great about it, frankly. Most of those jet jocks wouldn't hold still two minutes for what you've asked of Griff, Dana. Russian hands and Roman fingers—you know the type."

Maggie was right about jocks thinking they could stake a claim on any woman. "He is different," she admitted, putting the lid down on the small wicker basket.

Maggie giggled. "Dana, you kill me. You're so cautious!"

"It's my nature."

"I know, I know. Griff's demonstrated that he respects your needs. I think it's about time you two had an official date, don't you?"

"It's not a date," Dana protested quickly. "Just a picnic."

"Go and enjoy yourself, Dana. Griff makes you happy, and vice versa. Explore what you have on whatever level makes you comfortable." Maggie looked pointedly at the watch on her left wrist. "And I won't wait up for you. Believe me, if Molly was here, she'd be up waiting like a mother hen."

Molly had been gone two weeks, and they missed her terribly. Blushing, Dana picked up the basket. "You're right," she said, and then laughed with Maggie. In Molly's eyes, the world was idealistic. Maggie was much more pragmatic. So, where was Dana? Frightened as never before. Leaving the apartment, Dana plunged into deep thought. Griff was forcing her to look at issues she'd never had to confront before. Perhaps she could discuss some of them with him. Perhaps...

Griff sat on the pale blue beach blanket, the opened picnic basket between him and Dana. They had watched the sun set as they ate dinner. The roast-beef sandwiches laced with creamy horseradish had been delicious. Thoughtful little touches such as sweet pickles and black olives rounded out the tasty meal. The company, however, was even better in his opinion. At first Dana had been nervous. Now she sat cross-legged opposite him, the tension gone from around her mouth. He liked the gauzy lavender blouse she wore, and the white slacks and sandals. Taking the bottle of wine, he poured a little more into the plastic cups Dana had provided.

"This was a great idea," Griff congratulated her, and lifted his cup in a toast to Dana.

"Thanks, Griff." Lulled by the lap of water against the beach, she sipped the light, dry wine. "There's something I wanted to talk about."

Venturing a smile, Griff knew he'd been right to believe that something was on Dana's mind. "Sure. What is it?"

Licking her lower lip and tasting the wine on it, Dana said, "I'm going to miss you teaching me. No... It's more than that," she went on in a whisper, and stared down at the cup in her hands. "This is so hard. I've never done this before, Griff." Taking a deep breath, Dana dived on. "You're the first man who's been good to his word. You didn't chase me or make me feel pursued. I've relaxed and gotten used to you." Lifting her eyes, she held his dove-gray gaze. "I like what we have, Griff. I—I've never had a man who was a friend, before."

"The only kind of man you knew was Lombard's type," he said quietly. Dana's eyes were huge, mirroring her array of emotions. Griff stopped himself from reaching over to pull her into his arms and kiss her. Something far more important was happening, and he tabled his desires.

"Yes..."

"I've liked becoming your friend, too."

"You have?"

"I've never had a friend who was a woman." With a shrug, Griff stretched out and propped himself on one elbow. In the dusk, Dana's features remained delicate and beautiful. "I always saw women as potential bed partners." When Dana wrinkled her nose with distaste, he laughed. "Now I'm being honest, and you wanted that above everything else."

She smiled with him. "You're right."

"Well, as I was saying, women were great to make love with, but little else. Carol came along, and I discovered I wanted to settle down. I thought I had the right woman." Softly, he continued. "I didn't have, but it was as much my fault our marriage collapsed as it was hers. I projected what I wanted onto Carol, and she didn't have it to give."

"At least you don't blame Carol for all the problems."

"No, I wouldn't do that. Men aren't perfect. I'm certainly not, Dana. But," Griff added, holding her somber look, "I've learned a lot from it. I don't think I'll make the same mistakes again." He flashed her a grin. "Just new ones."

"What did you learn from your marriage?"

"Plenty. When I met Carol, I rushed her into marriage. We'd known each other just two weeks. I fell head over heels in love with her—or so I thought. She had—still has—some emotional problems that were brought into the marriage. In our last year, after I asked her for a divorce, she tried to commit suicide. The doctors told me her attempt wasn't serious. Carol was asking for help." Pain moved through him, his voice lowering even more. "She clung to me. I was her crutch, not her husband. I had a lot of guilt to work through after the divorce. I felt like I was abandoning her, but her therapist reassured me. Carol's doing better now. I stay in touch with her from time to time, just to see how she's doing. The suicide attempt brought things to a head, and she got help."

He managed a slight smile, holding Dana's compassionate eyes. "She's doing better now. Looking back on it, Dana, I was old enough to know I shouldn't have jumped into a marriage so fast. The raw chemistry was too much to combat, and I lost my normal ability to reason. I've learned to take my time with the woman who interests me. I want to know her for a long period and enjoy discovering her in all kinds of ways and situations. My marriage taught me that I need a friend in the woman I live with, not just a sex partner." His eyes crinkled when he looked at her. "Think I've learned some valuable lessons out of the mistakes I made?"

"I think so. I guess love does make you blind, sometimes," she ventured, moved by his ability to share his private life with her.

"So, what did you learn from your relationship with Lombard?" Griff probed gently. When he saw her grow uncomfortable, Griff added, "When you were unconscious in the hospital and your mother called, we were both shaken up. She was crying, and I was close to doing the same thing. Somehow, Lombard's name came up, and I let her talk about what he'd done to you, because she needed to."

"Oh." Dana set the basket to one side. Following her desire to be closer to Griff, she settled next to him. Resting her hands across her knees, she said quietly, "I learned that if a man chases you, he wants something from you. It might be sex, or it might be something else." With a shrug, Dana whispered, "Lombard had made a bet with his friends back at the academy that he could lay me. He even took me to his parents' home over the Christmas holiday to get me to believe he was interested in me as a person. I fell for it—all of it."

Reaching out, Griff captured her hand and squeezed it gently. Her dark eyes were filled with hurt. "I'm sorry, sweetheart. The bastard ought to be strung up for what he did to you."

His hand was warm and dry on hers, and it felt good. "Looking back on it, I was ripe for it, Griff."

"Why?"

"I was so afraid of men because of my father that I never dated through high school. I thought they'd all be like him. When I got to the academy, it really reminded me of him: all the yelling and screaming the upperclassmen do to a plebe. So, I hid in my books, the way I always had. It was safe there."

Stroking the back of her hand with his thumb, Griff held on to very real anger toward her father. "That's why you achieved a 4.0?"

"Sure." Dana managed a halfhearted laugh. "It's easy when you allow your world to revolve only around studies and block everything else out, Griff."

"Except that Lombard got inside your carefully constructed world."

"Brother, did he!" Dana placed her hand on top of Griff's, unconsciously running her fingers across its hairy expanse. "I guess I was a lot more lonely for companionship than I ever believed." Her hand stilled on his. "At the academy, they had a nickname for me."

The pain in Dana's voice brought Griff to a sitting position. Everything was happening naturally between them. Dana's reaching out to touch him had been an exquisite gift, sending such a protective feeling through Griff that he obeyed his next impulse. He settled his arms around her shoulders and caressed her back, to try to take away some of the pain she carried.

"What did they call you?"

Compressing her lips, Dana allowed his protectiveness to ease the tension gathered in her shoulders. "Ice Queen."

"Damn them," Griff muttered harshly. He leaned down and kissed her temple, feeling the silkiness of her hair beneath his mouth. Dana raised her chin, her lips bare inches away. Bringing his hands forward and cupping her face, Griff inhaled her feminine fragrance. "They were afraid of you, that's why. But they didn't see or understand your fear of them. You were withdrawn and cool because of your past experience with men."

Griff's understanding dissolved the last of her wary barriers. As his strong, capable hands cradled her face, Dana surrendered to her need of him. His mouth created a trail of lingering kisses from her temple along her jawline, and her breathing became chaotic. Her hands moved of their own accord, caressing his arms and broad shoulders. His breath was moist against her, and she risked everything, seeking his mouth, wanting to kiss him.

Groaning as Dana's lips tentatively pressed against his, Griff held himself in tight check. He realized that Dana was new at this, that Lombard had probably never invited her to explore him at her own comfortable pace. As she'd told Griff, Lombard had taken, not given. He smiled against her mouth, tasting the wine, tasting the sweetness that was hers alone.

"That's it, sweetheart," Griff whispered against her. "Explore me. I won't hurt you, I won't make you cry..." And the rest of his words dissolved beneath the bolder response of Dana's lips against his. Sliding his fingers through her thick, dark hair, he felt Dana ease down beside him, her body barely grazing his. Humbly, Griff returned her fledgling kiss, and tried to monitor his hunger. If he suddenly overpowered Dana, it would scare her and she'd retreat. Not wanting that, Griff forced himself as never before to remain in control of his tense, throbbing body.

The need to press herself against Griff was overwhelming. Dana didn't understand her own feminine instincts, but trusted herself enough to follow them. When their hips grazed each other's, he groaned. It was a delicious male sound that vibrated through her entire body like a song. As his hand settled against her hip, pulling her provocatively to him, Dana felt an ache begin to build between her thighs. As if understanding her needs, Griff's hand moved upward, cupping her breast. The sensation of his fingers curving around her was unexpected. Heated.

A little cry escaped her as his thumb moved in lazy circles around her nipple. It felt as if something were loosening inside of her, and it made her shaky with need. Dana felt his arms move around her, and he laid her back onto the blanket. As Griff settled down beside her, Dana opened her eyes, her breathing ragged. She stared up into Griff's darkened face. His gaze was narrowed with fiery intensity, his breath as chaotic as hers. Every time he caressed her breast, she moaned.

"You're so damned responsive, so hot," he rasped, running his tongue across her full lower lip. Her breasts were small and firm, with nipples that begged to be pleasured. "You're not made of ice, sweetheart. You're made of fire." The driving need to continue to explore Dana nearly overwhelmed Griff. Reluctantly he left her breasts alone and framed her flushed features. "Ice Queen, you're not," he told her, his mouth worshiping her lips, which had blossomed to life beneath his. With trembling fingers, he moved tendrils of hair aside and guided them around the curve of her small ear.

When Dana at last opened her eyes, Griff smiled down at her. Her mouth was wet and ravished looking, her gaze lustrous with pleasure and awe. "You see," he continued in a low voice, stroking the curve of her neck and shoulder with his thumb, "good things can be shared between a man and woman."

All Dana could do was stare up into his lambent gray eyes, lost in a warmth that washed through her like a heated tidal current. Raising her hand, she barely grazed his cheek. "You stopped."

A grin pulled at his mouth and Griff leaned down, nuzzling her earlobe. "Want me to continue?" Her little moan enticed him, but he kept his hands still.

"Yes...no...I don't know."

Lifting his head, he smiled at her. "That's why I stopped. I felt you start to tense."

Amazed that he could read her body language, Dana stared up at him. "I'm sorry...It wasn't because I didn't like it, I—"

"No apologies, sweetheart. I know you enjoyed it. So did I. It was time to quit. That's all."

Stymied by his statement, Dana gradually sat up. She was content as Griff brought her into the shelter of his arms, simply holding her. With a sigh, she leaned her head against his neck and jaw. "Lombard didn't quit. He didn't respect my fear of him, of something that was new to me."

Griff wanted to kill Lombard in that moment. He held Dana tightly, hearing the pain and confusion in her voice. "Some men take," he agreed. "But loving another person means involving them in the act, Dana." He tucked her in the circle of his arms and studied her shadowed features. "I wanted your participation just now. I wanted you to enjoy it as much as I was."

The quaver in his voice told her everything. Gently, Dana caressed his cheek and leaned upward, wanting the power of his mouth fitted against hers once again. "Kiss me?" She'd never been kissed like that, and she wanted to continue to explore the wonderful landscape of his body and what it did to her awakening body and five senses.

Griff smiled and leaned forward. "Anything the lady wants," he breathed.

Chapter Thirteen

Griff tried to wait patiently in the ready room for Dana. It didn't work, and he got up to pace, then sat back down. She was supposed to get off her Friday-evening training flight shortly. Where had the weeks gone? Already, Dana was in her ninth week, and doing exceptionally well. Sitting at one of the report tables, Griff tapped his fingers out of boredom. Time with Dana since that exquisite evening on the beach had become severely limited. He'd promised not to interfere with her schooling to the point of her risking her grades dropping because they were spending too much free time together. No, Dana's drive to graduate and get her wings was too important to her—and him.

The room was empty and quiet. Glancing at his watch, Griff chafed and began to pace again. Would Dana go along with his plans? The tenth week was coming up, a cutoff point in the course. By this time, the students who were going to make it had done so. The rest had been weeded out and reassigned to other Navy career slots and stations. He stared at the door he knew Dana would come through, his thoughts lingering sweetly upon her.

Since their heated kisses on the beach, Dana had surrendered the rest of her wariness of him. With a sigh, Griff was glad he'd been able to control his own needs for her sake. Gaining Dana's trust was everything to him. His commitment to her was for the long haul. They had the time.

Or did they? Griff scowled, not wanting to look at that question too closely. Dana had another seven weeks at Whiting before she graduated. Depending on her grades, which were academically brilliant, she would be assigned by Captain Ramsey. Probably to turboprop aircraft or jets. And, Griff was sure, to another naval air station—anywhere in the world. He was stuck at Whiting for another two years.

Dammit, he loved her! There, he'd admitted it to himself. Getting up, Griff paced the huge room, hands behind his back. He'd fallen in love with Dana at the airport. Only he hadn't realized it at the time. That partly explained why he had overreacted to her presence initially; unconsciously, he'd been fighting his powerful attraction to her.

Every moment he spent with Dana was precious. Over the past month, their intimacy had grown. Griff had never felt this close to another woman. There was such intensity between them. Was this real love? A quiet joy flooded him every time he thought of Dana, heard her voice or was with her. When she smiled, Griff's heart blossomed with such spiraling happiness that he stood in awe of his own feelings toward her. Yes, every day was a gift to them—and they both knew it. That was what made their burgeoning relationship so special and rare.

Dana's laughter preceded her entrance into the ready room. Griff turned, expectant. Her instructor, Lieutenant Jay Gardiner, followed her into the building. Dana's smile deepened when she saw Griff.

"Hi," she greeted. Griff was in a pair of dark blue slacks and a light blue short-sleeved shirt.

Griff smiled at her. "You look happy," he noted, giving a nod to Jay, who sat down at a report table. Dana sat opposite her instructor.

"I am. Mr. Gardiner just awarded me a 2.3 for this flight."

"Well deserved," Jay told Griff. "This will only take a few minutes, and then she's done for the night."

"Take your time." Griff sat down at the other end of the room. He hadn't tried to keep his interest in Dana a big secret, but discretion was warranted. Fraternization between student and instructor was frowned upon, but not illegal. He knew Jay, who was happily married, suspected something was going on, but he'd kept any questions he had about it to himself. Once, Dana stole a look in Griff's direction. Her azure eyes shone with such happiness that it stole the breath from Griff.

Signing off on the board, Dana rose and thanked Gardiner. The instructor smiled, waved goodbye to Griff and left. She picked up her helmet bag and logbook, and walked across the room to where he sat.

"This is highly unusual behavior on your part," Dana teased. She made sure no one could see them before leaning over and giving him a quick kiss on the mouth. The surprise in his eyes made her laugh as she straightened.

"I know this is erratic behavior for me," Dana said, "but you looked so good sitting there, I just had to kiss you."

Griff grinned. "I like your spontaneity."

Dana stood, wanting so badly to step into the circle of his arms but knowing she couldn't under the circumstances. She read the smoldering intent in Griff's gray eyes and felt her body coming to life beneath his smoky look. "It's your fault. You bring it out in me," she accused, smiling.

"I'm glad you're in a spontaneous mood tonight, Miss Coulter." Griff stood and walked with her toward the exit.

"How'd you like to grab enough clothes for the weekend and go deep-sea fishing off the coast with me?"

Stunned, Dana halted. Griff had stopped and placed his hands on his hips in a typical jet-jock pose. He looked impossibly handsome, a devilish glimmer in his eyes. "The whole weekend?"

"Yes, we'll be alone. I have a friend who has a fishing boat. It's got bunks and a galley." His heart beat harder. Would Dana say no? He saw her hesitate. "I don't know about you, but I need a break from this place. I thought you might like one, too." That was the truth. He hoped Dana wasn't thinking he'd planned the trip as a way of getting her to go to bed with him.

An entire weekend alone with Griff.... The thought was provocative, enticing. Where would it lead? Over the past month, how many times had she wanted to make love with Griff? Would it be the same as it had been with Lombard? Fear placed a wedge between Dana's need to share herself with Griff, and her past experience. "Griff...I don't know...."

Lowering his voice, Griff stepped over and barely grazed her cheek with his thumb. "Look, just because we're together on the same boat doesn't mean I expect anything from you, Dana. I'm not Lombard taking you home for a weekend and then trapping you in a room. Okay?" He held her luminous azure eyes, seeing desire in their depths, but also seeing the fear. Right now he wanted to strangle Lombard. The bastard had really hurt Dana with his selfishness. It did Griff no good to insist he wasn't like Lombard, he had to continue to prove it—one slow, patient step at a time.

Dana hung her head. "Thanks for understanding, Griff. It's not you...."

"I know." He leaned over, pressing a kiss to her cheek. "Want to come with me?"

Dana's mouth curved into a slight smile. "I'd love to."

Back at the apartment, Dana packed a small suitcase. Maggie wandered in a bit later and leaned against the doorjamb.

"Hi."

"Hi." Dana turned and smiled. Maggie looked as tired as Dana felt.

"Going someplace?"

Heat crept into Dana's face. "Yes."

"With Griff?" Maggie pushed away the doorframe and walked into the bedroom.

"Yes."

Maggie smiled, throwing her arm around Dana. "You're blushing. Why? It's not a sin to take some time off with someone you like."

"You're right." Dana went back to packing. Maggie sat down next to the luggage, and Dana told her everything.

"Do you feel like Griff's setting this up, the way Lombard set you up?" Maggie asked, stretching out on the bed.

Zipping her suitcase shut, Dana shook her head. "No... But I'm not sure what will happen."

"Welcome to the real world. Weird, funny, stupid and crazy things happen when you get a man and woman who like each other together."

With a laugh, Dana sat down and shook her head. "Good old pragmatic Maggie comes through again with one of her parables of wisdom."

"Experience speaking," Maggie reminded her archly, grinning. "Not a whole lot of it, but enough to be able to sit here and tell you to relax and have fun. Don't try to read anything into it, Dana. Frankly, I wish I had a guy like him, right now. I think he's trying to give you a break from this crazed training. Take it and run!"

Silence settled around them. Dana stared down at her clasped hands. Finally Dana whispered, "I guess I'm more frightened of my feelings toward Griff, than I am of him or this weekend alone on the boat. It's me I don't trust."

Maggie reached over, placing her hand on Dana's shoulder. "Take it one hour at a time, Dana. Don't expect anything of yourself. Just let things flow naturally between you. It's time you two tried being alone. Griff's serious about you, and vice versa. Just enjoy him without reading anything into it. Okay?"

Standing, Dana picked up her suitcase. "Thanks, Maggie. You're always the wise Celt."

Maggie grinned broadly and picked up strands of her red hair. "Druidic heritage, my dear. We Celtic women have the Sight. I'm right: You'll have a wonderful time."

Leaving the apartment, Dana thought how much she wanted Maggie to be right. Sometimes Maggie had a phenomenal intuitive ability that bordered on being psychic. Her heart moved gently and centered on Griff. Within an hour they would be on the boat, heading out to a small cay in the gulf. Excitement mixed with dread washed over Dana. Was she ready for this step?

When Griff shrugged out of his dark blue polo shirt and revealed his powerful chest, Dana's mouth went dry. They had just anchored the huge fishing boat—which looked more like a racing craft—on the leeward side of a small cay off Santa Rosa Island. Clad only in his tan shorts, Griff was the consummate male animal in Dana's eyes. She was amazed at his total lack of concern over his near nakedness. His natural acceptance of his body gave her the courage to shed her jeans and blouse.

Griff gave her an appreciative look. Dana wore a two-piece rose-colored bathing suit that lovingly outlined the firm contours of her body. "Want to swim before we settle in for the night?"

The cay, little more than an oval of coral-and-white sand the size of a parking lot, beckoned to Dana. "Sounds wonderful!"

The evening was drawing to a close, the horizon a flaming apricot color, while the sky above darkened. Griff placed the aluminum ladder over the side. "I'll join you."

"And then we'll eat?"

He grinned. "Yeah. I'll make noise in the galley tonight and see what I can scare up for dinner."

With a laugh, Dana moved down the ladder and into the warm, inviting water. "Maybe we ought to look for fish, huh? As I recall, you said your cooking ability was limited."

Griff joined her in the gulf, noticing how the water lapped at her skin. He wanted to skim his fingers across her sculptured collarbones. He capped his torrid thoughts. "I exaggerated my cooking inabilities," he informed her, starting to swim lazily toward the cay. "I can make more than beans and wieners."

Joining him, Dana grinned. "Exaggerated how much?"

"I cook a pretty mean T-bone steak."

Dana closed her eyes, rolled onto her back and began a freestyle stroke. "Mmm, that sounds better than beans and wieners."

On the cay, Dana walked around discovering and picking up small seashells that had washed up on the sand. Griff found a few more and gave them to her. They stopped, looking west toward the sunset. The cay was bathed in dying orange light. She leaned against Griff, feeling his arms go around her.

"You're happy," he whispered, leaning down and kissing the tip of her nose, tasting the brine on it.

"Very." Dana slipped her arms around his waist, closed her eyes and allowed him to take her full weight. She was aware of the coiled tension in his body. "This all seems like a dream to me."

"What does?" Griff kissed her slowly on the nape of her neck, then created a languid pattern around her earlobe.

"Mmm..."

Griff felt her press shyly against him and he found her parted lips. Her mouth blossomed with warm welcome beneath his. Heat, like a tidal wave, consumed him. The shells dropped one by one to the sand at Dana's feet as her arms slowly came up and around his shoulders. The eagerness of her mouth against his burned away at his control. Easing from her lips, Griff held her entranced azure gaze.

"Keep that up," he warned huskily, "and we'll have dessert before our meal, sweetheart."

Awed by what they shared, Dana thought a moment before Griff's meaning finally registered on her dazed senses. He wasn't made of stone. No, not by far. She was aware of his strength, his need of her. It wasn't fair to Griff for her to do what she wanted and not expect him to respond. Easing away from him, Dana whispered, "You're right." Crouching down, she picked up the shells she had dropped, embarrassed.

Griff joined her and captured one of her hands. He looked into her eyes. "What we have is good," he told her in a low voice. "It's just that you're such a hot, fiery lady that sometimes, I want to take you with me and love the hell out of you. Making love isn't wrong. It can be the most right thing in the world between two people." His fingers tightened around her hand. "I know you're afraid, and I know why. If only... if only I could convince you it doesn't have to be one-sided or painful, Dana. But you can't know that, and it's a bridge we're going to have to cross—together, someday." Griff managed a crooked grin. "You're worth waiting for, sweetheart, and I don't ever want you to stop kissing me or touching me when it feels right to you. I like it, too."

Touched by his deep, vibrating words, Dana hung her head. "You're being more honest than I am," she whispered. Sitting down on the sand, Dana was glad Griff joined her. His arms came around her, and she leaned her head against his shoulder and closed her eyes. "You don't know how many times I've dreamed of you...us, together. But every time that happens, I see Lombard and everything shatters. I wake up feeling so rotten, Griff," she said, lifting her chin and meeting his hooded gaze. "You've done nothing but make me happy and teach me that things between a man and a woman can be wonderful."

He caressed her sun-warmed arm. The dusk light touched Dana lovingly, accenting her delicate features. "With time, you'll lose that fear, Dana. Someday, your need to love me will outweigh the fear you're carrying."

She caressed Griff's rock-solid jaw and saw his eyes darken. "Will I know when?"

Catching her hand and pressing a kiss to it, Griff rasped, "You will. And when it happens, sweetheart, it's going to be the most beautiful thing that's ever happened to you or me."

Part of her cried out to love Griff now. The tenderness burning in his eyes made her want him in ways Dana had never known possible. The smile on his mouth deepened.

"Come on, let's watch this sunset together, and then we'll swim back to the boat and I'll fix us dinner."

The galley was small; almost what Dana would call "intimate." Griff worked at her side, their hips brushing from time to time. Tension was high, and Dana's hands shook as she prepared the salad to go with the steaks now being fried in the skillet on the stove. A huge part of her wanted to dispense with the sham of being hungry, or even preparing a meal. What she wanted—needed—was Griff.

On deck, they sat across from each other, eating their meal, as the darkness fell around them. The gentle rock of the boat took the edge off Dana's taut nerves. Her body wanted another kind of sustenance. The fear in her wary mind was gradually being eroded by her heart, which trusted Griff. Dana picked at her steak, barely touching it. Instead, she forced herself to eat the salad.

Griff didn't miss anything. He finished his meal and put his plate aside. The only light came from the cabin entrance that led back down to the galley. Toying with the idea of discussing Dana's nervousness, he decided not to. They'd already discussed it on the island. Frustrated, because it hadn't been his intention to make her uneasy, he didn't know what to do.

"I'm going to take my mattress and pillow and sleep up here on deck," he told her casually, rising. Picking up his plate and glass, he looked over to gauge Dana's reaction. She looked confused, not relieved. "I'll do the dishes and you can dry," he added.

Dana sat there, digesting his statement. She didn't know whether to be happy or sad. Such a huge part of her wanted Griff on so many other levels. Yes, it was physical, but the real hunger in her was one she couldn't define. Maggie had, at one time, confided to her that love, real love, according to her mother, was a spiritual need between two people. It transcended physical attraction, and was far more profound. Touching her heart, Dana frowned. Was that what she was feeling—this restlessness to absorb Griff into her body and soul? For the thousandth time, Dana was sorry she had no experience with which to examine her feelings.

With a sigh, she got up and went back down into the galley with Griff to finish the dishes.

Dana tossed restlessly in her bed at the bow of the boat, Griff's low, almost tortured words ringing through her head and heart. The door was shut, and the cabin was stuffy. Her watch read fifteen minutes after midnight. Dressed in a long white T-shirt that brushed her thighs, Dana struggled as the sheet became entangled between her legs. With a frustrated sound, she rose and quietly opened the door. Moonlight cascaded down the hatch and spilled like silvery liquid into the passageway between the bunks on either side of the boat. Her entire body screamed for Griff's touch, to have his lips upon hers. It was no longer impossible to ignore, and Dana felt driven beyond her fearful mind. Only her heart's crying need throbbed palpably through her. Every nerve felt stretched and taut. Automatically, she moved forward, each step bringing her closer to where Griff lay sleeping.

Gripping the teakwood rail, she slowly ascended the stairs. At the top, the fresh, salty air welcomed her. Her gaze went immediately to Griff, who lay on the oversize mattress. Moonlight pooled across his shadowy form, outlining his powerful, muscular body. Only a bit of the white sheet lay across his hips. Otherwise he was naked. Her mouth dry, her heart pounding in her throat, Dana slowly walked toward him. When she stopped beside him and lifted her eyes, she saw that he was already awake. In the darkness, his gray eyes were hooded, but filled with smoldering promise. Her throat constricted as she stood awkwardly before him.

"Can't sleep?" Griff asked, reaching out and capturing her hand. Dana barely nodded. He took in her uncertainty, her mussed hair. It was the gold in her eyes that told him what she wanted—needed. Her T-shirt was wrinkled and shapeless, but the curve of her legs flowed from beneath it. He ached to slide his fingers across her thigh and feel its firm silkiness.

"I couldn't sleep, Griff." The rest of her words jammed up in her throat. The mattress was large enough for both of them, and he moved to one side, gently tugging on her hand.

"I haven't been able to sleep, either," he admitted. "Come on. Lie down next to me. I'll just hold you, Dana."

His words were dark with promise. Dana came wordlessly, slipping into the makeshift bed. He gathered her into his arms and brought her gently against him. Only the thin barrier of a sheet separated them. Heat pooled in the area of her belly and hips where his body barely grazed hers. Griff began to stroke her shoulders in slow, light circles, easing her tension. After a few minutes, Dana relaxed, resting her head in the hollow of his shoulder.

"I was so scared to come up here. I didn't know what to do."

"You did the right thing. You followed your heart."

The gentle rocking of the boat further soothed Dana, and her senses focused on Griff's hand splayed against her back, feeling his fingers caress the length of her spine. She tensed slightly as his hand moved across her hip, but his touch remained light, not demanding, and gradually Dana accepted his intimate exploration. His hand slid along the curve of her thigh, brushing the moist juncture. A small, ragged sigh escaped her.

"That's it," Griff coaxed, resting his mouth against her brow. "Just lie there and enjoy it. If you get frightened, all you have to do is tell me to stop, sweetheart. Just one word. That's all."

Reassurance riffled through Dana, and she shook her head. "I—I want you, Griff. I want to share with you...."

Nestling his head beside hers, he concentrated on her slender neck. After each small kiss, he ran his tongue tenderly over the area. "So do I. I'm as scared as you are, Dana. I'm afraid of hurting you, of doing something wrong...."

She gazed in awe up at his shadowed features, his eyes vulnerable with the admission. Whatever fear was left in her dissolved beneath the warmth and concern in his gaze. "You could never do anything wrong," she whispered unsteadily, tears forming in her eyes.

He laughed huskily, and gave her a fierce embrace. "Oh, yes I could. Look what I did the first month we were together." With his hand, he caressed her upturned face. "No, sweetheart, I am capable of hurting you again. I'm human. I want you so damn badly I don't know if I can control myself for your sake. And if that happened—" He groaned and shook his head.

"I like your human side, faults and all," Dana murmured. "More than anything, I trust you, Griff."

Realizing the gift she'd just given him, he wanted to cry for the sheer joy of her softly spoken words. Some of the fear he was feeling abated. "The night's ours," he promised thickly, feeling her arch against him, a soft sound escaping her as he moved his hand downward and cupped her breast.

The wonderful sensations of his fingers curving around her breast chased away the last of her fear. A soft cry vibrated in her throat as his mouth captured the budding nipple hidden beneath her T-shirt. The moist heat drove her into a wild mindlessness as he worshiped her like some fragile, beautiful vessel. Dampness collected between her thighs, and she sighed as Griff moved the cotton material aside. Sliding his hand beneath the T-shirt, he followed the line of her rib cage.

"You're so beautiful," he rasped, tracing the outline of her small, firm breasts. Dana's eyes were languorous, her lips parted, telling him she was enjoying his sweet assault as much as he was. Griff tried to ignore the spasms creating pain in his loins. He'd wanted Dana for so long that he felt as if he were tied in a white-hot knot. One wrong move on his part could scare Dana and make her cringe away from him. Griff broke out in a sweat, unsure whether it was out of need or fear that he would accidentally hurt her. So much was on the line. Was he capable of walking that fine line with her?

As Griff coaxed the T-shirt off Dana and she lay naked and unguarded before him, he saw the gold of desire in her eyes. With equal deliberateness, he removed the thin sheet from between them. He could feel the heat radiating from their bodies, hear her ragged breathing and see the pleading look in her eyes.

Dana clung to Griff's gaze, not knowing what to do next. She needn't have worried, because Griff leaned over, his strong, hard body warm and stabilizing against hers. It was a pleasant shock to feel his strength pressing and molding to her. He fitted his mouth to her mouth, his tongue caressing hers, making her wild with need of him. Moaning, Dana automatically drew her arms around his tense shoulders, and she pulled him across her.

Griff's weight felt good and right. He plundered her mouth, which was now moist and willing. Sliding his hand along her small but incredibly strong spine, Griff cupped her hips, deliberately bringing her against his hard maleness. Momentarily she tensed, and he leaned down to suckle her nipple. A quiver raced through her, dissolving the tension, and she felt like melting honey between his hands. The firm curve of her thigh met his, and he moved his hand in slow, teasing circles, approaching the juncture between them. Lightly stroking her with his fingers, Griff heard her give a startled little cry, but it was one of surprise and utter pleasure, not of pain or denial.

"You're so wet and hot," he rasped unsteadily against her ear. "Give yourself to me, Dana, just melt into me. Let me give you all the pleasure you can stand. Trust me, just trust me...."

With each loving stroke of his fingers Dana felt her thighs open of their own accord to his tender, exquisite exploration. She was a flower opening before the light, feeling her beauty as a woman in touch with the deep responses within her body. As Griff lay above her, moving more deeply into her, giving her exquisite pleasure that throbbed like white liquid heat through her, Dana's head thrashed from side to side. Her fingers opened and closed spasmodically against his damp, tense flesh.

"Just feel it," he rasped against her lips, unable to believe how moist and welcoming she had become. Meeting her eyes, Griff saw her begging him for more, and he smiled. "Tell me when, sweetheart. When do you want me? You're so ripe, so ready right now...." He caressed her intimately, feeling her arch suddenly against his hand, a gasp escaping her. Prolonging the sensation for Dana, Griff wanted to cry for the sheer joy of being able to give her the gift of the shattering climax. She fell back into his arms, her eyes dazed and filled with wonder.

Griff kissed her tenderly and felt Dana's trembling hand on his shoulder, asking him to cover her, to become one with her. He shook his head and rolled over onto his back, bringing her across him.

"This is the only way, sweetheart," he rasped, his hands fitting along her hips. When he saw the confusion in her eyes, he gently guided her against him. Dana's lips parted, her fingers digging into his arms. "Take what you want, when you want. That way, you'll get used to me, and there won't be any pain—I promise you."

Trembling badly with need, Dana barely nodded, feeling his hard, demanding length caressing the entrance to her moist womanhood. "Help me," she pleaded. Griff lifted her hips slightly. His lips pulled away from his clenched teeth as he barely entered her slick, heated darkness.

Dana threw her head back as he rocked his hips against her. The sensation was explosive, and she moaned, arching her back and taking more of him into herself. He filled her, but the sensation was one of utter fulfillment, not pain. Each rocking motion made her feel as if she were deliciously flying apart in all directions. As he raised his head, his mouth finding her nipple and suckling her, fire zigzagged up through the center of her. Griff had promised her it would be good, but Dana was dazed by the pleasure he was wreaking from her untutored body. With each rocking motion, he thrust deeper, until Dana experienced the oneness she'd never realized could exist. Griff's hands tightened along her hips, almost painful in intensity as she increased the ragged, urgent motion. And then, an explosion started low within her and spiraled upward like a blazing whirl of sparkling light.

A cry tore from Dana as Griff prolonged the sensation. Mindless, she felt his entire body tense—felt the clean, strong power of a man completing her. In moments the beautiful song they'd created together dissolved into a quiet liquid pool of wonder. Dana lay on him, her head on his shoulder, simply absorbing the beauty of their mutual act. Only when Griff's hand gently explored her shoulders and back and began wiping away the dampness, did she slowly start to return to reality.

Griff sighed, feeling her begin to move. "No," he whispered hoarsely, "stay. I want to be inside you. I want to feel you breathe. You're so passionate, sweetheart...."

Each caress made Dana feel more languid. Weakly she moved her hand across his darkly haired chest. She traced one of his prominent collarbones. "I don't think I could move," she admitted softly.

"Kind of nice, isn't it?"

"You're wonderful, Griff."

It was his turn to laugh. "*We* were wonderful. Sweetheart, you could bring a man to tears with the way you love."

Dana absorbed his fervent words. Finally she said, "It was so different with Lombard."

"He only wanted to take," Griff said huskily, "not share. You can see the difference now."

There was a catch in her low voice. "You've shared so much with me, Griff. You took away my fear and pain."

"When it's right between two people, that always happens, sweetheart." He smiled tenderly into her eyes and saw tears stream down her cheeks. With his thumbs, he gently caught them and brushed the liquid against his chest. "I like what we share. Even tears."

"I want them always to be tears of happiness between us, Griff."

He threaded his fingers through her short, ebony hair. Dana's face was flushed, but the soft smile pulling at the corners of her mouth humbled him. "Things won't always go smoothly between us. You've already seen that. But, if we talk, if we share, we can always repair and build on what we have, Dana."

Lifting her head, Dana swam beneath his stormy gray gaze. Even now, he was filling her again, making her vibrantly aware of his maleness, his power. Yet, Griff's touch, his eyes, spoke only of the tenderness he held for her. "I like lying this way with you."

Griff moved his hips, and saw her eyes widen with surprise, then grow sultry with pleasure. He smiled, cupping her breasts, feeling them grow firm within his hands once more. "I like it, too." The words *I love you* almost slipped out, but Griff bit them back. Dana's returning moan dissolved whatever worry hung over him about their future. "Tonight, and then tomorrow," he rasped, arching deeply into her, letting her know his hunger for her all over again, "I want to love you until you melt into my hands with pleasure. You're mine. I'm yours. All I want to do is bury myself in you, sweetheart. I don't want anything more."

His powerful thrust sent another spasm spiraling through her, and Dana gripped his arms, arching her back in response. Physical sensation dissolved her functioning mind, and Dana, because she utterly trusted Griff with all her being, sank back into the building caldron of heat he was creating for them. The moonlight had shifted, flowing across them, outlining them, lending a sheen to their flesh. The boat rocked gently with the breath of them, lending a sheen to their flesh. The boat rocked gently with the breath of the ocean, and Dana's breathing synchronized with Griff's as they sought and found their way through the ancient rhythm. This time Dana felt not only Griff, but a vibrant awareness that all things moved with a flow, a pattern.

She became one with him, and gloried in her strength as a woman coming to her man as an equal, absorbing his power into herself and sharing the primal pleasure with wild, hungry intensity.

Chapter Fourteen

Dana awoke with a start. She felt Griff's arms tighten around her for a moment to reassure her she was safe. Blinking, Dana realized that sometime in the night, she had turned over, her back against Griff. She savored the way he folded and followed her curves, providing a protective, loving sensation.

"It's all right," Griff reassured her in a husky voice. "Go back to sleep."

The gray light of dawn was invading the sky. "I'm not used to sleeping with someone. When I woke up, it startled me," Dana admitted. His arm was curled around her waist, and the sheet covered their lower bodies.

"You don't want to go back to sleep?" Griff inhaled the scent of her hair next to him, and he playfully nibbled at the nape of her neck.

Giggling, Dana dodged his tongue and felt that familiar heat collect immediately between her legs. What had happened to her? Griff lightly caressed her shoulder and arm, and already she hungered for him as a man. "No," she murmured. "I'm not sleepy anymore."

"I like waking with you in my arms, Danielle." Griff smiled and rose up on his elbow, urging her to turn onto her back. Her blue eyes looked incredibly happy, and he leaned down to caress her smiling mouth. "Danielle. That's who you are, you know. Not Dana, but Danielle. The name's provocative, like you...."

Simmering within Griff's embrace and heated gaze, she whispered, "When you say my name, I feel different—like a whole, complete woman."

Moving his hand in lazy circles across her rounded belly, Griff nodded. "You survived as Dana. The rest of you—the woman you're learning to become—is Danielle."

"With you, I can be both," she whispered unsteadily.

Griff kissed the tears away, tasting the salt of them. "Sweetheart, I like you any way you want to be for as long as you want it that way."

A tremor fled through Dana, and she held his serious gray gaze. "What will happen to us after I graduate, Griff?"

His hand stilled against her belly. Dana was incredibly small, yet strong in surprising ways. "What do you want to happen?" he asked, fighting his own fear at what her answer might be.

Placing her hand over his, Dana sighed. "We've gone through so much in such a short period of time, Griff. What we have is good...wonderful. And we've seen each other at our worst and at our best."

"And still, we've managed to keep what we have alive and well."

Reaching up, Dana cradled his cheek against her hand. She felt the stubble of his beard prickling her palm, hotly aware of small but delicious sensations as never before. "What I want...what I wish for, Griff...is that we keep what we have."

"And build on it?"

"Yes."

Relief flooded through Griff. "I want the same thing, sweetheart."

"What will we do when I graduate?"

Caressing her wrinkled brow until it smoothed out, Griff kissed her gently. "Let's take it one step at a time." He held her gold-flecked azure gaze. "I'm not losing you. Not to orders, not to a change of stations. Understand?"

His commitment stirred her belief that no matter what happened, their relationship would survive. "Yes, I understand." Dana sought his embrace, and pressed herself against him, her voice muffled against his chest. "Still, I'm afraid, Griff."

"So am I. We'll be afraid together, okay?"

Dana managed a partial laugh. "I like being scared with you, Griff Turcotte."

"Seven weeks, sweetheart. We've got seven weeks together." Kissing her long and hard, drowning in the sweet warmth of her welcoming mouth, Griff wanted a hell of a lot more than that. He wanted a lifetime with Dana—not less than two months.

"This should be the happiest day of my life," Dana told Griff. She had just graduated with honors from the sixteen-week flight course. On her uniform, above the left breast pocket of her summer dress-uniform was a new set of gold wings. Her mother, Ann, had proudly pinned them on her. Griff stood between them, a crowd of nearly three hundred family members of the graduating class milling around them on the parade ground after the ceremony.

Ann Coulter slipped her hand around her daughter's arm, giving her a small squeeze. "I'm sorry Molly wasn't here to celebrate with you and Maggie. I know how close the three of you have grown over the years."

Griff saw the pain in Dana's eyes. "I heard from a friend of mine, Lieutenant Cameron Sinclair, who's a test pilot instructor at Patuxent, that she's hanging in there and learning to be a flight engineer,'' he said.

Ann smiled at her daughter. "See? I told you Molly would pick up the pieces and move on.''

"You did, Mom.'' Dana hugged her mother tightly, fighting back the tears. Hadn't they both picked up the shattered fragments of their lives and moved on to something better, more positive? Sniffing, she took a handkerchief from Griff, who stood protectively at her side. A fierce love of him welled up through her.

Maggie came over to them with her parents and three older sisters. It always amazed Dana that Maggie's sisters had gone into the service, too. As Maggie so aptly pointed out in their plebe year together at Annapolis, her family could trace its roots back to the famous line of Celtic warriors descending from Queen Boudicca. Dana had spent many holidays with Maggie's family, who were fiercely close, and she knew the other sisters well. Caitlin, the oldest at thirty, had copper hair much the same color as Maggie's. Although dressed in civilian clothes today, she was a major in the Air Force. She flew the huge C-130 cargo transport planes all over the world and exuded a quiet confidence that Dana hoped someday to possess. Next to her was black-haired Calista, whom everyone called Callie. At twenty-seven she was a Navy intelligence officer stationed at the Pentagon. Callie resembled their mother a great deal, Dana thought: small, dark-haired and with flashing blue eyes. Dana liked Callie's quiet intensity. And auburn-haired Alanna, one year older than Maggie, was a radar officer aboard a Navy sub-hunting airplane, a P3. Dana hoped that she, too, would be assigned to flying a P3. If her grades stayed up, she had a good shot at it. Who knew? Perhaps she would be flying with Alanna! The thought made her grin. Keep it all in her extended family, she thought happily.

Maggie came forward and threw her arms around Dana.

"We made it," she whispered, hugging her friend tightly, then stepped back, wiping her eyes.

Dana sniffed. "I can't believe it," she said. "I just wish Molly were here."

"Listen, Dana, she was happy to quit. We both knew she wasn't crazy about flying like we were." Maggie smiled softly. "Hey, she's going to be a test-flight engineer! That ain't hay, you know. She's going into a very elite field. Molly's breaking new ground for all women. You ought to be a little happier for her."

With a nod, Dana admitted Maggie was right. She wondered nervously when the loudspeaker would boom out that they were to line up and receive their orders. Where would the Navy send her? As much as she wanted to, Dana couldn't seek the safety of Griff's arms. He stood next to her, dressed in the white dress uniform traditional for graduation ceremonies. How handsome he looked. The corners of his mouth curved upward and he glanced down at her, conveying so much in that one, heated look. Dana closed her eyes and took a deep breath, trying to steady her torn emotions.

Her mother slipped her hand around Dana's waist. "You look worried, honey."

Dana put her arm around her mother's small shoulders. "I am, Mom."

"Griff said you'll get a good assignment, with your grades."

"That's not it," Dana managed. She glanced back at Griff. His gray eyes conveyed his own worry. "We don't want to be separated from each other, and I'm sure it will happen."

"It will just be a question of distance," Griff informed Ann. It could be halfway around the world once Dana completed the second phase of her training at Pensacola.

"I think the love you have for each other is wonderful." Ann sighed.

Guilt needled Dana. She'd never told her mother that Griff wasn't her fiancé. When her mother had arrived the day before to stay at her apartment, she'd choked on the admission. A call to Griff hadn't helped. He felt it was a white lie; something that hurt no one. Why ruin her mother's happiness? Why indeed, Dana thought, and had let it go. "We've got something special, Mom."

"Very special," Griff added. "I see Captain Ramsey coming up to the podium. He's going to hand out the orders."

"At least, with my last name starting with *C,* I'll be one of the first to get mine," Dana whispered unsteadily.

"We'll handle it, whatever it is," Griff told her quietly. "I love you, Dana. Orders aren't going to change a damn thing about the way I feel about you."

Startled, Dana stared up at Griff. He loved her! He'd never said it before. Dana heard her mother sigh and move over to Griff, giving him a smile.

"Dana deserves someone as fine as you, Griff."

He grinned. "I know she does." Not caring whether his commanding officer was watching or not, Griff leaned down and kissed Dana's flushed cheek. "We're in this together," he told her huskily, his voice filled with emotion. "Go on. Go get your orders."

In shock over his admission, Dana did as he coaxed. How many times had she ached to tell Griff that she had fallen in love with him? The forthcoming orders had hung over her head like a sword, curtailing so much of what she dreamed of sharing with Griff. Dreams, he had told her one night after a tender session of lovemaking at his apartment, were to be worked toward, to be held close to their hearts, and most of all, made to come true.

Well, she thought shakily as she moved into line to receive her orders from Captain Ramsey, her dream was to remain with Griff. But that was impossible.

Griff stood with Ann Coulter and watched as Dana received her orders. Her salute was crisp. She was so strong and beautiful. He was glad he'd finally admitted his love to Dana. It was too bad it couldn't have been in more private circumstances, but Griff wasn't sorry he'd said it. The look on her face had told him something he'd known all along: She loved him, too.

"Oh, I'm so excited, Griff," Ann said, clutching his arm. "Where do you think they'll send Dana? I hope it's near San Francisco where I live. Are there any air stations in that area?"

"Yes, there's Moffett Field, at the tip of San Francisco Bay." Griff hoped just the opposite—wanting Dana stationed on the East Coast. As Dana approached, Ann clasped her hands in expectancy.

"Have you opened them yet?" Ann asked breathlessly.

Dana glanced over at Griff as she halted between them. "Uh, no, Mom. Not yet." Why delay the inevitable? The orders were bound to send her somewhere other than here. With shaking hands, she opened the official envelope, her breathing suspended as she unfolded the crisp white paper.

"Oh, my God!" Dana choked.

Griff's heart slammed against his ribs. Had she been sent overseas? Trying to sound steady, he placed his hand on Dana's arm. "What?"

Tears streamed from her eyes as she showed Griff the orders. "I don't believe this, Griff. Look. Look!"

Griff's mouth dropped open as he slowly and carefully read her orders. "You're going to be assigned as a flight instructor at Pensacola!"

"Oh, Griff," Dana cried, throwing her arms around his neck.

Overwhelmed, Griff embraced her hard, not ever wanting to let her go.

"My dream was to stay here," Dana sobbed. "I didn't want to leave here after finding you...I love you so much!"

With a laugh, he lifted Dana off her feet—a totally un-military maneuver, but he didn't care. "God, I love you too, sweetheart."

Dana's feet touched the ground physically, but her heart and spirit were still flying high. "I didn't know they let flight students become instructors!"

With a shake of his head, Griff held on to her hand, re-reading the orders in disbelief. "Sometimes, but it's rare." Why hadn't he thought of this? Dana had graduated with honors, number two in her class.

Maggie came hurrying back over to them, along with her ecstatic family. "Look, Dana! Look at my orders! I don't believe this! I think I'm going to faint. Look!"

Dana read Maggie's orders: She was to report to Mira-mar air station out near San Diego, California, to take advanced fighter training in the F-14 Tomcat. "What does this mean? I didn't think they would allow a woman to fly a combat jet?"

"I don't know. But I *love* it!"

Griff studied the orders. "There's been a lot of scuttle-butt about training women to fly combat jets, ladies. It looks as though the Pentagon and Navy are going to test out the theory."

"To see if we can fly combat jets as well as the boys?" Maggie drawled, barely able to suppress her smile.

Dana laughed at the challenge glinting in Maggie's eyes. If anyone could be a combat-jet pilot, it was Maggie. She saw the pride mirrored in the faces of her family who surrounded them. "You'll fly the pants off those boys at Miramar."

"That's where they train the Top Guns," Griff reminded them. "I went through there two years ago." He smiled over at Maggie. "Obviously they think you have what it takes to play with the big boys."

Grinning, Maggie said, "I'm ready for them, Griff."

"I feel sorry for them." He laughed, holding out his hand to congratulate her. Maggie had been number one, and had gotten her wish to fly planes on and off carriers. Gazing at Dana's ecstatic features, he added with feeling, "But then, you're a rare lady, too, sweetheart. Not many students get to become instructor pilots." *Rare and so damned loving.*

Ann smiled up at them, hiding her disappointment that her daughter wouldn't be stationed on the West Coast. "So this means you'll be close to each other."

"In more ways than one." Griff laughed. He saw Ann's sadness. "I'll take good care of her for you. I promise."

"I know you will, Griff."

"I'll be out on leave to visit you, Mom, next year," Dana said, wanting to ease her mother's disappointment.

"*We*'ll be out there," Griff corrected.

Dana could hardly wait to be alone with Griff, to talk, to celebrate their good fortune. First, they were having dinner with Maggie's entire family at their apartment, then she would go over to Griff's bungalow for an hour or so. Dana desperately needed to talk with him, and she saw the look of longing in his eyes, too.

"Did you mean it? You love me?"

Griff glanced over at Dana as he drove them back to his apartment after the celebration dinner. "Yes, I did." His hands tightened briefly on the steering wheel. Dana's face remained contemplative.

"Wow! That was a heck of a time to tell me."

"I know. It just kind of slipped out. I saw the panic in your eyes and I wanted to let you know that no matter what happened, it wouldn't hurt what we have, sweetheart." Griff smiled and reached over, gripping Dana's hand.

"I love you, too."

"I was hoping you did."

She gave him a flat look. "Is there anything you don't know?"

With a laugh, Griff brought her hand to his lips, kissing it. "Lots of things."

"You're so arrogant sometimes, Turcotte, you drive me crazy." Dana smiled and relaxed against the seat. The residential streets were quiet and well-lit, casting rays of light into the dark interior of the sports car.

"But you love me anyway?" he ventured.

"You know I do."

"I'm not taking anything we have for granted," Griff continued seriously. He pulled into the driveway of his bungalow. Shutting off the lights and engine, he absorbed in the gathering silence. "It's been one hell of a day, hasn't it?"

"Yes. Mom's so happy—about everything. I got my wings, and orders to stay here." Dana shook her head. "I can hardly believe it, Griff." Dana turned and placed her arms around his shoulders. Holding his dark gaze, she whispered, "It's been the most wonderful—and worst— sixteen weeks of my life. Talk about ups and downs."

Griff sighed and cradled her face between his hands. "The worst is over," he promised.

Leaning forward, Dana pressed a kiss to his mouth. She became lost in the heat, the strength and tenderness that was only Griff.

"This is what I was waiting for," Griff whispered as she fitted against him, her head on his shoulder. Absently stroking her arm, he said, "We've got the time we need, now."

"For what?"

"Well," Griff hedged, "we're both coming out of some hellish circumstances. You, with your father, and me, with my divorce from Carol. With you being stationed here for the next two years, we'll have time to properly heal ourselves and get to know each other even better." Griff knew Dana wasn't ready to be asked for her hand in marriage. Age and experience had taught him that when people were seriously injured, they needed time to recover before entering a relationship with any amount of stability. Dana still reacted out of the old conditioning she'd grown up with, and she needed more time to continue to realize that although Griff was a man, he wasn't her father. Time would be on his side on that issue.

"I like what we've started to build together," Dana began quietly. "And I feel you're right."

"Our love will stand the test of time," Griff agreed.

"After such a rocky start, I'm sure it can survive anything," Dana said with a muted laugh. Nuzzling against Griff's neck, she sighed contentedly.

"You know, with Maggie leaving, you're going to be stuck in that huge, three-bedroom apartment by yourself. It's going to be mighty lonely to come home to every night."

"I never thought about it, but you're right."

"I have a possible solution."

Dana lifted her head, a grin pulling at her mouth. "Griff Turcotte, every time you take on that tone of voice with me, it means you're up to something."

He smiled broadly. "Caught in the act."

"Again."

"That's okay. I was thinking that since we love each other, we could live together and see how it works." Griff knew it would, without a doubt. This way, Dana wouldn't feel pressured into anything. Glancing down at her shadowed face, he prompted, "Well? What do you think?"

"I like the idea."

"How much?"

She shook her head and laughed. "A lot, Turcotte. Satisfied?"

"I feel like a cat who's just stolen all the cream from the saucer."

"I imagine you do."

Griff was more than contented. He knew they should go inside, but having Dana in his arms gave him everything he'd ever wanted—ever dreamed of—so he was satisfied to remain in the car with her. Dana would be getting thirty days' leave, and he'd ask for and be granted the same amount of time. They would have one beautiful, long, uninterrupted vacation together. He nuzzled her cheek and kissed her lips tenderly.

"I like what we have, what we're growing toward, sweetheart."

Dana closed her eyes and savored his arms around her. "I do, too. I love you so much, Griff...."

Tipping his head back, never wanting the moment or the feelings of utter happiness to end, he whispered back, "I know...."

*   *   *   *   *

Bestselling author NORA ROBERTS captures all the
romance, adventure, passion and excitement of Silhouette in
a special miniseries.

THE
CALHOUN WOMEN

Four charming, beautiful and fiercely independent
sisters set out on a search for a missing family
heirloom—an emerald necklace—and each finds
something even more precious...passionate romance.

Look for THE CALHOUN WOMEN miniseries
starting in June.

COURTING CATHERINE
Silhouette Romance #801

July
A MAN FOR AMANDA
Silhouette Desire #649

August
FOR THE LOVE OF LILAH
Silhouette Special Edition #685

September
SUZANNA'S SURRENDER
Silhouette Intimate Moments #397

IT'S A CELEBRATION OF
MOTHERHOOD!

Following the success of BIRDS, BEES and BABIES, we are proud to announce our second collection of Mother's Day stories.

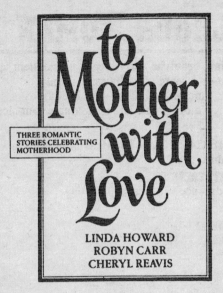
Three stories in one volume, all by award-winning authors—stories especially selected to reflect the love all families share.

Available in May, TO MOTHER WITH LOVE is a perfect gift for yourself or a loved one to celebrate the joy of motherhood.

Silhouette Books®

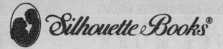
Silhouette Books®

SILHOUETTE BOOKS ARE NOW AVAILABLE IN STORES AT THESE CONVENIENT TIMES EACH MONTH*

Silhouette Desire and Silhouette Romance

> May titles: April 10
> June titles: May 8
> July titles: June 5
> August titles: July 10

Silhouette Intimate Moments and Silhouette Special Edition

> May titles: April 24
> June titles: May 22
> July titles: June 19
> August titles: July 24

We hope this new schedule is convenient for you. With only two trips each month to your local bookseller, you will always be sure not to miss any of your favorite authors!

Happy reading!

Please note: There may be slight variations in on-sale dates in your area due to differences in shipping and handling.

*Applicable to U.S. only.

Silhouette Special Edition

proudly hails

WOMEN OF GLORY

from Lindsay McKenna

Soar with Dana Coulter, Molly Rutledge and Maggie Donovan—Lindsay McKenna's WOMEN OF GLORY. On land, sea or air, these three Annapolis grads challenge danger head-on, risking life and limb for the glory of their country—and for the men they love!

May: NO QUARTER GIVEN (SE #667) Dana Coulter is on the brink of achieving her lifelong dream of flying—and of meeting the man who would love to take her to new heights!

June: THE GAUNTLET (SE #673) Molly Rutledge is determined to excel on her own merit, but Captain Cameron Sinclair is equally determined to take gentle Molly under his wing....

July: UNDER FIRE (SE #679) Indomitable Maggie never thought her career—or her heart—would come under fire. But all that changes when she teams up with Lieutenant Wes Bishop!

SEWG-1